The No-Fly List

Donna –
Thank you for your support of my work. Enjoy!

Lisa R. Schoolcraft

The No-Fly List

Lisa R. Schoolcraft

Printed in the United States of America

First Printing, 2020

ISBN-13: 978-1-7339709-2-1

Cover design by Brittany Jordan

Publisher: Schoolcraft Ink LLC

Visit the author's website at www.schoolcraftink.com

Dedication

To my family and friends, for always believing in me

Table of Contents

Chapter 1

Ravyn Shaw answered her phone to her sister's voice.
"I'm getting married!" Jane Shaw said with excitement.

"That's wonderful, Jane," answered Ravyn. "When did Nick pop the question?"

"Can you believe he did it on April Fool's Day? We had a nice dinner and were walking through Falls Park," Jane explained, describing the park in downtown Greenville, South Carolina, where she and Nick lived. "Then he got down on one knee and proposed! He said he'd be a fool to live without me. I can't believe it."

"That sounds very romantic," Ravyn said.

"It really was. And my ring is beautiful. I'll text you a picture."

"Have you told Mom and Dad?"

"I called them right before you."

"Have you picked a date for the wedding?"

"We're thinking about a fall wedding. Maybe mid to late October. It depends on how quickly we can pull it together, get the venues. I'd like to get married in the park where he proposed. Ravyn, would you be my maid of honor?

Ravyn was shocked. Jane and Ravyn were close, but Ravyn expected Jane would have asked her college roommate, Patti.

"Jane, I'd be honored."

"Oh, thank you. And will you come up and help me shop for my dress?"

"Of course, I will. You just let me know when I need to come up and I'll be there."

"Oh, Ravyn, I'm so happy!"

"I'm happy for you. And let me know when I need to come up. Love you, little sister."

"Love you, too, big sister."

"Tell Nick I said congratulations and he's getting a wonderful girl."

"I'll tell him. Love you!"

Ravyn hung up with her sister, a smile on her face. This was wonderful news for her sister, but it all seemed to be happening so fast.

She'd only met Nick, along with her family, at Thanksgiving. Jane and Nick had moved in together shortly after that and just a few months later Nick had proposed.

Then a feeling of sadness overcame Ravyn. She lifted herself off her sofa and walked into her condo's kitchen. Filling a glass with cubed ice, Ravyn poured herself an iced tea.

She sat at her breakfast bar and thought back at her recent relationships. A handsome entrepreneur whom she'd fallen in love with, a hot Italian man with whom she'd had a vacation affair, and a very nice special agent with the Federal Bureau of Investigation's Atlanta office.

The FBI agent hadn't really been a romance as much as a series of dates before it all fizzled out. Still, Luke had been a nice distraction and for a few short weeks, she could say she was "dating" someone.

Now there was no special someone on the horizon, and no real prospects, either. Where were the single men out there? Ravyn wasn't one for bars or nightclubs. At least not now. In her younger days, yes.

She certainly wasn't meeting anyone through work. She'd met entrepreneur Marc Linder through work, but that was when she was a freelancer. She'd been assigned to write a profile of him and then fell for him.

Ravyn was managing editor of *Cleopatra* magazine now, a fashion and lifestyle magazine in Atlanta. It meant a steady paycheck, but not the ability to meet single men.

So how could she go about meeting new people? she wondered. She could join some meet-up groups, maybe learn some Italian. She could take a yoga class, but there were probably more women in a yoga class than young hot men. Maybe she should try online dating.

She'd heard of some friends who had met their significant others that way. But which one should she try?

Tinder? Bumble? Plenty Of Fish? Match? eHarmony? Which one was the best? Which one wasn't filled with creepy dudes? Which one was for women in their early 30s?

Ravyn would have to do some research online, but she was sure she could find one that was right for her. She'd tried online dating when she was new to Atlanta, but that had been several years ago and her experience had been one of blind dates until she'd made friends at the daily newspaper who had been able to introduce her to their single friends.

She'd heard good things about Tinder. Her friend Rebecca had met her husband Chris that way. Maybe she'd try that first.

She opened her laptop and found Tinder's website. She read the overview, downloaded the app, created a profile, and uploaded some photos.

Because she had such a distinctive first name, Ravyn decided she'd use a "username" rather than her real name. She decided on Mizzou Gal since she had gotten her journalism degree at the University of Missouri. That wasn't a lie. Just not her real name.

It wasn't long before she got confirmation that she was live on the dating site. She was excited and a bit apprehensive about it.

But maybe this was the story she would tell her grandchildren: That she had met her future husband online.

It wouldn't be as good of a story as her parents' "how we met" story. But these were modern times. Modern times call for modern technology.

While she waited to see if she got any "likes" on the site, she decided to call her best friend Julie Montgomery and tell her what she'd done. Julie would probably have some good advice, too.

"Hey girl," Julie said.

"Hey yourself. Guess what I've done?"

"What have you done? Gone blonde, gotten a tattoo? What?"

"I set up an online dating profile."

"What?! Why did you do that? What about that Luke fellow? Is that over?"

"That never really started," Ravyn sighed. "It's hard to find people to date. I decided to let the internet help me."

"Really? You think the internet will help?"

"Hey, thanks for the vote of confidence!"

"You know what I mean. You are a smart, professional woman. I don't think you need the internet. Just get out there. Go to some of those parties you get invited to."

"I get invited to parties that are PR events. Mostly women are invited to those. I'm more interested in meeting men. Single men."

"And you think a dating site will help?"

"Well, I hope it won't hurt. I've signed up for three months. I hope I find someone in 90 days. Otherwise, I'm joining a convent."

"You aren't joining a convent. Why are you really doing this?" Julie asked.

"Jane's getting married."

"She is? That's great!"

"And I'd kind of like to be dating someone so I have a date for the wedding."

"That's really not a good enough reason to try online dating, if you ask me."

"I'm not asking you. And I want someone stable in my life. You have to admit the past year has been a bit of a roller coaster in the romance department."

"That's no lie. But let me ask you, did you ever call Marc Linder? Didn't he want to have lunch with you? I think he's still stuck on you."

"Stuck on me? Are we in middle school?"

"You know I have tween girls. I think they still say stuck on you. Maybe they don't. Anyway, did you go out with him?"

"No. I kind of blew him off."

"Well, call him and give him a second chance. Maybe he'll be your date for the wedding."

"Julie, I don't think I can. I keep thinking of how he treated me. He should have believed me when I said I hadn't switched the numbers in his fourth-quarter numbers. I would never do that."

"Laura Lucas would."

"Well, yes. And Laura Lucas did. I can't believe that bitch was so desperate to break us up that she'd sabotage Marc's company."

"That's Laura. If she couldn't have Marc, she didn't want you to have him either."

"It's over with Marc."

"OK. I take your word for it."

What did Julie mean by that? Ravyn wondered. She decided to change the subject. "I'm a little nervous about going on blind dates, though."

"Well. you let me know where you are going. And always meet the guys in public places. Like the police station."

Ravyn burst out laughing. "I'll be sure to do that."

"Hey, I think I hear the girls. Rob took them to soccer practice today and I was supposed to be cleaning the house. Oh well!"

"Any plans tonight?"

"No. And Rob and I are overdue for a date night."

"I can always babysit."

"Ravyn, you said yourself, you are trying to meet single men. You will never do that babysitting my daughters."

"But I love your daughters! See you soon, for lunch maybe?"

"How about next weekend?"

"Done. See you then."

Ravyn returned to her smartphone and was pleasantly surprised to see she had several profiles waiting for her approval on the app. She began to peruse profiles of the men. A few of them seemed promising. She swiped right for the ones she was interested in and left for the ones who didn't catch her eye, or who she thought were too old. What did a 60-year-old man want with a 34-year-old woman? She rolled her eyes. She knew what he wanted.

Ravyn did notice that there were a lot of shirtless profiles and some men who were upfront about being in "open marriages." Ravyn wondered if their wives knew since several of those profiles said they wanted discrete connections.

She felt good about the profiles she had approved. Maybe this online dating thing would be a breeze! One man, Scott, was a match and messaged her immediately. Ravyn was surprised.

Hi Mizzou Gal. Is that your real name? How are you this evening? his text read.

I'm very well. My name is Ravyn, she replied.

Why are you on Tinder? You are beautiful, Scott said.

I'm very new to Tinder. You are the first guy I'm chatting with.

I'm pretty new as well. Are you looking for love? For a long-term relationship? his text read.

I'm looking to meet some new people and if there is a connection, to date, she responded. Scott was pretty forward, she thought. Why are you here?

I'm divorced. And then my long-time girlfriend and I split up. We were together for four years. What was your longest relationship?

I've never been married and my last long-term relationship ended last year. We were together for several months.

Why did it end? Scott asked.

How to tell Scott that she and Marc ended because he hadn't believed her when she said she hadn't sabotaged his business. That her rival, Laura Lucas, had done that.

Even though she and Marc had tried to make it work after the deceit was discovered, Ravyn hadn't really believed he wouldn't do it to her again. She felt there would be some other crisis and Marc would blame her.

He said he wanted to date another woman, Ravyn lied. She figured it was easier to lie about Marc and Scott wouldn't ask more questions about her relationship with him.

How do you feel about sex in a relationship? Is that an important part of a relationship to you? Scott asked.

Scott was certainly being direct. Ravyn took a breath and blew it out.

I certainly think sex is an important part of a relationship, but there is far more to a relationship than sex, she responded. Where was he going with all this?

How do you feel about 420? Are you 420 friendly? Scott asked.

Ravyn had no idea what he was talking about. She quickly Googled 420 friendly and found out it referred to marijuana.

Ravyn wasn't necessarily opposed to marijuana use. She had done some smoking in college, but it wasn't her thing now.

I'm not a real fan. I need to keep my girlish figure, she joked. She hoped Scott had a sense of humor.

Hey, I'd like to chat more with you offline. Do you use Snapchat?

I have an account, but I hardly ever use it, she replied. Thankfully, her username was just her first name, no last name. Scott still wouldn't know her last name. She was leery of letting someone she'd only met online know her full name. She gave him her Snapchat name and waited.

Suddenly, the entire Tinder text messaging conversation disappeared. What happened? Ravyn wondered.

Then she heard a ping from her phone. Her Snapchat account had alerted her.

Do you think this will satisfy you? The text and the image Scott had sent was a very large, erect penis. In the new age of online dating, Ravyn had just gotten her first dick pic.

"Eww," Julie said as Ravyn recounted her first online dating experience. "What happened after that?"

"Nothing. The photo disappeared from Snapchat, too. I didn't respond. What am I supposed to do? Send him a boob shot? I don't think so."

"Well, you can't let one bad apple spoil the barrel. Have you found any other cute guys on the app? Anyone interesting?" Julie asked, biting into her rainbow roll. Ravyn and Julie were at their favorite Buckhead restaurant, Twist.

"There are a couple of guys I'm texting pretty regularly. I'm having lunch with a guy named Joe tomorrow."

"Where are you going?"

"I don't know yet. He said he has to work right after our lunch and could we meet in the Georgia Tech area. That's close to my condo, so that should be OK."

"Do you want me to call you about 10 minutes in, in case you need to say an emergency came up and leave?" Julie said, putting her chopsticks down and leaning in conspiratorially.

"What?"

"You know, if Joe is a troll living under a bridge, do you want me to call you so you can excuse yourself?"

"Excuse myself?"

"You know, say you've got to take this call and walk out of the restaurant?"

"Julie, it won't come to that."

"I'll do it if you need me to."

"Julie, it will be fine. And we'll be in a public place."

"Well, call me right after the date," she said, picking up her chopsticks and resuming her meal. "I want to hear all about it."

"You are enjoying this, aren't you?" Ravyn asked, surprised.

"I have to live vicariously through you! And I didn't get nearly enough detail with that Italian stallion you were with last year."

Ravyn could feel her face blushing. "That was just a vacation fling. It was nothing."

Ravyn had taken a wonderful trip to Rome, attending a cooking school, and ended up having an affair with Luca, who unbeknownst to her was an undercover police officer keeping tabs on some jewel thieves. Those thieves had been classmates in the cooking school.

When a nearby jewelry store had been robbed, Luca's job had required him to investigate the case, but he'd essentially ghosted Ravyn, never contacting her until the case was nearly closed and she was back in Atlanta.

Ravyn had never told Julie how much she'd fallen for Luca, and how his deception had hurt her. Even though he'd reached out to say he was sorry for how he'd left her, Ravyn hadn't forgiven him.

"Who are the other guys you are texting? Other than this Joe person?" Julie asked.

"There's Al," Ravyn replied. "He's in real estate, but I think he lives in the north part of metro Atlanta. He works in Buckhead, though, and I think we're going to try to have lunch next week at Houston's."

"The one in Buckhead or the one on Peachtree?"

"The one on Peachtree. It's a little bit between us since I'll be coming from downtown."

Ravyn's office at *Cleopatra* was in downtown Atlanta. She'd been at the job for a little over a year and had enjoyed it when she first started. But a new boss, Jennifer Bagley, had arrived months earlier and the pair had clashed several times.

For now, there were calm waters at the office, but Ravyn never knew when rough waters would return.

"Well, keep me posted," Julie said. "And if you get frisky with Joe or Al, I'll expect some details."

Ravyn just shook her head and smiled at her best friend.

Joe texted Ravyn that he had to be at work right after their lunch and asked if she would mind meeting him at a casual restaurant.

She didn't mind. It would get her in and out quickly, she thought, so if there was no connection, she wouldn't have to suffer through painful conversation.

He said he knew he'd asked if they could meet near Georgia Tech, but could she meet him elsewhere?

Where? she asked.

Do you know the Chick-fil-A at North Druid Hills and I-85?

I think I do.

Can you meet me there? I have to work at the airport and can head down right after lunch.

Sure, Ravyn replied. But she didn't expect he meant a fast-food restaurant when he asked if she would meet him at a casual restaurant. She'd gotten dressed up that day, wearing a skirt and a nice top. She'd gotten dressed up for Chick-fil-A?

See you at noon, was Joe's reply.

Ravyn drove north on Interstate 85 and got off at the North Druid Hills exit, turning right to get to the chicken sandwich chain. She could see the restaurant on the corner of Briarcliff Road and North Druid Hills Road. Pulling into the parking lot she knew she'd made a mistake.

There, in front of her, was a large indoor playground for kids behind a plexiglass wall of the restaurant. Not only was it a fast-food place but it would be noisy with children. She tried to tell herself maybe this was what she and Joe would tell their grandchildren: That they had met at Chick-fil-A.

She opened the door to the noise and long lines and felt her heart sink. She just didn't have a good impression about this date.

Tall and lanky, Joe was near the door, clearly scanning for her. Ravyn recognized him immediately since he was so tall. He'd said he was 6-foot, 3-inches and he towered over most people next to him.

"I'm so glad you made it," he said. "I was worried you wouldn't come."

Ravyn wanted to say she wished she hadn't but decided she needed lunch anyway, so she'd try to make the best of it.

Joe stood behind her as they waited in line. Just then, a new cashier opened a register and waved her over. Ravyn took a sidestep over to greet the cashier, just as Joe stepped forward in line. They were now in two separate lines.

Ravyn didn't think it could get much worse. Great, Ravyn thought. Now I don't even have the chance to get a free meal out of this crappy date.

She ordered and looked over to find Joe waving at her from a table near the indoor playground.

"I'm sorry," Joe said. "I meant to pay for your lunch. I'll make it up to you next time."

Ravyn doubted there would be a next time.

She and Joe kept up the small talk, however, and she discovered he worked in customer service for Delta Air Lines at Hartsfield-Jackson Atlanta International Airport. He worked the afternoon shift in the Sky Club.

Suddenly, a boy's voice shouted "No!" by the playground and a shoe came flying toward the table where Joe and Ravyn were sitting, hitting Ravyn squarely in the chest and knocking the soft drink from her hand and down her blouse.

Ravyn jumped up, the cold and wet drink startling her.

"Oh, let me help you with that," Joe said, reaching for paper napkins and beginning to dab the front of her shirt.

Ravyn looked down at what was now her see-through shirt. Her bra showed clearly through the blouse.

Suddenly Ravyn felt a little squeeze on her right breast. She looked up to see Joe looking at her with a little smile on his face. She was so shocked she could only open her mouth before she said, "No!"

She took the napkins from him, grabbed her purse and walked away from the table, heading out the door to her car, never looking back.

"He did what?" Julie asked.

"Basically, he copped a feel."

"What do you mean?"

"I mean he was dabbing the front of my shirt and his hand gave my breast a little squeeze," Ravyn recounted. "He had a napkin under it. He was trying to wipe up the drink all over my shirt, but he definitely copped a feel."

"Jesus. Did you slap his face? Kick him in the balls?"

"No, I would have thrown my drink in his face, but I just had my own drink dumped on me by some kid who threw his shoe. It was so humiliating. And then I found out what he did for a living."

"What does he do for a living?" Julie asked, worried.

"I don't mean to sound snobbish, but he's a glorified waiter at Delta's Sky Club at the airport."

"What? What do you mean?"

"He works in the Delta Sky Club refreshing everyone's drinks."

"I'm sorry, sweetie," Julie said. "Maybe this Al person will be more of a gentleman."

"Lord, I hope so. If this is what online dating is all about, I'm going to have to become a nun," Ravyn lamented.

"You are not becoming a nun. You've had too much hot sex to become a nun. So, what are you going to do about Joe?"

"I blocked him from Tinder and I blocked him from my phone."

"Good for you. What an asshole."

"And that's not the worst of it," Ravyn said.

"There's more?"

"I bought my own damn lunch at Chick-fil-A. He copped a feel without buying me a chicken sandwich!"

Chapter 2

Marc Linder could not stop thinking about Ravyn Shaw. He was trying not to become obsessed with her. He'd tried calling her and asking her to lunch but gave up after she'd turned him down twice.

He'd even driven past her condo, hoping he'd see her on the sidewalk.

How pathetic was that? he wondered. This is getting unhealthy.

Marc wanted to talk to her so badly. Tell her he knew he'd fucked up and wanted to try again. They had tried again, actually, but he knew he'd fucked that up, too. He should have been paying more attention to her.

Now that LindMark Enterprises had its funding and some solid investors were interested in possibly purchasing the company outright, he realized he was missing what he wanted and needed to make him happy in life: Ravyn.

Maybe this is just a midlife crisis, he thought. He had just turned 41.

No, this was not about age. He was missing having a woman in his life and he wanted that woman to be Ravyn. Her easy smile, the smell of her floral perfume, her blue-grey eyes, her warm, supple body, the way she curled into him when she was in his bed.

If he kept thinking of her, he was going to have to go home to take a cold shower.

Marc got up from his desk and stretched, then walked down the hall. He wanted to be ready for his video conference with the Black Kat Investors team, but he was too keyed up. A quick walk around the block of his office building should do the trick.

Marc stepped outside into the May warmth. He was glad he left his sports jacket behind. He'd better keep the walk short or he'd be sweaty. He walked out of his Midtown office and turned left onto Peachtree Street. He'd walk down a couple of blocks toward 12th Street and then over to Juniper Street and back again.

As he re-entered Colony Square, Marc was surprised to run into Julie Montgomery, Ravyn's best friend. She was sitting at a table in the office building's food court.

"Julie," he called out and waved.

Julie stared at Marc before she recognized him.

"Oh, Marc. I wasn't expecting to run into you."

"Me, neither. What are you doing here? Some shopping? Lunch? Is Ravyn with you?" Marc asked, looking around for her.

"No, she's not here, Marc. I'm waiting for one of my tennis partners."

"Oh," he said, trying to keep the disappointment out of his voice.

"Hey, you're still into her, aren't you?"

Marc was silent for a moment, trying to think of how to respond. He decided to be honest.

"Yes. I've tried calling and texting her. I'd like to see her again, but she's not responding. I don't want to come off as some sort of stalker."

Marc was silent for a moment, then asked. "Is she seeing someone?"

Julie gestured for Marc to sit at her table. "Well, not really. But she is online dating. She's on Tinder."

"Tinder?"

"You know, swipe right or swipe left?"

Marc looked at Julie blankly. "I've never done online dating."

"Really? I'm surprised. How do you meet women?"

"At the gym. Through work."

Julie made a face. "Laura Lucas."

Now it was Marc's turn to make a face. He grimaced. "Not my proudest moment. But it's because of Laura that I met Ravyn."

"That's true. Well, to make a profile on Tinder you'd have to be shirtless, show off your sports car or boat, and hold your trophy fish."

"What?" Marc asked, looking perplexed.

"Oh, Ravyn showed me some of the profiles of men on Tinder. Half of them are shirtless and the other half are holding fish. Don't ask me why."

"And she's dating these guys?"

"She's dated one guy and it didn't go well."

"What happened?" Marc asked.

Julie thought it over. She didn't want to tell Marc about Joe being 'handsy.' "Ah, never mind. It just went badly. But she's supposed to go out with another guy, Al, this week."

"She's seeing someone else?"

"Well, Marc, that is the point of online dating. You keep dating until one sticks."

"Oh."

"You love her, don't you?"

Marc looked away before looking at Julie. "I do. I've tried to forget about her and I can't."

"What happened, Marc? Why did she break up with you?"

"I thought we were getting back together. We were together for a while. Then she just kind of…"

"Stopped. Turned her feelings off. Right?"

"Right."

"I've known Ravyn for a long time. I've seen her do it to men. She kind of gets scared and shuts her feelings down."

"I'd like to try it again. Let her see I'm serious about us. About making us work. I know I made a mistake. With Laura Lucas and with that whole fourth-quarter report. God, I wish I could go back in time and just believe her. Ravyn I mean."

"Yes. You should have believed her. You hurt her, Marc."

"I know," he said quietly. "I'd give anything to take it all back."

"Listen, I wish I could help you…" Julie started to say. Then her eyes got wide. "Hey, maybe I can help you."

"What do you mean?"

"Why don't you create an online profile on Tinder and I'll encourage Ravyn to swipe right."

"I don't understand how to do a profile. And wouldn't Ravyn reject me because she'd see my face?"

"Oh, that's probably true. Could you use a friend's picture?"

"I'm not sure…"

"Hey, don't you have a brother?" Julie asked excitedly.

"Um, my brother isn't really…"

"Do you look like him? Even a little bit? We could use his photo and put all the great stuff about you and I'll get Ravyn to go through profiles with me so she picks you." Julie was talking quickly, excited by her plan. "Oh, but we can't use your real name. What's your middle name?"

"Edward."

"We'll use that."

"But I don't…"

"Listen, I see my friend Abigail," Julie waved at a woman with long blonde hair walking toward her. "What's your number? I'll call you and help you set up your profile. Your homework is to get some photos of your brother."

Marc gave Julie his number. "Thanks. Thanks for your help with this. I hope it works."

"It will. You'll have me to help give her a little push in the right direction."

Marc got back to his office unsure that Julie's plan would work. First, his brother Bruce didn't look that much like him. And his brother was once again being scarce. He got that way when he was using and abusing drugs and alcohol.

Marc didn't even know where his brother Bruce was, let alone to get a recent photo of him. He shook his head. This isn't going to work, he thought.

Ravyn was lucky she didn't have to valet park at Houston's. She got the last spot in the small lot right next to the restaurant. She was nervous about meeting Al since her date with Joe had not gone well.

She walked into the small foyer and saw several people sitting on benches, waiting to get tables. She hadn't thought to make reservations. She hoped Al had made them.

Ravyn queued up in line for the hostess stand and when she got to the front, she gave her name.

"Oh, your party is waiting on you," the woman said. "Please follow me."

Ravyn followed the dark-haired woman to a booth where Al, who had sandy brown hair and a neatly trimmed goatee, was waiting. He stood up as she approached the table.

"Ravyn?"

"Al?"

Ravyn extended her hand. "Nice to meet you."

"Likewise."

Al motioned for her to sit down. A menu and a glass of water waited at her seat.

Ravyn sat down and an awkward silence settled in at the table.

"How was the traffic?" Al asked.

In Atlanta, traffic was an easy ice breaker. It was always horrible, but Atlantans were used to it.

"It wasn't too bad. I'm in downtown, so Peachtree was a little rough."

"Yeah. Same for me," Al said. "How is your day going?"

"It's going OK. I've been doing a lot of editing for the June issue."

"June issue?"

"I work for *Cleopatra*, the fashion and lifestyle magazine."

"Oh, the media," Al said dismissively.

"Yes, the media," Ravyn said rather defensively. "I was a reporter for a lot of years before I worked at the magazine."

"At the *Atlanta Daily Tribune*?" he asked, incredulously.

"Yes, what's the matter with that?"

"That liberal rag. I can't believe you worked there."

Ravyn frowned. This date was not going well either.

"Hey, I did a good job there. I worked to let people know what was going on in the city."

Al threw his hands up defensively. "No need to get your panties in a wad about it."

The waitress appeared. "Hi, I'm Brittany. I'll be your server today. Can I get you a beverage other than water?"

"Oh, I'm going to need some bourbon," Al said. "What about an Old-Fashioned."

"Same," Ravyn said, feeling the need to meet Al on his turf.

"I'll get those right away," Brittany said. "But let me tell you today's specials."

She went through a litany of specials, including a salad with ahi tuna, a filet with blue cheese crumbles, and a lump crab-based appetizer.

If Ravyn was having an Old-Fashioned, she wanted red meat with it. She might have to sleep under her desk after lunch, but she didn't care.

"I'll take the filet," she said. "That sounds good.'

Al raised his eyebrows at her choice.

"We can split the bill," Ravyn said.

"No, no," Al said. "I invited you. I'll take the burger with fries."

Al handed over his menu and Ravyn did the same.

"So how long did you work at the lib rag?" Al asked.

Ravyn tried to keep her temper. "I worked there for several years, but I got laid off in 2009. Then I went to work for myself."

"That's great. I'm all for entrepreneurs."

"Well, it was hard. And I was glad to get the job with the magazine. I got full benefits again."

"But it's a 'lifestyle' magazine," he said, raising his hands to make air quotes. "It's all soft news with local celebrities, right? It's a glorified People magazine."

"It is not!" Ravyn said, raising her voice. She lowered her voice. "It is not."

"Come on," Al said. "You are writing about what the latest fashion is, what the latest kitchen design trends are, what the latest trendy restaurant is. It's hardly Fox News."

"Fox News?" Ravyn asked.

The server brought their drinks to the table and Ravyn took a large sip of her Old-Fashioned.

"Yes, Fox News," Al said. "That's the only real news station. You know that don't you?"

"No, I don't know that. I know I worked very hard at the daily newspaper when I was there and I work very hard at the magazine now. How is the commercial real estate business?"

"It's great! The market is coming back. It had been really bad for a while, but it is coming back. I've got some great deals in the works."

The waitress appeared with their food and Al ordered another Old-Fashioned. Ravyn raised her glass as well, even though she wasn't finished with her first drink.

Ravyn began cutting into her filet, the juices running out just the way she liked it. She took a bite. "Wow, this is good," she said.

Al bit into his burger and shook his head in agreement.

"So, what are you working on at the magazine?" Al asked.

Ravyn was feeling a bit defensive again but felt a bit emboldened by her first bourbon drink.

"We are about to get started on our back-to-school issue. Our July/August issue is all about back-to-school."

"Back to school?" Al asked. "That's soft news shit. Next thing you know, you'll be writing about what private school celebrities send their kids. Who needs that shit? That's not news."

Ravyn dropped her fork and knife. "Really? Back to school is not news? For someone in commercial real estate, I'd think you would sing the praises of retail. Back to school sales drive consumers to the stores."

"Somewhat, yes," Al said, taking another bite of his burger but continued talking with food in his mouth. "As long as the stores are in a good location and a great market. Otherwise, shoppers will just go online."

The waitress arrived with their second drinks, and Ravyn drained the last of her first one, her tongue reaching the cherry at the bottom of the glass. She pushed her empty glass toward the end of the table. She reached for her second drink but put it back down again.

"Hey, I'm not trying to argue with you," Al said. "I'm sure you're good at what you do. But in the scheme of things, it's not all that important, is it?"

"And commercial real estate is?"

"Well, my job contributes to the economy here in Atlanta. I'm not trying to be insulting, but your job doesn't."

"Yes, that is insulting."

"You just said yourself you are writing about back-to-school stories. That's fluff. My job means people go to work. I'm working on office building deals."

Ravyn wanted this lunch to be over and to block Al's phone number forever. She concentrated on finishing her steak.

"Hey, don't be that way."

"What way? Don't be insulted by you?"

"You are too sensitive."

"No, I don't think I'm being too sensitive, Al. You are being very condescending. I appreciate that you enjoy your job and congrats that you build buildings that people can work in. I happen to love my job. It's creative and satisfying."

"Well, OK."

Al didn't speak again until the meal was over. The waitress reappeared to clear their plates and asked, "One check or two?"

"Two checks, please," Al said, holding up two fingers.

Ravyn tried to hide the shock on her face. For the second time in one week, her date was not paying for her lunch.

The check arrived and Ravyn slid her credit card on her bill. Al did the same, but he was sure to let Ravyn see he'd pulled out a platinum American Express card.

As they left the table, Ravyn said, "Well, enjoy the rest of your day."

"Yeah. Have a nice life," he responded.

"Julie, he was insulting what I did," Ravyn said into her cell phone driving back to her office.

"I'm sorry. God, you've had a tough time with this, haven't you?"

"I mean, I realize I'm not going to meet someone on a first date and fall madly in love right away, but why have my first two dates been so shitty?"

"I don't know. Hey, I wanted to see if you are free next weekend. The whole weekend. Lynne and Celia have the lake house and wanted to know if you want to go up."

"Oh my God! That would be great. I could roast a chicken like from my cooking school in Italy. That would be fun. And maybe the lake house would take my mind off these miserable men."

"You should let me help you with the profiles. I'll be your wingman this weekend. Don't make any more dates until I help you."

"Believe it or not, I'm supposed to meet one more guy next week."

"Who?"

"His name is Tony. He's an architect."

"Where are you going for lunch?"

"We're meeting for drinks at the Sun Dial," Ravyn said.

"The revolving restaurant at the Westin?"

"That's the one. Hey, I'm pulling into the parking garage. I'll lose my cell signal."

"OK. Talk to you later."

Ravyn popped two breath mints in her mouth as she waited for the elevator to stop on the eighth floor. She hoped no one could smell the bourbon on her breath.

She exited the elevator and headed toward her office.

"Ravyn, there you are," said Jennifer Bagley, Ravyn's editor and direct superior. "I've been looking for you."

"I stepped out for lunch. I got stuck in traffic. What's up?"

"Have you worked up your budget for the back-to-school issue? Joel says ad sales are a little soft for the issue. Frankly, I don't think that man could sell space heaters to Eskimos."

Ravyn giggled. It was not a secret that Joel Greenberg, the ad director, and Jennifer Bagley didn't like each other. They tolerated each other and acted professionally toward each other. But they constantly took swipes at each other when the other wasn't around.

"So, you need me to trim the budget?" Ravyn asked.

"Let's be a bit conservative with this one. It's getting into the summer months selling season and ad revenue is usually down. If the sales pick up and Joel miraculously hits his goal, we can hire a couple more freelancers for stories."

"They'll want a rush fee if I don't get the stories assigned out in the next week."

"We're not paying a rush fee," Jennifer said. "Don't promise it. I'll let you know Monday if you can assign anything extra."

"OK. That's good."

"And Ravyn."

"Yes?"

"Please don't drink at lunch when you are working again."

Chapter 3

Ravyn was nervous about meeting Tony. Since her first two blind dates had gone badly, she felt like her footing was a little off when it came to first dates. Was it her? Was she giving off undatable vibes? She hoped not.

She was meeting Tony shortly after work. Ravyn thought she would walk over to the revolving restaurant on top of the Westin and save herself having to valet in the hotel's underground parking deck.

Ravyn got to the ground floor elevator to the Sun Dial, which was on the 73rd floor of the hotel, and looked around for someone looking for her. She didn't see anyone.

She thought she might be late, but she was right on time. Maybe Tony was running late. Just then her phone pinged an incoming text message.

Parking. Be there soon.

Ravyn was relieved. He wasn't standing her up.

Tony was tall, fair-haired, wearing khaki pants and a sports coat. He had come from work too.

"Ravyn?" he asked as he came closer to the queue to go up to the restaurant.

"Hi, Tony," Ravyn said, sticking out her hand.

"Sorry I was late. I took a last-minute call."

"No worries. I just got here. I walked over from my office."

"Oh, you're downtown too?"

"Yes."

"Shall we go up?"

"I'm looking forward to it. I haven't been here in a long time."

"It is nice at sunset, too. Not sure that we'll be here that long, but you never know," Tony smiled a big smile, showing perfect teeth.

As the couple approached the elevator door, Tony asked the woman taking the fee to go up to the restaurant whether the elevator would be full. "I have a little bit of claustrophobia," he admitted.

"It shouldn't be too full," the hostess said.

"Great. I just get a little nervous in small spaces," he said, turning to Ravyn.

The elevator opened and Tony, Ravyn, and another couple entered.

With a whoosh, the elevator began its ascent. Within a moment, the elevator abruptly stopped.

"What was that?" Tony asked.

"I'm not sure. We've stopped," Ravyn said.

Tony looked down. They weren't quite at the top. He looked up, then back at Ravyn. Tony was trying to keep his face neutral, but Ravyn could see he was uncomfortable.

"It will be OK," she said, trying to be comforting. "I'm sure it will only be a second before we start moving."

But Ravyn looked at the other couple in the elevator. They had a slightly worried look, too.

"This happened last week," the gentleman said. "They said they fixed it."

"This happened last week?" Ravyn asked.

"Yes. I'm one of the bartenders at Sun Dial. This happened last week."

"Oh my God," Tony said. "How long was the elevator stopped?"

"About an hour," the bartender said.

"Oh God! Oh God!" Tony said. He was looking panicked and then pressed the emergency button. "We're stuck! We're stuck in the elevator!" Tony shouted.

A disembodied voice came through the elevator's intercom. "Just a moment. We'll have the elevator moving shortly."

Tony took off his sports jacket and undid his collar. He was beginning to sweat.

Ravyn felt sorry for him. This couldn't be easy if he was afraid of tight spaces. And with the elevator stopped, she didn't feel like air was moving. It was beginning to feel close and uncomfortable. Or maybe that was Tony's reaction rubbing off on her.

Tony began pacing the small space. "I've got to get out of here. Why aren't they doing anything?" He pressed the emergency button again.

"It's OK, Tony. We'll be out of here soon." Ravyn looked to the bartender, who just shook his head slightly.

The other woman in the elevator looked exasperated. "Will you please stop pacing?" she asked Tony. "You're freaking me out. Just stand still. It will be OK. They will get us out of here."

Tony tried standing still but began tapping his foot rapidly.

"Stop that!" snapped the woman.

"Listen, we might be here a little while, so let's try to calm down," Ravyn said, evenly. She was trying to think calm, soothing thoughts herself.

"Can't you get your boyfriend under control?" the woman hissed.

"He's not my boyfriend," Ravyn snapped back. "We're here on our first date."

"Sucks for you," the bartender said. "Not a good way to get started, eh?"

"No, this is not an auspicious start."

Tony continued tapping his foot. "God! I need to get out of here. I need air! I need this to move!"

"Tony, why don't you tell me about your work? Are there any buildings you've worked on I'd know about?" Ravyn asked, trying to distract him.

"I'm an architect," he said.

"Yes, but what do you work on?"

"Bridges. I work on bridges," he said, but it came out more of a pant.

Ravyn was worried about him now. He'd gone pale.

"I think I'm going to be sick," Tony said. He crouched down, then sat on the elevator floor.

"Put your head between your legs," Ravyn said, trying to be helpful.

"I just want this elevator to move," he said. It came out in a whine.

The other woman in the elevator rolled her eyes, then said, "You better not be sick. I don't want the smell of vomit in here. Then I'll puke, too."

Ravyn was trying not to check her watch every minute, while Tony moaned in the corner of the elevator. He had laid his head against the elevator wall, turning slightly from everyone else. This was certainly not the date she had expected.

After 20 minutes, the elevator lurched, then came to another stop.

"Oh, God! Are we going to crash?" Tony exclaimed, his eyes wide.

"No, no," Ravyn said, putting her hand on the top of Tony's head. "Looks like they're working on the elevator. It will be OK soon."

He looked up at her, his eyes pleading. She felt so sorry for him.

The elevator lurched again, then began moving upward.

"Oh, thank God!" Tony said, standing on wobbly legs.

Ravyn could feel her ears pop as they went up. When the doors finally opened, Tony bolted out of the elevator and rushed to find the men's restroom.

Ravyn exited the elevator and stood still for a moment.

"Hey, you look like you could use a drink," the bartender said. "After what you've been through, it's on the house."

"Thanks. I hope my date is OK," Ravyn said, sitting down at the bar.

"He didn't look so good," the bartender said, walking around to the working area. "What will you have?"

"A glass of dry rosé, if you have it."

"Coming right up."

The bartender placed the glass of wine in front of her. "I'm Sam, by the way."

"Ravyn Shaw. I'd say it's very nice to meet you, Sam, but it sure was unusual."

"It was," Sam said, coming back to the seating area and taking a seat next to Ravyn. Sam and Ravyn chatted for about five minutes before Ravyn felt her phone vibrate in her purse and hear the ping of an incoming message.

She took it out to see the text from Tony: I'm sorry. I can't do this. I have to go home. Sorry.

"Bad news?" Sam asked.

"Tony's not feeling well. He's bailed."

"I'm not surprised. He looked terrible. Well, his loss is my gain. Would you like to have dinner with me?"

"What about your girlfriend?" Ravyn asked.

"Girlfriend? Oh, that chick in the elevator? I don't know her. And she was being a real bitch."

"Yes, she was," Ravyn frowned, then smiled up at Sam. "Sam, I'd be delighted to have dinner with you."

"Let's get a table."

Ravyn smiled as she drove home after her spontaneous date with Sam Alexander. They'd had a nice dinner, and he paid for her meal, although she did offer to split the bill since it "wasn't a real date."

"Why not?" Sam had asked. "I invited you."

"I really enjoyed this. You saved my evening."

"I'd love to see you again."

"I'd like that, too," said Ravyn, and she and Sam exchanged phone numbers.

Ravyn threw her keys on top of her breakfast bar and sorted through her mail. Mostly junk. She bent down to pet her gray tomcat, Felix, who was doing circle eights between her legs and meowing loudly.

"I know, big boy. You want some food."

She took the cat food bag out of the kitchen pantry and filled his bowl, then filled his water bowl. "There, all set."

Ravyn sat down on her couch and looked at her phone. There were several texts from Tony, apologizing for the evening. She didn't respond. And she didn't plan to tell him that she'd ended up on a date with Sam, the bartender.

She took out her phone to send Sam a text to thank him again for dinner.

Just got home. Thanks for the dinner date tonight and for saving my evening.

Ravyn waited to see if a bubble reply was coming.

Who is this? was the reply.

Ravyn was confused. She'd texted Sam, right? She looked at the phone number to be sure before answering.

This is Ravyn, we had dinner tonight.

Well, this is Sam's wife. Don't text my husband again.

Ravyn was shocked. Sam didn't say he was married. He didn't say he was single, either though. Ravyn had just assumed. She felt tears welling. Ravyn then put her head in her hands and cried.

Julie waved at Marc from a booth at Marlow's Tavern in Midtown. Marc was glad Julie had agreed to meet him for lunch to help set up his Tinder profile.

He'd managed to find some old photos of his brother Bruce at his parent's house in Dunwoody. They'd have to do. They might be from a few years ago, but at least Bruce didn't look drunk or strung out in them. If Marc managed to find out where he was, he was unsure he'd get a decent photo of him now.

He'd simply taken a photo of them with his cell phone. He'd hope they'd do.

"Thank you so much for meeting me," Marc said, sliding into the booth opposite Julie.

"Well, I had to do it before we head out to the lake over Memorial Day," she said. "I told Ravyn I was going to help her with Tinder. I want to be there to swipe right on your profile."

"You think this will work? I only have old photos of my brother. He looks more like my mother than me, which is good. I take after my father."

"All the better. And these photos don't have to be perfect. I'm going to know it's your profile and I'm going to make her swipe to like you. Then you just have to message her and set up a date. Just remember you're Edward."

Julie took Marc's phone and began setting up the profile.

"Do you want to use your real age?"

"Yes."

"What is it? How old are you?"

"I'm 41."

"And we're putting in that you live in Buckhead. What are we going to say you do for a living?"

"They want a company name? I can't say LindMark. She'll know it's me."

"No, we can't put that. What does LindMark do?"

"We create software that helps retailers track inventory, essentially."

"Hmm. Let's say you're an IT guy. That's not really lying."

Julie typed furiously to create a profile of Marc. He was divorced (true), no kids (also true), and a non-smoker. She put in that he worked out at the gym and was looking for a serious relationship. She turned his phone back to him to let him read what she had written.

"Anything else we need to add?"

"That about covers it."

"Do you want to say any other hobbies or activities? Like you enjoy golfing or tennis or boating or whatever?"

"I don't do any of those things. Other than the gym, I just work, work out, and go home."

"We can't put that in. That's kind of boring. Oh, sorry," Julie said when she realized what she had said.

Marc sighed. "No, I am kind of boring. What in the world do I have to offer to someone like Ravyn?" he asked rhetorically.

"Listen, you offer a lot," Julie said, trying to be supportive. "You have a job, you are emotionally stable, you have your own hair and teeth."

Marc snorted a laugh at that.

"And you are working to show her you love her," Julie said matter of factly.

"Yes," Marc said.

"Then let's make this a profile she's going to want to swipe right, OK? Let's put you like movies, you like to cook, enjoy good wine, stuff like that."

"That's true. Say I can grill a mean steak."

"Oh, that's good. She'll like that."

The waitress came over and they ordered burgers. Julie also ordered two glasses of red wine. Marc raised an eyebrow, but when the glasses came to the table, she set them close to each other and took a photo of it.

Julie chose three of the profile photos of Bruce, then decided to add the wine photos, adding the text "All that's missing is you" to the photo.

She uploaded all of them and hit send for the profile.

"OK, you're in business," she said. "You might want to play around with the app to get the hang of it. Oh, and she's not using her real name on her profile. She said her name was too identifying. She's using Mizzou Gal. Just don't swipe right on any women unless you want to get matched with them. Go through the profiles and if you find Ravyn's be sure to swipe right."

"I don't want to be matched with anyone but Ravyn," he said. "Thanks. I appreciate this."

"Well, I'm getting a great burger and a glass of wine for my trouble," Julie picked up her wine glass and clinked Marc's glass. "Cheers. To a perfect match."

Ravyn's cell phone rang as she worked at her desk.

Surprised, she answered it to hear Rob Montgomery's voice, Julie's husband.

"Hey, Rob, is everything OK?"

"I'm looking for Julie. I got a call from school that Lexie isn't feeling well. I can't go get her. Julie's not answering her phone, but she said she was having lunch with you today, so I thought I'd call you. Can you put her on?"

Ravyn was silent. She wasn't having lunch with Julie.

"Uh, Rob, she just went to the ladies' room. I'll have her call you when she comes out."

"OK, great. Thanks."

Ravyn quickly dialed Julie's phone. "Julie, pick up, pick up," she said into the phone.

The call went to voicemail. "Julie, I don't know where you are, but Rob is trying to get you. Lexie's sick and he said you were having lunch with me. Don't know what's going on, but call Rob."

Then Ravyn texted her friend. Julie, Lexie is sick and needs to be picked up from school. Rob thinks we're having lunch and called me trying to find you. Call him.

Ravyn was relieved when she saw text bubbles in reply.

Did you tell him I wasn't with you?

No, I said you were in the restroom. Is everything OK?

It's fine. I'll call him now. Thanks. I owe you one.

Ravyn didn't like the sound of that. Julie and Rob had been through a rough patch in their marriage. Julie had caught Rob cheating on her a little over a year ago. They'd gone to couple's therapy and Ravyn thought they were going to be OK. Now she wasn't so sure.

Why did Julie say she was having lunch with her? Who was she having lunch with?

Ravyn was worried for her friend. She'd have to question her when they were alone at Lake Lanier next weekend.

Late in the afternoon, Ravyn looked up to see Joel Greenberg leaning against her office door jam.

"Hello, Mizzou Gal," he said in a throaty voice.

Ravyn could hardly suppress the look of shock on her face. "Excuse me?"

"I said, hello, Mizzou Gal," Joel said with a sly smile. "I saw your profile on Tinder."

Was Joel on Tinder too? How had he seen her profile?

"Oh," was all Ravyn could say.

"Your profile is nice. I liked the photos of you in the pretty dresses. Most of the women's profiles I've seen, they are in tiny bikinis, or their boobs are falling out of their tops. Lots of cleavages. I guess we know what they are selling, right?"

Ravyn didn't know what to say to that. She didn't want to tell Joel about all the shirtless men or bare backsides she'd seen in some of the men's profile photos.

Was Joel's profile like that? She had to force herself not to shudder at the thought of Joel shirtless, or with a bare backside.

"Are you having any luck? Most of the women I'm finding seem to want me to be a sugar daddy. They want me to take them to all these fancy restaurants in Buckhead or buy them expensive gifts."

"I've gone on a few dates, but nothing's serious, yet."

"Just playing the field, eh?"

"No, I'd like to meet someone who ends up being a boyfriend," she said, although why she was telling Joel this she couldn't imagine. This was the most personal conversation she'd ever had with him. "I'd like to find someone special."

"Wouldn't we all, Ravyn? I'm just looking for some gal that won't take me to the cleaners like my last wife. Someone I can have a little fun with, if you know what I mean."

Ravyn didn't want to know what he meant.

"Well, good luck," Joel said, turning from her office.

"You, too."

Chapter 4

Ravyn's Honda Civic headed north on Interstate 85 toward the lake house on Lake Lanier in Gainesville. She had been to the lake house once before, not quite two years ago with Julie and two sisters Ravyn now considered friends, Lynne and Celia.

That first trip was a fun girls' weekend, with lots of cocktails, dancing on the outside deck, and racing jet skis in the lake. It also had an unfortunate episode with a glass eyeball from a stuffed bison head that hung over the flagstone fireplace.

Ravyn felt sure there would be more drinking, dancing, and shenanigans over Memorial Day weekend. She just hoped "Tom" the bison remained unmolested this time.

She pulled into the driveway behind Julie's SUV, got out of her Honda, and knocked on the front door.

"Hey! Welcome to party central!" Lynne said, opening the door with a glass of wine in her hand. "We're going to have so much fun this weekend. Like the last time we were all here."

"I'm looking forward to it. Let me get my bag. Should I leave my car here, or do you want me to move it somewhere else?"

"No, you're good there. Come in and get a drink. I think Julie is making some sangria."

Ravyn followed Lynne into the house, which had a large open living room. She glanced to the right and saw the large bison head. "Hello, Tom," she said.

Lynne laughed. "No climbing Tom this trip!"

"You're here!" Julie squealed, opening her arms to give Ravyn a big hug. "Ready for a drink? We're getting the party started!"

"I see. Yes, I'd love a glass," Ravyn said. To Lynne, she asked, "Where shall I put my bag?"

"I've put you in the bedroom you had before."

"Lovely. Back down to the left, correct?"

"Yes, just down the hall," Lynne said, pointing.

Ravyn opened her bedroom door, placing her bag on the huge queen bed. She almost started to unpack her bag but heard Julie call from the living room. "Hey, the pigs in a blanket appetizer are done! Come get them while they're hot!"

Ravyn would unpack later. Appetizers and sangria were calling her name.

Celia stood at the breakfast bar, which was off of the large living room. "Hey, Ravyn! I'm glad you could come."

"Me, too. Thanks for having me again this weekend. I'm looking forward to relaxing. My work has been a little stressful with my new boss."

"Oh yeah? What's he like?"

"It's a woman. And she's a bit of a control freak."

"Oh, yeah. That can be bad."

Julie handed Ravyn a large glass of sangria. "And Ravyn is on Tinder! Tell them about your date with the claustrophobic architect. That's hysterical."

"Julie, that was not hysterical. He was really freaked out." Ravyn turned to Celia and Lynne, who were listening intently. "We got stuck in an elevator. He had a bad time. He got sick after the elevator ride."

"Oh, that's rough," Lynne said.

"No, what's rough is what happened after Ravyn met another guy in the elevator and he took her out to dinner and he was married."

Ravyn rolled her eyes. That was a very painful experience and she didn't want Julie making light of it, but Julie's eyes were glassy. She looked like she'd had a couple of glasses of her concoction.

"Oh, that sucks. Do you see all the guys on Tinder who say they are in open marriages?" Celia asked.

Ravyn shook her head. "Makes you wonder if their wives know."

"So, you ended up with a player," Celia said. "It happens. Swipe left."

Ravyn laughed.

"Here, have some apps," Lynne said, presenting the pigs in a blanket on a plate.

"Speaking of apps, let me see your phone," Julie said. "I want to see this Tinder app. I want to see these men who have open marriages."

"Oh, Julie, I don't want you screening my Tinder dates."

"Why not? I'm your bestie. I should be your best wingman. Or wing woman."

Ravyn reached for her phone and opened the Tinder app. The profile of a man named Brad popped up. There were photos of Brad laughing, Brad with a puppy, Brad in front of a motorcycle, and then a shirtless Brad.

"Well, hello, Brad!" Julie exclaimed. "But no. Next," she said, swiping left on Ravyn's phone.

"Hey! Don't do that. You didn't even read his profile!" Ravyn tried to grab her phone back from Julie, but Julie spun around and looked at the next profile.

"Oh, hey, all this profile is me looking up Steve's nose," she said, turning the phone so the women could see a man's profile that was at an odd angle so that his nose looked prominent. Julie turned the phone back so she could see the rest of his photos, including him with a young girl. "Oh, she's cute."

Ravyn tried to grab the phone again, but Julie turned and showed them the photo of Steve with what appeared to be his daughter of about five. "Are you ready to be a stepmother?"

"Maybe. I'm not sure," Ravyn admitted.

"Swipe left," Julie said, swiping left on the profile. "That didn't sound like you are."

Ravyn grabbed for her phone a third time and managed to get it. "Stop it, Julie. We're not here to go through my Tinder dates. We're here to have fun."

"Oh, OK. But really, let me help you this weekend. Let us all help you. We can vote on who you pick next."

Ravyn rolled her eyes. She didn't want to date by committee. "We'll do that later. Pour me another glass of your sangria. It's delicious."

That Friday night ended with dinner out on the back deck, after all of the women had naps following the three pitchers of sangria.

With the dinner plates cleared, the women sat out on the deck drinking more wine, a fire in the fire pit.

"How do you like Tinder?" Celia asked. "Are you meeting lots of eligible men that way? And you know, decent men?"

"Well, I've only been on three dates and none of them will be getting a second date," Ravyn admitted.

"I'm not sure that is encouraging," Celia answered.

"No. It's not. But when I get to Atlanta after this weekend, I have another date with a guy named Jeremy. We're meeting at the Vortex in Midtown for lunch."

Julie seemed a little alarmed. "Who's this Jeremy?"

"Jeremy Stephens. He's a police officer with DeKalb police. He lives in Decatur, but he said he'd meet me near my condo, so we're going to the Vortex. I just hope we can sit outside. I don't like all the cigarette smoke in that place," Ravyn said.

"Why'd you pick it then?" Julie asked.

"He picked it. I think he might be a smoker."

"That will be a deal-breaker for you, Ravyn, right?' Julie said. "You need to let me help pick some of these men. We all can. Let me have your phone."

Ravyn sighed and handed over her phone. "Now don't swipe anything without my approval."

"I won't," Julie said, holding her red wine glass in one hand and Ravyn's phone in the other. Julie was mentally crossing her fingers behind her back in her head.

The women giggled at the shirtless torso shots, the big fish shots, or the motorcycle shots. They swiped left of anyone who only had a photo but didn't write a profile.

"Never trust a man who doesn't write a profile," Lynne said. "You have no idea what he's like."

"And swipe left to all the ones with typos or bad grammar," Julie said. Julie was hoping she would find Marc's fake profile, but she didn't see it. How many of these profiles were there on Tinder? she wondered. This might take a while.

"I don't know," Celia said. "Grammar's not the measure of a man. He may have a lot of life smarts, but not book smarts. I'd rather have a man who can fix my car than can quote Shakespeare."

"I do kind of agree with that," Ravyn said. "But I want him to be able to converse. I mean, you can't just have great sex. We have to be able to talk."

"Oh, if I'm having great sex, he can be mute," Lynne said. "In fact, it might be better if he didn't talk. I want a man who's taken a vow of silence."

The women laughed deep throaty laughs. Ravyn felt so comfortable among these women. Julie was one of her truest friends, but she considered Celia and Lynne good friends now too. They were her girlfriend posse.

"Another bottle?" Celia asked, holding up the empty wine bottle.

"Yes!" was the response from the other three women.

"Another Cabernet or something else? Chardonnay?"

"I want to stick with red. Cabernet is fine for me," Ravyn said.

"Same," Julie replied. "But bring out the bug spray, will you? The mosquitoes are getting thick."

"I'm so glad we're here. This is fun," Ravyn said, turning to her friends. "We need to make this an annual event."

"I'm in!"

"Me, too," Lynne said. "Maybe I can get the lake house later in the fall, like last year."

"Oh, my God. That would be great!" Ravyn said. "That was so much fun. And there won't be as many bugs and mosquitoes."

Celia returned with an open bottle of wine and placed it on the patio table. She also dropped a can of Deep Woods Off on the table, and the women began spraying arms and legs.

The sky had gone pink, then orange. It was a warm night, the humidity on the rise for late May, but the breeze off the lake kept the women comfortable. None of them wanted to move inside.

As the evening darkened, fireflies began their mating flashes in the trees surrounding the lake house. It made the evening fairy-like and magical.

The women sat silent, drinking in the wine and evening.

"But if that man was going to talk to you after great sex, what would he say?" Celia asked her sister.

"Want to go again?" Lynne deadpanned.

The women howled with laughter.

Julie began swiping through the Tinder profiles, showing the other women the faces. Some men were frowning, some were smiling.

"You know what you have there?" Lynne asked.

"No, what?" Julie asked.

"You have a lot of men who are on the No-Fly List," she said.

"What's a No-Fly List?" Ravyn asked.

"They are men who are trolling for women. They aren't going to treat their dates well. They just move on to the next one," Lynne said. "We should keep a list and put them on the No-Fly List, just like the airports do."

"I've got a couple we can add to the list," Ravyn said, giggling. "Sam the bartender, Tony the architect, Joe the sky waiter."

"What happened with Sam the bartender? You didn't tell us about him," Celia said.

"That was the guy I met in the elevator while on my almost-date with Tony the architect. Sam was the perfect date," Ravyn said, voice flat. "Until his wife told me not to contact him again."

A collective groan went out from the table.

"Sam's definitely on the No-Fly List," Lynne said.

"Then there was Joe who managed to cop a feel while 'helping' me," Ravyn said, making air quotes, "mop up a spilled drink on my blouse."

"Oh my God," Celia said. "I hope you punched him."

"That's what I said!" Julie exclaimed.

"He's now on the No-Fly List with a bullet," Lynne said, refilling her wine glass.

Eventually, the women moved inside, the mosquitoes getting thicker. Plus, the bottle of recently opened Cabernet was empty.

"I'll open another bottle," Lynne said. "I think this is the last one. We'll have to go into town for more tomorrow."

"I did bring rum for rum punch," Julie said.

"Oh boy, I'll have to wait until tomorrow for that," Ravyn said.

Julie and Ravyn sat on the couch in front of the unlit fireplace, alone for a moment while Celia and Lynne were busy elsewhere in the house.

"Hey, who were you with at lunch last week that you didn't tell Rob?" Ravyn asked.

"Oh, it was nothing. He's being paranoid," Julie scoffed.

"Are you seeing someone?" Ravyn asked bluntly.

"No," Julie replied, annoyed that her friend would think that. "Rob's the cheater, remember?"

"Julie, I'm not judging you."

"Feels like you are."

"No, I'm not. But I'm worried if you are out to lunch with some guy and using me as your excuse."

"No, there is no other man. I'm not stooping to Rob's level," Julie said sharply. Julie paused, thinking about what she'd said. "That came out a little harsh, sorry. It's just the wine talking."

"Is everything OK with you two? Really?"

"We're fine. I've forgiven him and the couple's therapy has helped. He's been going with me. Willingly even. But we're only going once a month now. I imagine we'll give it up soon."

"I'm glad it's worked out. It just caught me off guard when he called looking for you and thinking you were with me."

"I'm sorry. I should have used some other excuse. I was just out to lunch with a friend and I didn't want to explain."

"Explain what? Who were you with?"

"Just a friend."

"A guy friend?"

"Well, yes, but it's not like that. It's nothing. Nothing is going on with me and my guy friend. I'm not having an affair if that's what you want to know."

Ravyn was silent. She thought Julie was being evasive. If nothing was going on, why didn't she just say who she was having lunch with?

"OK. I was just worried about you."

"Well don't be. I'm fine. I can't have lunch with my tennis coach?" Julie said, thinking up a quick lie.

Tennis coach? Ravyn wondered. Julie never mentioned a tennis coach. She knew she was on an ALTA team, but didn't know she was taking lessons. Maybe that was all it was. But she still had doubts.

Celia re-entered the living room. "Anyone for a movie? Or cards?"

"I'm good. Just enjoying the wine and the friendship," Julie said.

"Same here," Ravyn said.

The women tucked themselves onto the leather couches and talked deep into the night, naming off past lovers or boyfriends to add to their collective No-Fly List and laughing at each others' stories. Shortly after 1 a.m., they drifted to their bedrooms, tipsy and sleepy.

Ravyn woke up Saturday to the smell of fresh-brewed coffee. She pulled on her pajama bottoms and straightened her T-shirt before wandering out to the open kitchen.

"Want a cup?" Celia asked.

"Yes, please. Do we have cream or milk?"

"We have some half and half."

"Perfect. Are Julie and Lynne up yet?"

"I heard the shower, so someone's up, but I'm not sure who."

Ravyn took a long drink of coffee. "That's better."

"Did you sleep well?"

"Like a rock. That mattress is great."

"Good. I'm glad you slept well. I'm starting to make a list of things we'll want for the weekend. I've got eggs and bacon for this morning's breakfast, but we'll need some things for lunch and dinner for the next couple of days."

"Great. I'll eat just about anything, but if you'd like I can roast a chicken tonight for dinner. It's a recipe from the cooking school I attended in Italy last fall. Then we could make chicken salad out of the leftovers for lunch tomorrow."

"That might work. I was thinking of getting some steaks too. The gas grill has a new tank."

"Yum. I love steak, but I live in a condo. We have some community grills, but they aren't cleaned well and are kind of gross."

Julie padded out in her robe, rubbing her eyes. "Coffee, please."

Celia poured her a cup.

"You sleep OK?"

"Yeah, but I had some trouble falling asleep. You'd think I would have slept well without Rob here to snore. I might have to schedule a nap this afternoon so I can party tonight," Julie said, wiggling her butt while sipping her coffee.

Lynne came out to the kitchen toweling off her wet hair. Celia poured her sister a cup of coffee. "I'm just putting a list together for food for the weekend. Ravyn's offered to roast a chicken and we can make chicken salad with the rest of it for lunch. I'm getting some steaks for Sunday. Any snacks we need?"

"We can get some chips, maybe a veggie tray and stuff for salad. Oh, and more wine," Julie said.

"I put wine first on the list," Celia said.

"You know us well," Julie laughed.

"For the chicken, we'll get some white wine. For the steaks let's get more of that Cabernet. That was good last night, right?"

"That was great. We better get more bottles than we think we'll need," Ravyn said.

"I'll go ahead and get a case," Celia said. "What we don't open we can take home."

"Do you want me to give you cash?" Ravyn asked.

"Let me go to the store and you can either PayPal or Venmo me."

"OK, great."

"What do you need for the chicken?" Celia asked.

"I've got the recipe in my bedroom. Let me get it and give you the list."

Ravyn walked into her bedroom and heard a chirp from her phone. It was a text from Jeremy, the guy she was meeting next week for lunch.

Hey, Ravyn. My hours got shifted. I'm free today for lunch if you are. I'm excited to meet you. You are gorgeous.

Thanks. But I can't meet today. I'm up at Lake Lanier this weekend with friends. But can you still make it next week?

I think so. My new schedule comes out Tuesday. I'll let you know. Lake sounds nice. Have fun.

I will. I'm looking forward to meeting you.

Ravyn went to the Tinder app to look at Jeremy's profile. He was cute. He had short-cropped brown hair and was muscular. She liked that. And he was a cop.

Ravyn had covered the police department when she was a reporter for the Atlanta daily newspaper years ago. She had known some police officers then. She'd heard the rumors about some of them, having affairs and generally being bad boys.

Jeremy looked nice. He had a nice smile. She hoped he was one of the good guys.

Celia returned with several bags of groceries and Ravyn was surprised that they'd need so much for the weekend. And then there was nearly a case of wine. Would they need that much? Well, maybe.

The women had sandwiches for lunch, then took the SeaDoos out on the lake. Celia drove one with Julie on the back. Lynne drove the one with Ravyn on the back.

They raced across Lake Lanier, Ravyn's ponytail snapping behind her.

Lynne throttled back to a stop in the middle of a channel. "Hey, do you want to switch? Do you want to drive?"

Ravyn did want to drive the jet ski, but she was a little unsure of herself. "Yes," she shouted over the noise of the engine. "But I might need some help."

"No worries," Lynne responded. "I'll help."

The pair gingerly changed places on the SeaDoo, Ravyn wrapping the emergency stop around her wrist.

Ravyn pulled on the throttle to give the SeaDoo a little gas. It leapt forward. Ravyn, spooked, pulled back, slowing the device.

"Go ahead and give it some gas," Lynne shouted in Ravyn's ear. "It will be OK."

Ravyn gave the SeaDoo another tug on the gas, and it pulled forward. This time, she didn't throttle back. She quickly picked up speed and felt a rush of adrenaline. They raced across the lake. Ravyn felt free.

Ravyn and Lynne eventually caught up to Celia and Julie, and the four women slowed in an inlet.

"Race you back to the house," Celia called out. "I'm ready for happy hour!"

Celia roared off. Ravyn opened the throttle and chased after her.

Julie stirred a pitcher of rum runners, then checked the oven to see if the pizza rolls and mini quiches were done.

Ravyn popped a quiche in her mouth and immediately regretted it. She began blowing through her teeth and waving her hand but knew she had burned her tongue. She quickly grabbed a glass of the rum punch and took a long swig. Her eyes began to water.

"That's strong," she choked out.

"Should I add more orange juice?" Julie asked.

"If you don't, I won't be able to stand up and cook dinner tonight. I'll be passed out."

"Party pooper," Julie laughed, as she reached for the orange juice and poured more in the concoction.

"Hey, what smells good?" Lynne asked.

"The appetizers," Julie answered. "Careful, they're hot. Ravyn learned the hard way."

Julie poured Lynne and Celia drinks and the four women clinked glasses.

"Ravyn made me put more orange juice in, but if you want the rum runner's stronger, there's more Captain Morgan over there," Julie teased.

"I didn't make you," Ravyn protested. "I should have just added the orange juice to mine."

"Oh, yeah, oh well."

Celia took a sip and reached for the rum. "Well, I'm not driving tonight and I'm not cooking dinner. Let's spice this up just a bit."

"I'll start dinner in a little while," Ravyn said. "It should be ready by about 7, so don't eat too many appetizers."

"Sounds good. I'm looking forward to it," Lynne said.

"Hey, show us the cute cop you are meeting next week," Celia said.

Ravyn walked back into her bedroom to get her phone from the charger. She opened up the Tinder app and showed the match to Celia.

"Oh, he is cute. Jeremy?"

"Yes. That's him. He works for DeKalb County police. He lives in an apartment in Decatur and I think he's got a roommate."

Celia handed the phone to Lynne. "He is cute," Lynne agreed. "What's your profile look like? Can I see it?"

"Sure." Ravyn took her phone back and opened her profile. She'd put several photos on it. Ravyn on top of Stone Mountain. Ravyn after some 5K races. Ravyn on vacation. They were pretty standard photos.

Ravyn put her phone down, but Julie immediately picked it up. She hadn't been able to find Marc's fake profile and needed an excuse to search for it with Ravyn's unlocked phone.

"Hey, no swiping on anybody. I don't want to find I'm matched with random men," Ravyn admonished.

“Come on,” Julie said. “Some of these guys are so not you. Look at this guy. He’s got lots of tattoos. You don’t like these flashy large ones. I know you.”

“I like tattoos,” Ravyn protested.

“You liked Luca’s tattoos because they were attached to Luca,” Julie said, grinning slyly.

“Well, you’re not wrong there,” Ravyn admitted, feeling the warmth of the rum cocktail running through her.

“Luca had tattoos?” Celia asked.

“He had one of those armbands on his upper arm,” Ravyn said, wrapping her hand around her upper arm, about where Luca’s tattoo had been, “and he had a dragon tattoo on his hip.” Ravyn touched her left hip.

“On his hip?” Lynne asked.

Ravyn blushed. “Well, yes.”

“You lucky, lucky girl,” Lynne said, giggling.

Chapter 5

The weekend seemed to fly by, with the women enjoying the sun, the water, and each other's company.

Julie was getting panicked, not having found Marc's profile on Tinder. She kept trying to think of excuses to look at Ravyn's phone but hadn't gotten a chance to do any more sleuthing.

But Julie caught a break Monday morning, finding Ravyn's phone on the kitchen counter. Now, what was her password? On a whim, she typed in the numeric code for "Felix," the name of Ravyn's cat.

Bingo! The phone unlocked.

Julie quickly opened the Tinder app and sat on the couch with her coffee, swiping left of anyone who wasn't Marc. She swiped probably a dozen profiles and was feeling doubtful when she found "Edward." Julie recognized the photos of Marc's brother, Bruce.

Julie quickly gave him a "Super Like," ensuring that Ravyn would be a match. She watched as the app alerted to a match. Julie clicked on the app to accept the match. At least Ravyn wouldn't notice the new match right away, Julie thought.

She then pulled out her cell phone to text Marc to let him know she'd found him and made the match.

Marc, I found you on Tinder and matched you with Ravyn. Why don't you message her?

Julie waited to see if he got the message, but no response bubbles appeared.

Julie could hear her friends stirring and quickly got up to start another pot of coffee in the kitchen, replacing Ravyn's phone on the counter.

Ravyn came out of her bedroom to the smell of freshly brewed coffee.

"Julie, you're up early," Ravyn said.

"I think it's ingrained in my head to get up early. I'm always up early for the girls."

"I get that. I'm up almost earlier on the weekends to go run before it gets too hot or to get ready for a 5K race than I am when I get up for work. Hey, I'll take a cup of that coffee."

"Sure," Julie said, handing over a cup.

"Oh, I didn't realize I left my phone out here," Ravyn said, looking at the iPhone on the kitchen counter. She turned it on but didn't see any messages. She was hoping Jeremy had sent her one, but there was none.

Ravyn put her phone face down and sipped from her coffee. "What time are we leaving today?"

"I'm guessing just after lunch," Julie replied. "Do you have to be somewhere this afternoon?"

"No, I was just hoping I'd hear from Jeremy. I've got my neighbor Jack watching Felix, so I don't have to get back right away."

"Jack who ordered up porn on your cable while you were on vacation in Italy?" Julie asked, sarcastically.

"That's the one."

"I don't know why you let him in your condo again."

"He did apologize and pay for the porn charge."

Julie rolled her eyes. "Listen to what you are saying."

Ravyn's neighbor Jack had helped himself to a porn movie on her cable TV while she vacation was in Rome last year. He had apologized, but Ravyn felt bad that she'd had to keep the secret from Jack's girlfriend, Liz.

"Yeah, I know. I better not have another porn movie on my credit card bill this trip."

Celia and Lynne came into the kitchen, both reaching for coffee cups. Celia looked a bit hungover. They had all danced and drank late into the night, but Ravyn had turned in after midnight. The sisters had stayed up a little longer.

"Good morning," Julie smiled. "You look like you need a little more than coffee. A bit of the hair of the dog?"

"What do you have?" Celia asked.

"I can whip up some Bloody Marys," Julie said.

"Dear God, yes," Celia said.

"Oh wait? There's stuff for Bloody Marys?" Lynne asked. "Why didn't you say that yesterday?"

"Because we had mimosas!" Julie exclaimed. "We finished up the orange juice, or I'd offer those."

"Is there Prosecco left?" Lynne asked.

"Nope. Remember we drank the rest of that after the orange juice was gone," Julie said.

"Oh, right," Lynne said.

"OK, bloodies it is," Celia said. "I'll take one."

Lynne and Ravyn looked at each other and nodded. Maybe there would be time for a quick nap before they left the lake house, Ravyn thought.

Julie was pretty generous with the vodka, but the Bloody Mary mix, celery stick, olives and slice of cold bacon worked wonders on Celia and Lynne. Ravyn, who wasn't hungover, relished the drink.

Suddenly, Julie's phone trilled a text message. She looked at it and smiled, texting back. It was from Marc.

Thanks for that. I'll message her.

Don't do it now. She's here in the kitchen and might hear the alert. Do it later.

Oh, OK. Thanks again

No problem

Want to have lunch this week to plan what's next? Marc asked.

Sure. Let's do that.

"Is that Rob?" Ravyn asked.

Julie looked up, surprised.

"Oh, yes. He was letting me know about the girls," Julie lied.

Ravyn took another sip of her morning cocktail, eyeing her best friend. Why didn't she believe her?

"I'm going to need another one of these," Celia said, draining her glass.

"Oh yes," Lynne said.

Ravyn shook her head no when Julie began another batch of drinks.

"What are we doing today?" Ravyn asked. "Do I need to strip the bed?"

"You don't have to do that," Lynne said. "I've got the cleaning woman coming tomorrow to do all that and clean the towels and all. Just leave the old towels on the floor of your bathroom."

"OK. Can I help with the cleaning woman's fee?" Ravyn asked.

"Nope. My treat. This has been so much fun this weekend," Lynne said. "I needed a weekend like this."

"Let's take the SeaDoos out for one last spin," Celia said.

"I'm game," Lynne said. She turned to Julie and Ravyn. "You two up for one last ride?"

"Hell, yes!" Julie said. "I'll just leave these drinks for when we come back." Ravyn nodded in assent as she drained her Bloody Mary.

The women quickly got into their bathing suits, strapping on the life vests, and waited for the SeaDoos to lower from the lifts into the lake.

"Do you want to drive first?" Lynne asked Ravyn.

"Yes. Thanks to all the experience on the lake, I feel ready."

Ravyn climbed into the driver's position, while Lynne climbed on back. They slowly rode out to the no-wake buoy.

Suddenly, Ravyn had a memory of her time with Luca, her Italian lover, holding on to the back of Luca as he zipped all over Rome on his motorcycle.

She smiled. Now she was in the driver's seat. She almost wished he could see her, taking control.

"Ready?" Celia asked from her driver's seat.

"Ready!" Ravyn answered back.

Celia roared off, Ravyn right behind.

Ravyn had driven out first, but Lynne had driven next and pulled into the lift that would store the SeaDoos. Ravyn wasn't quite ready to maneuver the SeaDoo into the lifts and was glad Lynne had done it.

Ravyn felt the sting of the hot water in the shower, enjoying the warmth after the rides on the SeaDoos.

The water ran over Ravyn's skin, and she began to think of Jeremy Stephens. She'd never even met Jeremy, but she was fantasizing about him. She thought about what he might look like naked. His hard body. His harder erection.

Ravyn was aroused just thinking about him. She moved the warm soapy washcloth between her legs and moaned, feeling her legs go weak. Ravyn nearly called out.

She held onto the shower door and quickly rinsed off. Panting, Ravyn turned off the shower and reached for a soft towel. Whew, she thought, I hope Jeremy is worthy of that.

The women ate leftovers for lunch and then cleaned the kitchen. Ravyn packed her weekend bag, then her car. She was sorry to be saying goodbye to her friends. The lake weekend had been refreshing.

Ravyn turned her Honda Civic south on Interstate 985 toward Atlanta, her car packed with a few of the groceries they hadn't eaten at the lake house that weekend. She even had one bottle of wine they hadn't drunk.

She pulled into her condo parking lot about 4 p.m. She dragged her luggage and hauled the bag filled with groceries to the condo elevator and dropped everything just inside her front door.

Felix, her gray tomcat chirped his hello.

"Hey, Felix. How's my big boy?" Ravyn said, scratching his blocky head. "You didn't watch any porn while I was gone, did you?"

Ravyn would be sure to check her credit card bill next month, just to be sure.

Ravyn put the groceries away and lugged her bag into the bedroom.

She then checked her text messages, hoping to find one from Jeremy. There were none. She decided to send one to him.

I'm home from the lake. Hope you had an uneventful weekend. Was it busy?

She didn't see any text response and then checked the Tinder app.

Ravyn saw one for a guy named Evan. He was a new match. She remembered swiping right on him a few days ago. But she was surprised to see a match with a guy named Edward. Who the hell was that? Ravyn wondered.

Ravyn immediately texted Julie.

Hey, were you messing with my Tinder app? I have a match with a guy I don't recognize.

Sorry, Julie responded. I might have accidentally touched something.

Well, at least he's cute.

Who is he?

His name is Edward. He has nice eyes.

Why don't you give him a chance?

Well, I won't unmatch him right away. I'll see if he messages me.

Right.

Julie immediately texted Marc to go ahead and message Ravyn on Tinder.

The Tuesday after the Memorial Day holiday seemed to drag on.

Ravyn got to work and rushed to assign out freelance stories for the next issue.

Jennifer Bagley breezed into Ravyn's office about mid-morning.

"What has Joel been telling you about his ad sales for the month?" Jennifer asked.

Ravyn looked up. "What?"

"What has Joel told you about his ad sales? Have they been on target for the month?"

"He hasn't talked to me about that. Why do you ask?"

"I think he's lying to me about ad sales," Jennifer said, crossing her arms and frowning. "I think he's trying to undermine me. You will let me know if he says anything to you, won't you?"

Ravyn knew not to say no to Jennifer. "Of course. I'll let you know if Joel says anything."

Jennifer turned to leave Ravyn's office, then turned back to face her. "I knew I could count on you."

Ravyn wasn't quite sure she could help Jennifer. She knew Jennifer and Joel weren't friends. They seemed to tolerate each other for the sake of work. But there seemed to be an undercurrent of veiled hatred between them.

Ravyn returned to her work when she looked up and noticed Joel at her door.

"Can I help you?" Ravyn asked.

"I saw Jennifer in your office earlier," he said. "What did she say to you?"

"Joel, she was asking about you," Ravyn said. "What is going on with you two?"

"She's just being a bitch. She'd been hounding me about ad sales. I'm on target, but she wants more. Seriously, I think she just needs to get laid."

"Joel, you don't have to be crude," Ravyn said.

"No, I'm serious. You know she's single. She's been single for a long time, divorced or something. Although who would marry her is beyond me. I think she just needs a boyfriend. That will take her mind off work."

"Joel, I don't think we should be talking about Jennifer's personal life," Ravyn started to say.

"Why not? Don't tell me you're one of those feminists. Or feminazis. Don't be so uptight, Ravyn."

Ravyn squirmed in her chair, uncomfortable with Joel's conversation.

She took a deep breath. "Joel, I don't appreciate your tone. You should not be disrespectful to me or Jennifer."

Joel grimaced and muttered as he left Ravyn's office, "Just as I suspected. A fucking feminist."

Ravyn was happy for the workday to end. She threw her mail on the kitchen counter, Felix winding around her feet as she walked to get his cat food for the evening.

After Felix's needs were met, she pulled off her work clothes, changing into yoga pants and a race T-shirt. She tied her brown hair into a ponytail and returned to the kitchen to fix dinner.

With a chicken breast sautéing in a pan, Ravyn checked her mail. There was a letter from the investor who owned her condo.

Dear Ms. Shaw,

As a reminder, your lease will be up Sept. 1, 2015. I have decided to sell the condo. I am giving you the first option should you choose to purchase the condo at market rates. My real estate agent believes the unit will command a price of $250,000. Please let me know by June 30, 2015, if you intend to buy the condo and we can begin the internal purchase process. If I don't hear from you by June 30, I will place the condo on the market and you will have until Aug. 31, 2015, to vacate the property.

Please let me know if you have any questions,

Sincerely,

Keith Spanner

Spanner Properties Inc.

Ravyn's hands began to shake as she finished the letter. Selling her condo? Where will she live? Could she afford to buy this place she'd called home for more than six years? She loved this place. It was in a great location and perfect for her. What was she going to do?

Ravyn immediately called Julie.

"Hey, bestie, what's up?" Julie asked.

Ravyn could hardly keep her voice from cracking. "I just got a notice from my landlord. He wants to sell my place!"

"What? What did he say?"

"He sent me a letter that I got today. He wants to sell my place. He's giving me 30 days to either say I'm buying it or I have to get out."

"Thirty days? That's not enough time."

"No, if I'm not buying, I have to be out in 90 days."

"Wait, what? What does the letter say? Read it to me."

Ravyn pulled the letter and read it to Julie.

"OK. Let me run it by one of my tennis partners. Her husband is a lawyer. And my other partner is a real estate agent. She can help you with the buying process if you need that."

"Julie, I'm not sure I can afford a mortgage payment. I don't have much savings. I could make my rent, but it's always been a bit tight. I'm just glad I don't have a car payment on top of it."

"Well, let's run the letter by a lawyer first, and I'll have my friend Cindy Freeman call you. She's the real estate agent. You should probably call your bank to see about a mortgage. You may be surprised. You may qualify. And can you ask your parents to help you with a down payment?"

"I'm not sure, Julie. My parents are pretty much footing the bill for Jane's wedding. I don't think they'd be able to help with a down payment on top of that."

"Oh, right. What's new with the wedding?"

"I'm supposed to go up to South Carolina at the end of June to help Jane pick out her dress. But that will be too late to talk to my folks. I have until the end of June to let my landlord know if I can buy it."

"Well, why don't you call your mom tonight and ask if they can help. Then call your bank tomorrow and get that started."

"Thank you, Julie. Thanks for helping me. I'm scared. I don't want to lose my home." Ravyn's voice broke. She didn't want to cry, but a sob came out.

"Honey, you won't lose your home. We'll figure this out. Love you, Ravyn. It will be OK, OK?"

"OK," Ravyn squeaked. "Love you, too." She hung up and cried.

Ravyn dreaded the call to her parents. She'd always been independent, not ever asking for help, even when her freelance work fell far short of her monetary needs. She'd always managed to eke out the rent, even if her diet had to be peanut butter and ramen noodles.

"Mom?" she asked.

"Ravyn? What's wrong?"

Ravyn knew her mother could hear the distress in her voice. "Oh, Mom," Ravyn began to cry again. Through her tears, she explained what was happening with her condo and how she would have to move out if she couldn't buy the unit.

"I don't know what kind of down payment I'll have to make. I'll go to the bank tomorrow to see if I can even qualify for a mortgage," Ravyn said.

Her mother Kaye was quiet, then asked, "Ravyn, are you sure you want to buy the condo? You will end up tied to that property for several years. What if you meet someone and want to get married? That place is too small for two people. It's perfect for you, but not another person. Maybe you should look for an apartment, or at least another condo to rent. Have you thought about that?"

Ravyn knew her mother was giving sound advice. She hadn't thought about renting another place, and there could be other units in her condo tower for rent. She didn't know. But she knew she loved the place where she lived. She loved looking south toward downtown Atlanta, seeing the skyline lit at night. She didn't want to give that up. She didn't want to move. She wanted everything to stay the same.

"Honey, are you there?" Kaye asked gently.

"Yes, Mom. I'm here. It's just…"

"I know, honey. Change is hard."

"It's just, my job has been stressful, and now this!"

"What's up with your job? I thought you loved it."

"I do love it, but my new boss is a bit hard to work with. She's a real micromanager, and it sort of rubs me the wrong way."

"Ravyn, you know you've always been stubborn and independent. You might have to look at yourself and how you are reacting."

"Yes, Mom."

"Don't 'Yes, Mom' me. You need to see how you may be contributing to the situation. I love you, honey, but you need to look within, too."

"OK, I will. But if I decide I want to buy the condo, would you and Dad be able to help me with the down payment if I need it?"

Kaye was silent again. "Ravyn, you know we are helping Jane with the wedding," she began.

"I know. And I don't want to have to ask for money. I just want to know if there was a way you could help if I needed it."

"Honey, we'd try our best to help you, but we may not be in a position…" Kaye paused.

"I understand," Ravyn said, a bit angry that her parents were helping Jane and would not be able to help her. "I'll go to the bank tomorrow. I've probably asked too soon. I might not need any help at all."

"Honey, you know we'd want to help you, too. It's just with the wedding," Kaye said, trailing off.

"No, I understand," Ravyn said, trying not to sound angry.

Kaye could tell she was. "Ravyn, we love you and your sister. This is her time now."

"I know, Mom," Ravyn said. "I love you, and I'm sorry I even had to ask for help."

"Ravyn, you are my stubborn and independent daughter. I'm glad you are asking for help. If we can, you know we will. Let me know what you find out from the bank. And reconsider buying. Maybe a new rental will be just the thing for you right now. Love you."

"Love you, too, Mom."

Ravyn hung up feeling unsettled. She knew her mother's advice was probably sound. Maybe she should just find another rental until her finances were more secure. She might be able to find another condo to rent in her building. That would be ideal.

She'd hate to have to give up her view, but if it meant moving from one floor to another, it would be better than moving to a new building entirely. She'd have to rent a moving truck for that. If she found a new place on another floor, she could just move a bit at a time.

She'd meet with the property manager tomorrow to see what might be available. For the first time since getting the letter, Ravyn felt a little bit better.

Chapter 6

Ravyn went online and filled out the loan forms before she made an appointment to meet with a loan officer at her bank on Friday. She had a list of documents she needed to bring. The loan officer seemed to think that she could come up with a way for Ravyn to purchase the condo if she wanted it.

Jeremy Stephens also had texted and they were planning on having lunch Thursday. She was looking forward to it. It would keep her mind on something other than her housing situation.

Work also took Ravyn's mind off her condo. She worked later than normal Wednesday night so she could take a longer lunch with Jeremy. She got home with a bag of takeout, kicked off her shoes, and reached for a bottle of white wine to go with her chicken curry.

She opened the wine and then fed Felix. Two glasses in, she was feeling relaxed. She reached for her phone to text Jeremy.

Hey, looking forward to lunch tomorrow. Are you working tonight?

There was no response. He must be working, she thought.

Ravyn then checked the Tinder app, finding a message from the match named Edward.

Hi Mizzou Gal. Do you have a real name? I'm Edward, but my friends call me Ed. You have beautiful eyes.

Ravyn hesitated. With Jeremy, Evan and Edward, she didn't want to have too many Tinder matches going at once. She hoped she could quit after meeting with Jeremy.

She decided to answer Ed.

Hi Ed. My real name is Ravyn. How long have you been on Tinder?

Ravyn waited but didn't see a response. She put her phone down and washed her dinner plate. Soon she heard a buzz from her phone. Ed had responded.

I've only been on here a couple of weeks, Marc said, answering as his profile Ed. How long have you been on?

About a month, Ravyn responded. What are you looking for here?

I'm hoping to find a long-term relationship. And you?

Same.

Are you divorced? Marc asked. He'd been glad he'd been poking around the Tinder profiles, reading those of other women. He knew to ask if Ravyn was divorced, even though he knew the answer.

No. I'm single. No kids. And you?

I'm divorced, Marc responded. No kids.

Any pets? Ravyn asked.

No pets. I had a dog as a kid. How about you?

I have a cat, Felix. Are you allergic to pets?

No. I'm not allergic to pets. And I like cats.

Ravyn gave a smiley face emoji. She liked a man who liked cats. Where do you live in Atlanta?

Marc was caught off guard. Where was he supposed to say he lived? It might tip Ravyn off if he said he lived in the Garden Hills neighborhood of Buckhead.

I live in an apartment, not far from Lenox Square, he lied. He'd seen those apartments, but he had no idea if an "IT guy" could afford one.

I'm in Midtown. What do you do for a living?

Marc almost responded that he was an entrepreneur, but caught himself, remembering the fake profile he had created. I'm in IT, he responded. What do you do?

I work as an editor at a lifestyle magazine, she responded.

Cool, Marc responded, as Ed, certainly knowing full well what Ravyn did for a living. Have you been an editor for a long time?

No, Ravyn responded. I've been at the magazine for about 18 months. Before that, I had my own freelance business.

That sounds exciting, Marc said.

Not really. It was hard to be my own boss.

Marc nearly replied that he understood, but quickly deleted what he had typed. He needed to keep to the script of the fake profile he and Julie had created. He was finding it a bit hard since he wanted to tell Ravyn who he was. But he played along as Ed.

So, what are you doing tonight? Marc asked.

I just finished dinner. Take out. It's been a long day.

Do you work long hours? Marc asked.

No, not often. But I did tonight. Ravyn didn't want to tell a new match she had stayed late so she could have a longer lunch with another match. What are you doing tonight?

I just got home from the gym. I'll fix dinner in a little while.

Can you cook? Ravyn asked.

Well, I can boil water and make ramen noodles, Marc answered, thinking he was being clever as a classic geek.

Ravyn frowned. Ramen noodles?

Marc looked at his phone. Maybe he wasn't as clever as he thought. Oh, no. I'm grilling some chicken tonight. I was trying to be funny. Guess I wasn't.

Ravyn sighed. This conversation was going nowhere, she thought. Well, Ed, I've got to go. Have a good evening.

You too, Marc said, although he wanted to keep talking to Ravyn. He wanted to talk to her all night.

Ravyn looked at the Tinder app and Ed's match. She contemplated unmatching him. She didn't feel a connection with him. But her finger hesitated on the unmatch icon. Just in case it didn't go well with Jeremy tomorrow or the other match, Evan, she'd keep Ed's match open. He still looked pretty cute to her. Maybe he was more personable in real life.

Ravyn had parked her Honda in her condo's lot and walked down to The Vortex when she saw Jeremy Stephens, with his dark hair in a military haircut, waiting outside.

"Hi, Ravyn?" he asked.

"Yes. Am I late?"

"No, I got here a little early. I was coming from Decatur." Jeremy held the door for Ravyn as they went inside. He held up two fingers, indicating it was the pair of them for lunch.

"Oh, right. I haven't been here in a while. I live right down the street."

"Really? You must make a mint. I can't afford to live in the city on a cop's salary," he said. "That's why I'm in an apartment with another cop as my roommate."

The comment struck Ravyn as rude. She didn't make a mint. She had been fortunate to have found her condo and that her landlord, or maybe ex-landlord, had given her a break on the rent for all these years.

"Do you like being a cop?" she said as they were shown to their table. It was in an area with scorpions under glass on the wall. Ravyn gave an involuntary shudder.

Large stuffed animal heads hung above them and the music was loud. The restaurant was also smokey. Now Ravyn remembered why she hadn't been to the restaurant in a long while.

"I love it," Jeremy said. "Kind of an adrenaline rush when we go out on a serious call."

"So, it's dangerous?" she asked.

"Not always. Mostly it's routine. Driving around the county and answering pretty mundane calls. Neighborhood noise complaints, stuff like that. But at night you get the drunk and disorderly calls. That can be kind of wild. People who are chill by day become obnoxious when they are drunk or high. Then they want to fight you."

"You've gotten into fights at work?"

"Oh, yeah. Comes with the territory. What are you having? I'm thinking about a burger," Jeremy said, looking over the menu.

"Burger sounds good."

The waiter arrived sporting two sleeves of tattoos and several piercings. They placed their orders and continued to talk.

Ravyn learned Jeremy had done a short stint in the military out of high school, married his high school sweetheart before entering the military, and then divorced shortly after coming out of the military. Jeremy's having been in the military before he became a cop made sense to her now.

"The military and marriage didn't mix for me," he said. "I was always gone. When I came back stateside, we were strangers."

"I'm sorry to hear that."

"I'm just glad we never had kids."

"Do you want children?"

"Yeah, eventually. What about you?"

"I'd like children one day. But I'd like to get to know the person I marry first. I don't want children right away."

"Right."

"And you joined the DeKalb police right after the military?"

"Yeah. My brother was living here and I just got divorced. I thought I needed a fresh start, so I moved here. I was lucky I got hired. There were all those hiring freezes when I first got here."

"Oh, right."

"I thought I was going to have to join a really small department and then work my way to a larger one. But I got hired."

"And you seem to like it."

"I do. It has its moments. People can be awful to each other. But I like helping people, too. Last week, I got a call about kids being loud in a neighborhood. I pulled up and they were trying to play basketball with a crappy ball. I went over to Walmart and bought them a new one."

Ravyn was touched by this small act of kindness. She was liking Jeremy even more for his big heart.

"That was nice of you," she said, smiling at him.

"It was nothing."

They finished their meal, and Jeremy quickly took the check.

"We should split it," Ravyn protested.

"Absolutely not," he said. "My treat."

"Well, thank you. I've enjoyed this lunch and I've enjoyed meeting you."

"Yeah. I'd like to do it again."

"That would be lovely."

"Maybe dinner? A movie?"

"Sure. I haven't been to a movie in a while. I don't even know what's playing."

"I'd like to see the new Avengers movie," Jeremy said. "Do you like the Avengers?"

"I think I saw the first one, but I haven't seen any of the others. Can I see it without watching the others? Will I get it?"

"I think so."

"I'll check my schedule and then see when the movies are playing. Can I text you?"

"Sure. That will be great."

They started to leave the restaurant, walking toward a giant wooden phallus near the hostess stand. Jeremy reached out and rubbed the top of it, ran his hand down the shaft, and grinned at Ravyn. "For luck."

Ravyn was nervous as she waited at the bank to meet with the loan officer.

A tall brunette woman, slightly older, came forward to shake Ravyn's hand. "I'm Mrs. Melcher. But please call me Jill. Ravyn, is it? That's an unusual name. I don't think I've ever had a client named Ravyn."

"I bet. My parents were really into J.R.R. Tolkien," she answered reaching out to shake her hand, almost dropping the folder that held all of her financial documents she was told to bring.

"Ah," Jill said. "Please come this way." Jill Melcher led Ravyn back to a glassed office and shut the door. "I understand you are interested in purchasing a condominium?"

"Yes. I've been renting it for years and my landlord now wants to sell it. He's giving the option to buy, but I don't know if I can afford a mortgage. I just don't know. I hope this will help me find out."

"We're certainly here to help people into their dream homes."

Ravyn sat down in the chair opposite Jill's desk and handed over her folder.

"OK, let's get started," she said. "You said you've been steadily employed for about 18 months?"

"Yes," Ravyn said.

"Is there a reason for the short employment history?"

"Well, I got laid off several years ago from the daily newspaper, so I opened my own freelance business. I was working, but it wasn't always a steady income."

"So, you do have tax records for those years?" Jill asked.

"Yes. I do," Ravyn said. "They are in the folder."

Jill Melcher looked through the documents, pulling out Ravyn's most recent pay stubs and her last W-2. "And you own your car? There's no loan on that?"

"I have a loan on my Honda, but it's nearly paid off."

"What about student loans?"

"Those are paid off."

"Do you have any down payment to apply?"

"I don't. I've asked my parents, but they are paying for my sister's wedding. They can't help."

"That's understandable."

Jill Melcher typed on her computer. "Well, based on the preliminary figures, with an ARM loan, and a second mortgage to cover the down payment, you could probably afford something in the $130,000 range."

Ravyn's face fell. "$130,000?"

"I know that's a little low for the Midtown market. You could probably afford something in the suburbs though, maybe a townhouse?"

"The suburbs? I want to keep living in Midtown."

"You might find something in that price range in Midtown. You never know. I just meant you'll get more house for your money in the suburbs."

"Oh, oh yes," Ravyn said, trying to keep her voice steady. She didn't want to cry in front of the loan officer.

"Shall I start the paperwork?" Jill Melcher asked.

"Let me check out what I can afford in my price range first. I'll call you then to start the paperwork. You said it would be better to be pre-approved, right?"

"Yes, if you are pre-approved it can make the home buying process easier. It shows you are a serious buyer. And you are a serious buyer, correct?"

"Yes, I hope so. If I can find a condo for that price."

"You don't think your condo is that price?"

"I know it's not. The investor wants to sell it for $250,000."

"Oh, I'm sorry. We couldn't approve a loan for that."

Ravyn blinked back tears. "I understand."

"Ravyn, I know you are disappointed. But we don't want you to be in over your head with the loan. I'm sure you remember the housing crisis and mortgage defaults that led up to the Great Recession."

"I was laid off because of the Great Recession. I struggled to survive after that. I remember very well."

Jill Melcher shifted uncomfortably in her chair. "Well, yes. And today's loan standards mean we won't put our customers in loans they can't afford. It's for your protection as well as ours."

Jill Melcher handed Ravyn's folder back to her. "Please let us know when you find a potential home and let us know right away so we can get your pre-approval ready."

"I will."

Ravyn walked back to her car, trying not to cry before she got there. She shut the door to her Honda and sobbed.

Marc waited at the hostess stand at El Scorpion in Midtown. The hostess wouldn't seat him until Julie arrived.

When she got there, they got a table inside the restaurant. The hostess had offered the one table still on the outside patio, but Julie shook her off. "I'll be too hot," she explained to Marc.

"So, how has your day been going?" Marc asked.

"Good. I had my tennis lesson this morning. I'm getting better. But I had to make an excuse to my husband that I was meeting a tennis partner for lunch. I couldn't use Ravyn as an excuse again. My husband called her the last time we had lunch. I had to make up an excuse that I was with my tennis instructor."

"I don't want to get you in trouble."

"Don't worry. Trust me, my husband would do well to think I'm off to lunch with a sexy man."

Marc smiled. He liked being called sexy.

"What's the smile for?"

"No reason. How long have you been taking tennis lessons?"

"About two months. And my instructor isn't a man, it's a woman. But I told Ravyn it was a man so I had an excuse to have that lunch at Marlow's Tavern with you. Don't let her know."

"She won't even take my calls or texts. Believe me, she won't know."

"Oh right. But you said she texted you on Tinder, right? That's a good sign."

The waitress arrived. Julie immediately ordered a margarita and the taco plate special. Marc did the same.

"I almost forgot I was supposed to be Edward, or Ed. I nearly gave myself away. But I caught myself, so I'm keeping to the fake profile. But I haven't heard from her in a few days. Should I text her?"

"Marc, she's been a bit preoccupied. The investor who owns her condo wants to sell. She either needs to buy or get out in three months."

Marc was silent. "But she loves that place."

"She does. She met with a loan officer to see if she could afford her condo for its market price. She can't."

"Oh. What is she going to do?"

"Well, she's on a waiting list at her condo's property management office to rent another place. And she's looking for other properties to buy in Midtown. Now, how has your day been going?"

Just then the waitress arrived with the drinks order. Julie had the margarita with salt on the rim. Marc had his without salt.

"It's going well. Can I tell you something in confidence?"

"Of course."

"I have someone interested in investing in LindMark."

Julie's eyes grew wide. "Really? Marc, that's huge!"

"Hey, quiet. I can't talk about it, but I'm excited. If this happens, I can clear a lot of personal debt."

Now Julie was surprised. "I thought you were doing well. What debt do you have?"

"I've had to borrow from my parents to keep my company afloat. Things are going well now, and I'm paying back my parents. But if these investors buy into my company, it will be really great."

"I'm happy for you. I hope it happens. Now, what is your next plan with Ravyn?"

"Well, I guess I'll text her again. I just liked talking to her. I miss her."

Julie frowned. She knew Ravyn had had a good date with Jeremy and planned to see him again. She didn't want Ravyn to fall for this cop and miss out on Marc. Julie smiled up at Marc and took another sip of her drink. He was beginning to grow on her.

The waitress arrived with their taco plates and Julie ordered another margarita. Marc signaled the same.

"I like a man who can match me in drinks."

"Your husband doesn't drink?"

"He gets drunk after one glass of wine. I'm the bad girl in our relationship."

Marc didn't know how to respond. Julie? A bad girl? Julie was revealing more than he'd expected to know about her.

"Do you have any siblings?" Marc asked, trying to change the subject.

"I have a brother and a sister."

"Are they here in Atlanta?"

"Oh no. One is in Charlotte and the other is in Boston. I know you have a brother. Any other siblings?"

"I have a sister, Brooke. She lives in Phoenix. You know my brother Bruce is, umm, problematic."

"Problematic?"

Marc grimaced. "My brother Bruce is a drunk and a drug addict."

"Oh."

"Yeah. It's hard. More so on my parents. Well, really my mother. She takes it hard, like she wasn't a good enough mother. My dad is just kind of mad. Sort of at Bruce and sort of at me. Like I didn't do enough to help Bruce from going down that path. I think my father likes Brooke. But it's just because she's never around."

Julie laughed, then thought maybe she shouldn't have. "Sorry."

"No, it's OK."

"No. I am sorry your family is complicated. But Marc, every family is complicated."

"What do you mean?"

"Well, you know Ravyn's sister Jane is getting married?"

"Yes. You told me that."

"Ravyn asked her parents if they could float a down payment on her condo and they said no. They are paying for Jane's wedding. Ravyn won't say so, but she is pissed."

Julie was talking louder the more she drank her second margarita.

"I wish I could help her," Marc said. "But I can't."

"I know. I can't help either."

"You'd help her?"

"Ravyn is my best friend. I wish I could help her with the down payment. But one, she'd never accept it. Second, I have two daughters. They've got activities and camps and everything else. I feel like any spare money I have goes right to them. Third, my husband would never go for that. He sort of holds the purse strings in our family, which is why it took me so long to catch him cheating."

Marc blinked at Julie, clearly uncomfortable with the way the conversation had shifted.

"He cheated?"

"Oh yes. I found our hotel points didn't add up. He said he'd gone on a work trip. Turns out he took an associate — a female associate — away for a weekend. But I caught him."

"But you're still together, right?"

"We're still together. We went to counseling."

"That's good, that you worked it out, I mean," Marc said, hoping to get off the subject of Julie's marital trouble.

"Well, we're working it out."

An awkward pause fell over the table. The waitress came over and began clearing their plates. "Can I get you any dessert?" she asked.

Julie shook her head no and Marc said, "Just the check please."

"One check or two?" the waitress asked.

"Just one," Marc said. "Julie, you are doing me a favor, helping me get back with Ravyn. Please let me buy lunch."

Julie thanked him, hoping that she was indeed helping him get Ravyn back.

Chapter 7

Jeremy Stephens reached over to hold Ravyn's hand during the movie. He gave her hand a little squeeze, then began to circle his forefinger in her palm.

Ravyn felt herself go flush in the darkened movie theater. Was Jeremy sending her signals he wanted to be intimate? This was only their second date. She wasn't quite sure she was ready to be intimate with him.

She tried to concentrate on all the action in the superhero movie. But Jeremy's finger made it nearly impossible. She squirmed in her seat, feeling her panties get wet.

Jeremy let go of her hand and reached his hand into the bucket of popcorn. Then he rested his hand on Ravyn's thigh.

Now he is sending signals, she thought. She put her hand on top of his and moved his hand off her thigh. No sense in giving him the wrong idea, she thought. She needed more time to get to know him.

Jeremy drove Ravyn home after the movie, lingering in her condo.

"Wasn't the movie great?" Jeremy asked. "I love the final fight scene."

"It was good," Ravyn said. "But I wish I'd seen some of the other Avengers movies. I kind of got lost with the story."

"Oh, I own the DVDs. You should come over to watch them."

"That would be great. I had fun this evening. Thank you."

Ravyn was trying to steer Jeremy toward the door.

"I had fun, too." He put his hand on Ravyn's shoulder and ran his hand down her arm, then moving his hand on her waist. "It doesn't have to end."

Jeremy looked into her blue eyes. Ravyn knew what he wanted. He wanted to stay the night.

"Jeremy, I had a nice time, but I'm just getting to know you."

She was trying to let him down gently. She didn't want to tell him no forever. She just wanted to tell him no for right now.

"We could get to know each other better," he said, leaning in to kiss her. He tightened his grip on her waist, pulling her closer. He kissed her deeply. She could feel his tongue probing.

Ravyn pulled away. "Jeremy, I'm not saying no. I'm just saying not right now. I'm not ready."

Jeremy gave her a pouty look. "But I'm ready for you. I really like you, Ravyn."

"I like you, Jeremy. Just give me a little more time to be sure of our relationship."

He kissed her again, his tongue thrusting in her mouth. He pulled back and whispered, "I can do great things with this tongue. To you."

Ravyn felt her breath catch. "Jeremy," she whispered.

"Let me stay," he whispered back.

Ravyn stepped back from him. "Not tonight. But soon I think."

"Soon?"

"Soon."

Ravyn met with Julie's real estate agent friend but also posted notices about renting a condo by the row of mailboxes at her building. It looked like one of those notices she'd seen in college, the information written out in big letters, then cutouts at the bottom of the paper with her cell number on each strip.

"I'm not quite sure what we'll find in Midtown at your price range," Cindy Freeman cautioned Ravyn as they sat at her breakfast bar. "Are you sure you don't want to widen your search? I'm sure we can find something suitable if we can cover more of Atlanta."

"I'd like to stay in this area," Ravyn said. "I'd like to stay here, but my landlord wants to sell and I can't afford it."

Cindy looked out toward the balcony, seeing the downtown skyline. "Yes, this condo can command a good price with the great views and upper floor."

Ravyn's face fell and she sighed.

"Well, I'll see what I can do. We might get lucky."

Cindy took some basic information from Ravyn, and Ravyn signed a contract that she wouldn't use another real estate agent during her process.

"Do you think we can find something in the next 60 days or so? I am going to have to be out on August 31," Ravyn asked.

"That's a little tight, but I'll start looking at properties today and I'll email you links to what I find. That way you can get an idea of what's available before we go out to visit the properties. I'd advise you to go ahead and get pre-approved for a loan. If we find something, we'll have to move fast, and being pre-approved will help. It will show you are serious about buying."

Ravyn nodded. "I have talked to my bank about a mortgage and I'll go ahead and finish the paperwork to get pre-approved. I just haven't taken that final step yet. My mother suggested maybe I go ahead and find another place to rent."

"But we can find you something and you can be putting equity into your own home, not paying rent." Cindy stood up to shake Ravyn's hand. "I'll work hard for you, Ravyn. Julie said I'd better take care of you or she'd wipe the tennis court with my ass."

Ravyn laughed. That sounded exactly like something Julie would say.

Ravyn and Jeremy texted throughout the workweek. His police schedule meant he was working when she was sleeping.

She woke up each morning to Hey baby. Did you sleep well? I can't wait to see you again.

She would send him selfies of her at her desk at *Cleopatra*'s offices, or when she got home. She even sent some of her and Felix snuggling together.

He'd send photos back of him working out at the gym or in his police uniform. She thought he looked really good in the uniform. He even sent a photo of him shirtless, flexing his biceps and texted, I'm bringing out the big guns for you.

She laughed at that. He'd finally sent the shirtless torso photo that she'd seen so many times on Tinder. But he was being silly and playful. She liked that in him.

When's your next day off? she asked.

I'm off Friday and Saturday. Can't believe I got part of the weekend off. Want to do something? Go out to dinner?

Why don't you bring one of your movies over Saturday and I'll fix dinner.

Can't wait.

Ravyn knew what she was doing by inviting Jeremy over. He'd believe this was an invitation to stay over. Ravyn took a deep breath and told herself she was ready to be intimate with Jeremy. What was she waiting for?

Ravyn decided to make Jeremy chicken piccata Saturday night before they watched one of the DVD movies Jeremy had brought over. Ravyn had gotten more confident in her culinary skills after the cooking school she had attended in Rome last fall.

The recipe had turned out well and she'd fixed a salad and steamed fresh broccoli to go with it.

When the movie finished, they went out to the balcony, sipped white wine, and watched the city lights.

Jeremy put his wine glass down on a small table outside and kissed Ravyn deeply, his arms running down her back before squeezing her behind.

"Ravyn, Ravyn," he whispered. "I want to make love to you."

"I'm ready." Ravyn took Jeremy's hand and led him to her darkened bedroom. She shut the door to keep a protesting Felix out.

Jeremy began unbuttoning Ravyn's blouse slowly. He kissed her neck, moving down to her collar bone. He moved her bra down and kissed her right breast, then sucked her nipple.

Ravyn groaned. Jeremy sucked her nipple again, then gave a little bite.

Ravyn gasped. Jeremy looked up and gave her a sly smile. "You like that? You like it when I bite you?"

"Jeremy," she whispered. "That feels good."

"I'll make you feel better."

Jeremy moved to unzip her jeans, pulling the material down. She quickly kicked them off. She was standing before him with her blouse open, her bra pulled down and in her panties. She was grateful she'd worn her nice underwear on her date tonight.

Jeremy slid down to her panties, breathing hard. He began to work his tongue over the outside of her panties then sucked hard.

Ravyn's head fell back. "Oh, God!" She moaned louder and fell back on the edge of her bed. Jeremy worked his tongue on her panties again.

She moaned again, louder.

Jeremy stood up and began removing his shirt and pants, revealing a large erection.

"You're making me so hard, baby. You want this, baby, don't you?"

Ravyn reached out for him while stretching over to her nightstand for a condom.

"I want you in me," Ravyn finally said.

"I want in you. Let me in you."

Jeremy pulled down Ravyn's panties and climbed on top of her, lowering himself down on her. She wrapped her legs around his torso.

"You want me, baby? You want me?"

"Yes," she moaned. "Yes."

Jeremy raised his body and entered her. Ravyn yelped and Jeremy began the rhythmic stroking inside her. Jeremy held onto Ravyn's arms, pinning her to the bed.

She almost screamed her pleasure as she reached orgasm. Jeremy's breathing got heavier and climaxed after Ravyn. He collapsed on top of her, spent. Then he rolled over, resting his hand on her breast.

Ravyn was trying to catch her breath. Her orgasm had been deep. She was feeling the post-coital glow. She pulled the sheets up around her as she began to hear Jeremy's even breathing. He was sound asleep.

Jeremy stirred early in the morning and Ravyn awoke, feeling the strange body next to her.

Jeremy rolled over, holding Ravyn close. "Good morning, beautiful."

"Hey," she whispered. Ravyn felt Jeremy's full erection against her leg. "You seem happy this morning."

"Why yes, I am," Jeremy said. "Are you ready for another round?"

He moved his hand between her thighs and Ravyn gave a throaty moan.

"Are you ready?" he asked.

"I'm not sure," she said.

"Well, let's find out."

Jeremy kissed her breast, then her stomach, and moved lower, finding Ravyn's pleasure spot between her legs.

Ravyn moaned. "Oh, Jeremy. Oh, God."

"Yes. I am your God. Tell me how much you want me."

"I want, I want… Yes, I want you."

Ravyn's hips twisted. She arched her back. She squeezed her headboard, feeling her body nearly explode. Jeremy put on the condom as quickly as he could.

Jeremy crawled on top of Ravyn, lowering himself down to enter her again. He thrust hard, Ravyn holding on to the headboard for dear life. Finally, they both came, spent with passion.

Ravyn rolled over, feeling sexually satisfied. She desperately had to pee and threw her legs over the bed and hustled into her bathroom.

When she came out, she saw Jeremy still laying in her bed. His left arm was thrown over his face.

She threw on her robe and padded out to her kitchen to start her coffee maker. Felix also made angry noises, having been left out of her bedroom all night.

She fed Felix and poured a cup of coffee, adding milk and sugar, then leaned against her kitchen counter. She blew on her hot coffee before sipping at her cup. She was glad it was Sunday. A lazy day. She looked out toward her balcony and the view of downtown Atlanta.

Ravyn felt tears come to her eyes, thinking about how much she would miss this view when she had to leave. She had not called her landlord to say she couldn't afford the condo, but she knew it was coming.

Jeremy padded out to her kitchen, scratching his head, wearing his boxers.

"Good morning, beautiful," he said, wrapping his arms around her. He kissed her neck.

"Good morning to you," Ravyn responded, giving him a quick kiss. "Coffee?"

"Yes."

"Cream or sugar?"

"A little sugar, please."

Ravyn poured Jeremy a cup of the aromatic coffee. He took it from her as she again pulled down the sugar bowl from her cabinet. She reached for the spoon on her spoon rest.

"Is this OK? It's my coffee spoon. I only use it to stir my coffee."

"Sure. That's fine."

Jeremy took the spoon from Ravyn and stirred one teaspoon of sugar in his coffee. He leaned against her counter. "I had fun last night. Sounds like you did, too.

Ravyn could feel herself flush. "I, well, yes."

Jeremy smiled a sly smile. "I'm glad." He took another sip of the dark, rich coffee. "I want to please you, baby."

Ravyn felt herself flush deeper and felt herself go wet again. But she took another sip of her coffee. "I was pleased. Very pleased," she said over her coffee cup.

"Want to be pleased again?" Jeremy said, raising an eyebrow to her. Ravyn looked down and saw the lump in his boxers.

"Well, then," she said. "Please, please me."

Jeremy smiled wickedly and put down his coffee cup, then took her cup and placed it on the counter. He took Ravyn's hand and led her back into the bedroom.

For the second time Sunday morning, Ravyn and Jeremy were in her kitchen drinking fresh coffee. This time they were both clothed.

Jeremy stirred some sugar in his coffee, using Ravyn's "coffee spoon."

"What are you going to do today?" Ravyn asked.

"I have a late shift. I'll go on at 10 p.m." Jeremy said.

"Oh. That's late."

"It is. I'll spend the rest of today sleeping to get ready for the overnight shift. What will you do today?"

"Sunday is laundry day. And I'll need to wash those sheets, for sure."

Jeremy smiled. "I guess you do. I hope you didn't have to sleep in the wet spot."

"I think there were several wet spots."

"I hope so."

Jeremy stood at Ravyn's door, unwilling to leave. "I had a great time last night. And this morning."

"Me, too."

"I'll call you tomorrow when I get off my shift."

"When is that?"

"I should be done by 7 a.m."

"OK. I'll look forward to it," Ravyn said.

Jeremy kissed Ravyn, sucking her tongue and lips as he left.

Ravyn shut her condo door and turned her back to the door. What had just happened?

The night had been so sensual. She had enjoyed Jeremy's body. She felt sure he had enjoyed hers.

She went into the kitchen for another cup of coffee. She reached for her coffee spoon. It was gone.

Ravyn met Julie at their favorite restaurant Twist at Phipps Plaza in Buckhead later that Sunday. It was a sushi place, and Ravyn and Julie had their favorite sushi rolls and a glass of wine.

"You look happy," Julie said.

"I am. I really like Jeremy."

"So, you've done the deed."

"Is it that obvious?"

"Well, when you practically glow, it does," Julie said, feeling sorry for Marc. She had tried to help him, but it looked like Ravyn was off the dating market.

"It was pretty great. He's a pleaser. Made sure I was satisfied first."

"Ah. That's nice."

"There's just one thing," Ravyn began.

Julie raised an eyebrow. Maybe Marc wasn't off the list just yet. "What's that?"

"OK. This is going to sound stupid."

"Spill it."

"Jeremy spent the night last night and we had coffee this morning," Ravyn said.

"So?"

"Well, you know how I always keep my coffee spoon on the spoon rest by the coffee maker?"

"No, I didn't know."

"Well, I do. I keep the same spoon next to the coffee maker. It's my coffee spoon. It's this cute little spoon with my initial 'S' on the stem."

"Ravyn, what's your point?"

"I think Jeremy took it."

"What? He took your spoon?"

"Yes, he took my spoon."

Julie shook her head. "Why would he do that?"

"I have no idea. We were having coffee, he had to leave because he is working the late shift and was going home to sleep for the rest of the day. When I went back to fix another cup, the spoon was gone."

"Maybe it just fell, or he put it in the sink. Have you checked the garbage disposal? Ashley dropped a fork down there once and I thought the kitchen was exploding when I turned the disposal on."

"I didn't check the disposal. I will though. But it's weird. I do think he took my spoon."

"Again, why would he do that?"

"I just have this creepy feeling. What if he's a collector?" Ravyn almost whispered the word, "collector."

"A collector?"

"You know, he collects things from every woman he sleeps with."

"Ravyn, where do you even hear about these things?"

"I look on the internet."

"I think you just better ask him. Ask him if he took the spoon. Or go over to his apartment and look for it. Or maybe not. If he's a sick bastard, I don't want you to go over there by yourself."

Julie took a sip of her white wine before asking, "So you have some doubts about this man? You're not going to see him again?"

"I think I'll see him again, but I don't think it will be at my condo. I may have to spend the night at his place from now on just so he doesn't take anything else."

Julie gave her friend a worried look. "You just be careful."

Chapter 8

Ravyn had looked at several links to condos on the market in Midtown, thanks to Cindy. She picked out three to check out the next weekend.

Ravyn was a little nervous since the condos were older and looked like they might need some renovation. She didn't have money for renovations. She was worried she'd find a place and never have the money to fix it up.

Ravyn was waiting outside her condo when Cindy pulled up to the curb in her silver Lexus SUV. Ravyn climbed in.

Cindy had a manila folder on the seat and Ravyn picked it up and put it in her lap.

"I took the liberty of finding a few more listings. I printed them out. If you like them, we can add one or two to our list to visit today," Cindy said.

Ravyn leafed through the pages. One was not far from Piedmont Park but was slightly more than she'd been told she could afford. "Can I afford to look at this place?" Ravyn asked, holding up the sheet of paper.

Cindy glanced over. "Well, that one has been on the market a while and they may be willing to accept a lower offer. Can't hurt to go look at it."

"OK. Let's add that to the list then."

"Oh, I saw Julie earlier today at lunch, although I don't think she saw me," Cindy said.

"In Midtown?"

"Yes. She was with some guy," the real estate agent said.

"Her husband, Rob?"

"No. I know Rob. This was some other guy. A handsome guy at that."

"Maybe it was her tennis coach. She told me she has lunch with him sometimes."

"No. It was definitely not our tennis coach. Our tennis coach is Sydney and she's a woman," Cindy laughed. "No idea who the other person was."

Ravyn frowned. Julie's tennis coach was a woman? That's not what Julie had told her.

"OK, here is the first property," Cindy said as she pulled into the small parking lot behind the building on Glendale Terrace.

They climbed out of the vehicle and buzzed into the small lobby of the three-story building. A central staircase led up to other floors, but the condo for sale was on the first floor.

They entered the condo and Ravyn couldn't help frowning her initial displeasure. The walls were painted a black matte, giving the space a dark and small feel.

Cindy looked around, trying to be cheerful. "Well, that would not be my color choice and walls can always be repainted. I'm surprised the agent listing this property didn't get them to paint the walls a neutral color."

"Yeah. This is kind of odd." Ravyn moved into the kitchen, with ancient appliances and rust on the refrigerator handle.

"Yes, well, we'd ask that there be an allowance to replace the appliances," Cindy said. "So that would drop our offer."

Ravyn moved to the tiny bedroom and bathroom. The tub had rust in the bottom and water damage was visible on the walls of the bathroom. The bedroom was also made dark by a deep navy blue wall paint.

Cindy could sense Ravyn's disappointment and would likely leave comments for the seller's agent to present the property in a better way.

"Well, this is just our first property. Don't be discouraged. At least you know what you don't like. We've got at least three more to look at this afternoon, right?"

"Right," Ravyn said, but she couldn't muster enthusiasm. If this was a sample of what was in her price range, she was going to have a hard time finding anything to purchase.

Ravyn had looked at a total of five condos with Cindy that afternoon. All of them had been older properties and a couple had the look and feel of being converted apartments because they were.

The square footage of most of the units she looked at were also smaller than the condo she was in.

One place had been a studio condo in Metropolis, where her bedroom and living room would essentially be one space. She wasn't ready to revert to a futon, where her couch would essentially become her bed at night. She'd done that right out of college and wasn't willing to go back.

Ravyn had climbed back into Cindy's SUV at the end of the day dejected.

"This is just our first day," Cindy tried to reassure her. "More homes come on the market every day, so I'll keep looking. Why don't you also do some internet searches, too? That way you can see what is in your price range. And you might want to extend your search. Are you opposed to Virginia-Highland, or Poncey-Highland? I might be able to find some properties in that area."

Those were neighborhoods not far from Midtown in Atlanta.

"I have looked online. And I guess I could extend my area of search, although I don't want to. What's in my price range depresses me," Ravyn said. "I was just hoping we'd find something great today and I could stop looking. I don't have much time before I have to tell my landlord I can't buy my unit."

"Ravyn, you might have to think about taking a short-term lease at an apartment while we continue your search," Cindy said, gently. "Or is there someone you can stay with while we still look?"

"My family lives out of state, so I don't have my parents or my sister to live with here. I'm not sure I could impose on a friend for that long, either."

"So, look at some apartments with six-month leases," the real estate agent said. "You'll pay a little higher price in rent, but then you won't be stuck with a year-long lease. I don't think it will take a whole year for us to find your new home. It probably won't even take six months, but you need a backup plan."

Cindy had dropped Ravyn off at the curb of her condo building and waved before she pulled onto Peachtree Street.

Ravyn could hardly keep from crying as she got to her front door. As she was putting the key in, her neighbor Jack Parker stuck his head out of his front door.

"Hey, Ravyn!"

"Hi, Jack," she said, wiping a tear from her eye. She didn't want him to see her crying.

"What's this I hear about your unit going up for sale? Are you moving out?"

How had he heard about that? She hadn't even told her landlord what her plans were.

"Ah, the guy who owns my unit wants to sell," she said carefully. "He's giving me first option to buy."

"Oh great, so you're not moving," Jack said, with what sounded like relief.

"I'm not so sure I can afford it, but I'm trying to work it out," Ravyn lied. "But if you hear of anything for rent in the building let me know. I asked the property manager to let me know, too."

"Yeah," Jack said. "That's who I heard it from. That you may be moving, I mean."

Ravyn shook her head. She might have known Patrick, the property manager, would say something.

"Well, if you hear of something I can rent, please let me know. I don't want to move out."

"I will. I promise," Jack said as he retreated to his condo.

Ravyn felt the tears rolling down her cheeks as she got her front door open.

Marc was sipping his second Scotch, not knowing if he should text Ravyn on Tinder. He didn't want to seem overly anxious, but he wanted to get closer to her.

He was halfway through his drink when he decided he would. What would it hurt?

Hi Ravyn, how was your day?

There was no immediate reply. Marc was still trying to figure out the app. He'd accidentally swiped the wrong way while trying to understand Tinder and got matched with a couple of women.

He'd tried to let the first match down gently, explaining his mistake. She had not taken it well. He'd simply unmatched the second woman. He knew Ravyn likely got an alert when he'd messaged her. Why wasn't she replying? Was she out with that Jeremy guy? That made him finish his drink in one gulp.

Marc was trying to unwind after a long week. Negotiations were going well with Black Kat Investors, and they were really interested in buying a majority share of his company.

He'd sent their proposal to his lawyer Dan Klein and was awaiting a response and possibly a counter-proposal. He didn't want to give LindMark Enterprises away. He wanted a good deal for his company.

Marc poured his third Scotch. Then he heard his phone ping. It was Ravyn on the Tinder app.

Hey, Ed.

Hi, how are you? How was your day?

Not so good. I am trying to find a condo to buy and I went out to look at properties with a real estate agent. I didn't find many things in my price range.

Sorry. Where are you looking?

I'm trying to stay in Midtown. But my price range is pretty low. I can't afford anything nice.

Have you thought about other areas? There are some great areas close to Midtown. Or you could rent.

Marc hoped it had seemed subtle. If Ravyn bought something, she might be stuck for a while in a condo. Could she afford the homeowners association fees? And what about having to call a plumber or repairman. Had she thought about that?

I may have to rent. My real estate agent even said I should look for a short-term lease while she keeps looking. I have to be out of my current home by August 31.

Oh wow. That's soon.

I know. I hate it. I hate this situation. I just want everything to stay the same.

Change is hard.

Hey, listen. I don't want to lead you on. I'm dating someone on Tinder. Perhaps we should part ways.

Marc was alarmed. He didn't want Ravyn to unmatch him.

I like talking to you, he said. Can we just talk sometimes? Would that be OK?

Ravyn shrugged when she got the message. Ed was probably just some lonely but cute loser. What did she care if he just wanted to talk? She'd told him she wasn't interested in dating him. She told him she was dating someone else.

OK. I guess that's fine.

Marc let out a breath he didn't know he'd been holding. If Ravyn had wanted to end their match, he didn't know what he'd do to win her back.

He wasn't happy she was seeing Jeremy. He'd have to meet with Julie again to enlist her help. He needed Ravyn and Jeremy to break up.

Suddenly he was worried Ravyn was sleeping with Jeremy. He tried to ask that question delicately.

Are you serious with this other guy?

Well, pretty serious.

Marc's heart sank and he gulped down the rest of Scotch number three. It made his stomach do a little flip and he thought he might be sick. He couldn't stand the thought of Ravyn sleeping with anyone but him.

I haven't met anyone yet that I want to date on Tinder. If anything changes with you, let me know.

Don't give up, Ed. Make more matches. Meet more women. The first five Tinder matches didn't work for me. Horrible dates. But then I met Jeremy.

My God, Marc thought. She said his name. He tried not to be jealous and changed the subject.

Why were your dates so bad?

Oh my God, they were awful. I got trapped in an elevator with one guy who freaked out, and one guy berated me for being a journalist.

Ravyn didn't even want to explain the Chick-fil-A date.

Oh, those don't sound so great. What are you looking for with Tinder though? To find true love?

Well, I hope so. My sister is getting married. That's what made me go on the app. I wanted to meet someone.

And you didn't have any boyfriends already? You are very beautiful.

Ravyn blushed. Well, I've dated some guys, even some I was very serious about. But they just didn't work out.

I'm sorry. Marc sighed. It was his fault it hadn't worked out with Ravyn. He'd screwed up.

Sorry for what?

Marc hesitated. He didn't know how to respond. Just sorry. Sorry that no man has lived up to your expectations.

Ravyn was shocked by Ed's answer. Did she have expectations that were too high? Was she at fault for her failed relationships?

It's OK. I've found someone on Tinder and I hope I've met my last boyfriend.

Marc really did feel sick. He didn't want Ravyn to have met her final boyfriend. He didn't want her to end up with Jeremy. He wanted her to end up with him.

Well, good luck, Ed. I think you should swipe right more. Good night.

Good night, Ravyn.

Marc switched off his phone and poured drink number four. He knew he was getting drunk tonight.

Ravyn hung up and reached for her bottle of red wine. She'd already had two glasses, but she was so depressed about the day's condo hunt and the texts with Ed depressed her further.

She couldn't text Jeremy. He was sleeping since he had an late shift. She wanted to text him though. She was missing the hot sex she'd had with him.

Maybe she would just text him so he'd have it when he woke up.

Hey Jeremy. Hope we can get together soon. Thinking of you.

Ravyn put her phone down and walked out onto her balcony with her wine glass. She looked out over the downtown skyline lit up. How could she ever give up this view?

Near 10 p.m., Ravyn got a text from Jeremy.

Hey babe. I miss you too. Can we get together tomorrow? Or Monday? I get those days off.

Can we meet at your place?

Sure. But why? Your place is more private. We can be noisy.

Ravyn blushed, but she didn't want Jeremy in her place again until she could be sure he hadn't stolen her spoon.

I'd like to see where you live.

OK. We can go out to dinner in Decatur Square. Then I'll show you my place.

See you at 6 tomorrow?

Yes.

Ravyn closed her phone suddenly feeling much better about the day. She had plans to see Jeremy again.

Ravyn and Jeremy met at his apartment off North Arcadia Road in Decatur. It wasn't too far from the Avondale MARTA station nor Decatur Square.

They drove to Raging Burrito in Jeremy's black Ford F-150 pickup truck, enjoying margaritas and burritos on the back patio of the restaurant. Ravyn couldn't even finish her burrito, asking for a to-go box.

Ravyn realized by staying over at Jeremy's on a Sunday evening, she'd have to pack a bag with a blouse and pants for work Monday, or else leave his apartment very early to go back to her place before going to work.

She hoped she could just get ready at his place, but she had no idea what his bathroom looked like, especially if he shared it with another guy. It might be really gross. She'd seen some ex-boyfriend's bathrooms.

In hindsight, they should have stayed at her condo, since Jeremy didn't have to work Monday. Oh well. She did want to see his place and see if she could find her missing spoon.

She never did find it at her condo. She even checked the garbage disposal as Julie suggested. It wasn't there either.

They got back to his apartment shortly before 8 p.m. It was too early for bed, although Jeremy kept moving his hand to cup Ravyn's butt as they got to the door.

"Where's your roommate tonight?" she asked.

"I told him to take another shift and I'd do the same for him later. We have the place to ourselves."

"Great. It's early. Do you want to watch a movie or something?"

"Or something," Jeremy smiled before kissing her. His hands went to her shirt, lifting it before moving to unhook her bra.

He cupped Ravyn's breasts kissing her collarbone and moving down to her left nipple. He circled his tongue around it, then sucked. Ravyn felt herself becoming aroused.

"Let's move into the bedroom," she whispered.

"No one is here. We could make love right here in the living room."

"I'd rather make love in the bedroom."

"Ravyn, you are so vanilla."

Vanilla? What did that mean? Ravyn wondered.

But Jeremy took Ravyn's hand and led her back to his bedroom.

Chapter 9

Ravyn arrived at work shortly after 9 a.m. She hadn't intended to be late but she and Jeremy had made love shortly after waking up. She had barely had time for a quick shower at Jeremy's place and never had time to search Jeremy's kitchen for her coffee spoon.

She was sorry she hadn't been able to stop at her condo, but she'd left some extra food for Felix. He'd be alright until she got home Monday evening.

Jennifer Bagley walked into Ravyn's office without even knocking. Ravyn looked up from her computer, annoyed.

"May I help you?"

"I wanted to make sure you saw the email about the time management meeting this week. You didn't sign up for an appointment."

"What email? What time management meeting?" Ravyn asked, surprised.

"Corporate sent it out two weeks ago. And you haven't signed up for a slot. The woman will be here Friday. Corporate is making the training mandatory."

"Even for you?"

"Yes, even for me. Why?"

"You seem very organized. I wouldn't think you'd need it. I could name people in this office who would need time management. Your name wouldn't be one of them."

"You mean Joel."

"I didn't say Joel," Ravyn hesitated, then nodded her assent. "But yes, Joel."

"That man will be late to his own funeral."

Ravyn laughed. She didn't even think Jennifer had a sense of humor. She was always so serious in the office.

"Please find that email and follow the link to make an appointment."

"I don't even remember getting the email," Ravyn said, peering at her computer screen and scrolling through her emails. "Did you send it?"

"No. It came from corporate. Or maybe it came from the time management firm. But I think we got the first email from Horizon Publications."

Ravyn's search proved no results. Then she searched her spam folder.

"Oh. There it is. Why are corporate emails landing in my spam filter?"

"I have no idea. Did you white list the emails?" Jennifer asked.

"I shouldn't have to. Our security feature seems set too high. Here is the email from the time management company too. Both went straight to spam."

"Well, you should be checking your spam filter more frequently. Otherwise, I would have had to mark you as not completing the mandatory training."

Ravyn stared at Jennifer. "Are you suggesting I waste my time going through hundreds of junk emails in my spam filter?"

"Yes. You might miss something important. Like the notice on the mandatory training. Case in point."

"And you would have marked me as missing this training?"

"Well, I wouldn't want to, naturally. But this is mandatory training. If you miss several it goes on your employment record. It shows you aren't a team player."

Ravyn could feel her jaw drop. What was Jennifer saying? That Ravyn wasn't a team player?

"I am a team player, Jennifer," Ravyn said, trying to keep the edge out of her voice.

"I never said you weren't. You are getting very defensive. You shouldn't take these things so personally."

Ravyn knew she would never win this argument. Jennifer had assumed the superior attitude and was making Ravyn feel like an underling, as she usually did. That was probably the entire reason for Jennifer's visit, Ravyn thought darkly.

"Well, I'll just get my appointment set up now. Wouldn't want you to give me a demerit for not being a team player."

Jennifer frowned but left Ravyn's office without saying another word.

Ravyn's only choice for the time management appointment was the very last one on Friday at 5 p.m. Ugh! Who makes or takes an appointment that late on a Friday? Apparently, I do, Ravyn said to herself. That would make for a long week.

She texted Jeremy next. She knew he was off today but they hadn't made plans to get together again. He'd probably be asleep since he was working late shift again. Dating a cop was tough with the crazy schedule he kept. She'd never dated anyone who didn't work regular office hours.

Hey Jeremy. Just wanted to see when you are off next. I've got a late appointment on Friday but wanted to see if you were free at all this coming weekend. xoxo

She got no reply, but she didn't expect to. Then she remembered Jeremy had called her vanilla. She Googled it. "Unexciting, normal, conventional, boring" is what she found on

Urban Dictionary. Then she found vanilla sex, which meant sex that involved no twists or kinkiness, and no S&M.

Ravyn didn't see herself as a prude. She liked to give and get oral sex, but she didn't think she'd want to do bondage stuff. She couldn't see herself being tied up. If that made her vanilla in Jeremy's eyes, she'd have to be vanilla.

She got a sudden ping on her iPhone. The text was from Jeremy.

Hey beautiful. I'm free Friday and Saturday. How late are you working Friday? Let's meet after that. I want to see you again. Taste you again. Do you want to taste me again?

Ravyn felt her panties go wet at his suggestions. She did want to do what he suggested.

I should be off work by 7 p.m. Friday. Can we meet back at your place? I liked Raging Burrito. I had the leftovers for lunch today. Made me think of you.

I like it when you think of me. And my big dick. Let's have some fun Friday.

I'm game.

Good. See you Friday at my place.

Ravyn found she was anxious for the end of the week.

Cindy Freeman texted Ravyn about some more properties to see on Saturday and Ravyn agreed.

Ravyn looked over the links to the properties Cindy had sent. She was disappointed again. Everything looked older.

Older properties that would need substantial upgrades that she didn't have money for. One of the properties was at Peachtree Walk. She knew her friend Mary Jane had bought a condo there when they had converted from apartments to condos.

She immediately texted her friend.

Hey, MJ. Hope you are well. What has been your experience at Peachtree Walk? I'm planning to look at a property there to buy on Saturday.

A few seconds later came the reply.

Hey, want to buy our place? We're looking to buy a house. I'm pregnant! This place will be too small for a family. It's one bedroom, one bath. But it would be perfect for you.

Is it on the market? Looking at a couple of units at Peachtree Walk. I can put yours on the list. Congrats on the baby!

Not on market yet. But soon. Let's do lunch next week and catch up. I can tell you about the condo and condo association. A bit of a strict condo board, if you ask me. And thanks. Not sure if I'm ready for diaper changes and 2 a.m. feedings, but then, who is?

You'll do great. You're going to be a great mom. Text me some dates for lunch next week. I'd love to take you out to celebrate.

Sure.

Mary Jane, pregnant! Many of Ravyn's friends were already married. She sighed and looked back at her computer. She could only hope she'd be among the married soon.

Ravyn's week seemed to drag on. Thursday morning the first of the time management meetings began. She'd had to watch a webinar on time management skills. Seriously, wasn't that enough? What more could she learn? She used several apps on her phone and used her calendar to keep herself organized.

Around noon she heard from Jeremy.

Still coming over tomorrow?

Yes. Can't wait.

I can't either. We're going to have some fun. Maybe something new for you. I've got plans.

Ravyn didn't know what Jeremy meant by that, but it made her smile.

She looked up to see Joel walking down the hall. He caught her eye and turned into her office.

"Well, that was a complete waste of time," he complained, leaning against Ravyn's door.

"The time management session? You had it today?"

"I did. I traded with Chase. He had an appointment tomorrow, so I took his slot."

"So, what happened in the session?"

"It was a joke. The woman went over the webinar and told us how to use our phones. Really? Like I don't know how to use the calendar on my phone?"

"Well, not everyone is technologically savvy," Ravyn said.

"You calling me old?" Joel said, but he was smiling.

"I'm not calling you old at all. But my parents, well, my mother, sometimes gets frustrated with her phone. She says she likes the ones where you just picked up the cradle and pushed buttons for the call."

Joel laughed. "Too late for that! It's a new world now."

"Yeah. Well, thanks for letting me know what to expect tomorrow."

"Your session is tomorrow?"

"Yes. I have the very last session at 5 p.m. Ugh!"

"You're kidding, right?"

"No. The corporate announcement got caught in my spam filter. Jennifer came by my office and let me know about it or I'd have gotten a demerit, for not taking the session and not being a team player."

"That bitch. That's just what she wants. She wants you to fail, you know," Joel said.

Ravyn was shocked. She didn't know that. "Really? Did she tell you that?"

"Oh, she doesn't talk to me, unless it is in a passive-aggressive way. But you can see the way she treats you and talks to you. She wants you to fail. She'd rather get her own hire in here."

Ravyn frowned. Was Joel right? Or was he just trying to stir up trouble?

"Well, I don't know..."

"Whatever," Joel said, straightening up and turning to leave. "You believe what you want to."

Ravyn tried to return to her work but couldn't concentrate. This week could not end soon enough.

Ravyn was relaxing on her sofa, enjoying a glass of wine when her Tinder app chirped.

She was surprised. She hadn't tried to get more matches on Tinder since she'd met Jeremy.

It was Ed.

Hi Ravyn, Marc texted.

Hi Ed.

How are you this evening?

I'm fine. I'm at home relaxing.

Busy day at work?

Stressful day at work, Ravyn answered, taking another sip of wine.

Why is that?

Oh, I've got a time management meeting tomorrow late in the day. I don't want to stay late on a Friday night, but I'll have to. It's some corporate-mandated training.

Sorry to hear that.

How was your week? I hope your IT work isn't as stressful.

No. My work isn't that stressful. And I like helping people. Marc was hoping he was giving all the right answers.

Helping people?

Well, a lot of my work is behind the scenes. Keeping people secure, you know.

Ravyn didn't understand, but said, Sure.

Do you have any siblings? Marc asked.

I have a sister, Jane. She's engaged to be married later this year.

That's exciting.

It is. I like her fiancé Nick.

Are you helping her with the wedding?

Yes, I'm her maid of honor. And I'll go up to South Carolina to help her pick out her dress.

That was news to Marc. He knew about Jane's engagement through Julie, but he didn't know Ravyn was the maid of honor. He was hoping she'd be through with Jeremy when it was time for her to bring a date to the wedding.

So you two are close? he asked.

We are.

That's good. I'm close to my sister, too.

You have a sister? Just one?

Yes, Marc lied. He wasn't about to tell Ravyn he had a brother. She might put two and two together and realize it was him. Then he thought he was being paranoid. She'd never guess it was him. But she doesn't live here in Atlanta. I call her every week, though.

That part was true. Marc did call his sister every week.

That's really nice. You obviously love her.

Marc realized he did. He probably loved her more than his brother and his father. He was sure he loved his mother most, though.

Ravyn's next text shook Marc out of his reverie.

Well, I hope you have a nice evening, Ed. I've got to get ready for bed, Ravyn lied. She didn't want to be chatting with Ed. She'd rather be chatting with Jeremy. Ravyn didn't want to lead Ed on.

Good night, Ravyn.

Good night.

Ravyn got a late start to work Friday morning. She had dropped her favorite coffee cup, filled with coffee, shattering it on her kitchen tile floor. The coffee had splashed onto her pant leg, forcing her to change clothes.

Construction on a water main down Peachtree Street meant a lane was closed, making her commute even slower. When she finally got off the elevator, she ran straight into Jennifer, wearing her cream-colored blouse and deep green skirt.

"Good morning, Ravyn," Jennifer said.

"Good morning. Didn't mean to be late. I spilled coffee down my leg and had to change clothes."

"Did you burn yourself?" Jennifer asked, concerned.

"No, but I did break my favorite coffee cup. I hope I can find a replacement for it on Amazon."

"Sorry about the mug. Don't forget about your session later today and I'd like to have the first draft of the cover story today, too."

"OK. I'll get that right to you. Just let me put down my things."

Ravyn hurried into her office, noticing three file folders on her desk that weren't there when she left the night before.

She glanced through them, realizing one was a contact sheet for photos for the cover. Gavin Owens, the magazine's photographer, must have left that. The other two were from Jennifer, some ideas for the back-to-school issue of Cleopatra.

Ravyn booted up her computer and checked a few emails, but she was antsy. She had a lot of nervous energy.

She checked her phone again. She was anxious to see Jeremy that night. She just needed to make it through the day.

Ravyn's day slogged on and her appointment with the time manager approached. She went to the conference room but found the door closed.

She peered in and saw a woman in the room with Chase Riley, the art director. Ah, she thought. I wasn't the only one who had a late appointment.

She returned to her office and waited another five minutes. Walking back to the conference room, she realized they weren't out yet.

Again, Ravyn returned to her office.

What kind of time management official is this late for an appointment? Ravyn grumbled.

Ravyn waited another five minutes and returned to the conference room. She returned several more times. At last, 30 minutes after her original appointment, Ravyn entered the conference room to greet the time management officer.

"Sorry to keep you waiting," said the woman, who extended her hand. "I am Lindy Lee."

"Ravyn Shaw," she said, accepting Lindy's hand.

"Let's get started. This is all about productivity. Horizon Publications wants to give you the tools to make you as productive as you can be."

Ravyn could almost feel her eyes begin to roll. Joel had been right. This was going to be boring and of no use.

Lindy Lee droned on. Ravyn nodded in all the right places, but she wasn't learning anything new.

Lindy explained how Ravyn's phone could be used to input calendar events, keep notes, and how to use apps to message her coworkers.

This was nothing she hadn't already understood or used.

In an hour, Ravyn could feel herself fighting to keep from yawning and her eyelids open.

"Are there any questions?' Lindy asked.

"Nope. No questions," Ravyn responded, hoping to sprint out of the office.

"Well then, if you'll just fill out this survey on the training session, and then this one on my evaluation," Lindy said.

Oh God, Ravyn thought. This was a waste of my time and this woman was late for my appointment! How can I be honest about any of this?

"Well, can I fill this out on Monday? I have a date tonight," Ravyn said, hoping to play on Lindy's sympathies.

"Oh! Well, of course. I don't want to keep you from your date."

Ravyn got out of the conference room as quickly as she could without appearing rude, returned to her office, gathered her belongings, and almost raced to her Honda in the parking deck.

Ravyn got home, fed Felix, changed clothes, packed an overnight bag she'd need and raced back to her car.

On my way, Ravyn texted Jeremy as she left her parking deck.

Come up when you get here, he responded.

She drove east on Sixth Street, then down Juniper Street and eventually back east on Ponce de Leon Avenue. She seemed to catch almost every traffic light, frustrating her as she slowed for the red lights.

Ravyn pulled up to Jeremy's apartment shortly before 7 p.m. and took the outside staircase two steps at a time.

Ravyn knocked on Jeremy's door, feeling aroused. She was kind of hoping they would forgo dinner and stay in, ordering take out. She wanted to be with him.

Jeremy opened the door, leaned in, and kissed her deeply.

"Hey baby," he said. "I have a surprise for you. A good surprise."

Ravyn entered the apartment. "Really? What is it?"

As she entered the apartment, she saw a petite red-headed woman just inside Jeremy's living room.

"I thought we'd have some fun tonight," he said, pulling Ravyn into the apartment by her arm.

Ravyn was confused. What was the other woman doing here?

"I want you to meet Tasha," he said.

Ravyn stuck out her hand, still confused.

"Hello," she said.

"Hi there," Tasha said, almost purring. "I've heard a lot about you." Tasha ran her hand through Ravyn's hair. "You are even more beautiful than Jeremy described."

Ravyn felt the hair on the back of her neck prick up. What was happening?

"I thought you, me and Tasha could have fun tonight," Jeremy said.

"What?" Ravyn asked, looking between Jeremy and Tasha. "You mean…"

"Yeah, Ravyn, let's have some fun."

"Oh, I don't think so," Ravyn stammered, looking toward the door.

"Come on, Ravyn," Jeremy said, grabbing Ravyn's wrist as she turned back toward the front door. "Don't be so vanilla. Explore. Live a little." He moved in to give her another kiss, but Ravyn pulled away.

"Let go of me!" Ravyn said, wrenching her wrist away from him. She pulled so hard, she hit her hand on the front door. "Ouch!"

Ravyn shook her hand from the pain.

Jeremy took her hand and kissed the top of it. "Are you OK?"

"I'm fine. I need to get out of here."

"Don't go," Jeremy pleaded. "Don't go. I think you'll enjoy yourself. Relax a little. Just sit on the couch. I'll get some wine. Get to know Tasha."

Ravyn looked over at Tasha, who was sucking her fingers.

Ravyn felt sick. This was not what she wanted to do. This was not what she was going to do. She was not going to have a three-way. She wanted Jeremy, and if she wasn't enough for him, she was out.

Ravyn opened the front door and fled down the stairs.

As she left, she could hear Tasha. "Jeremy, are we still going to have some fun?"

"Oh yes, baby, we are."

Chapter 10

Ravyn could not stop crying on her way home to Midtown. How could she be so wrong about Jeremy? And hearing him tell the other woman — Tasha was it? — that he still wanted to have 'fun' with her? Was he not even monogamous?

Ravyn wanted to get home and get in the shower. She felt so unclean.

She was too upset even to call Julie. Ravyn was afraid she wouldn't be able to talk, just blubber uncontrollably.

Ravyn pulled into her parking deck and got to the elevator, pushing the up button. She wiped her eyes with the back of her hand. She was embarrassed her eyes were so red and her nose was running. She just wanted to get to her condo without anyone seeing her.

Suddenly, Jack Parker and his girlfriend Liz got off the elevator.

Jack's face registered surprise as Liz exclaimed, "Ravyn! What's wrong?"

"I just broke up with my boyfriend," Ravyn croaked. "I don't want to talk about it right now."

"Understood," Liz said. "Come over tomorrow, if you want to talk. Or bash him."

Ravyn nodded. Liz hugged her, then Jack moved in for one. "Take care of yourself," he said.

Ravyn got in the elevator and pushed the button to her floor. She would miss her friends.

That just made her cry harder in the elevator. Her life felt like it was headed downhill.

Ravyn opened her front door and immediately headed for the red wine, pouring herself a large glass, drinking it down in almost one gulp. She poured another, this time sipping it as the first glass warmed her all over.

Felix wandered over and rubbed up against her.

She began crying again, hugging him against her. "Oh, Felix. You are the only man in my life who is loyal."

Ravyn woke up Saturday with a headache and a dry mouth. She remembered the second glass of wine and then a third. She looked down and realized she hadn't even made it out of her clothes. She'd just laid in the bed, crying.

Her eyes were all puffy too. She'd cried so much they hurt.

She looked at her phone and saw she'd done some drunk texting to Julie.

Are you OK? What happened? Julie demanded.

Jeremy wasn't what I expected, Ravyn had replied. He wanted to do a three-way at his place. He had another girl there and everything.

Are you kidding? You didn't do it did you? Do I need to come over?

I didn't do it. I got out of there as quickly as I could. How could I be so wrong about him?

How long did you know him?

About two or three weeks. Did I move too fast?

Julie tried to think how she would respond. Internally, she was jumping for joy that Ravyn had broken up with Jeremy, but she was also torn that Ravyn was hurting.

Well, that wasn't a whole lot of time. Not that I'm judging you. I love you and I don't want you to be hurt.

I did move too fast.

No, no! I didn't mean it like that.

I'm such a loser. I'm going to be single forever.

You will not! Don't say that. You will meet a man and get married and have children. You'll have all those things.

Ravyn wasn't so sure. She was feeling so alone, just so bereft. Her heart hurt.

Listen, just sleep on it tonight. And don't text Jeremy wanting to make up.

Oh, there is no chance of that. He's such a jerk.

He is a jerk. Because he didn't get to know the real you. He didn't love the real you. A man who loves the real you won't ask that of you. Love you.

Love you, too.

Ravyn reread the texts from last night. Julie was such a good friend. How did she get so lucky?

Ravyn shuffled out to the kitchen and made coffee. After the first cup, she began to feel better. She then moved to the shower, scrubbing herself with her loofah. Ravyn wanted to cleanse herself of the night before.

When she emerged from the shower, her pink bathrobe wrapped around her, she picked up her phone and texted Julie.

I'm alive, she texted. Ravyn waited for the text reply.

I'm glad. You OK?

I'm OK. Just embarrassed. I'll get over it.

You will get over it. This is just a bump in the road.

Coffee is my true love. It's always there for me and picks me up when I feel down, makes me feel warm inside.

Julie laughed. That was the Ravyn she knew. Joking through her pain. Ha ha. You need to put that on a coffee cup.

Maybe I do. Thanks for being such a good friend. What did I ever do to deserve you?

You'll be OK. Love you.

Love you, too.

Marc was surprised to get a text from Julie so early on Saturday morning. He had gone to the gym early that morning, needing to burn off some tension. Some sexual tension, if he was being honest.

Ravyn's relationship with Jeremy was eating at him.

Ravyn and Jeremy are over, Julie texted.

Marc sighed a deep sigh of relief.

How do you know? he asked.

She drunk texted me last night. It's over.

What happened?

Do you really want to know?

Marc hesitated. Yes, he answered.

Jeremy wanted her to have a three-way. He had another girl at the apartment last night when Ravyn got there.

Marc winced. He wiped his face with the gym towel he had in his hand. She didn't do it, did she?

Marc, you know Ravyn would never do that.

Thank God. But I know she wouldn't.

Marc could sense Julie was getting angry. Judging him for being doubtful and worrying about Ravyn.

I'm just worried about her, he texted back.

I'm worried about her too. I think you need to reach out to her, but don't do it today or tomorrow.

When should I text her?

Maybe Monday? Ask her how her day has gone at the end of the day? Make it a casual thing. You've been texting her, right?

Yes, I have. I've tried to text her every couple of days. I want to keep in touch with her. Are you sure I shouldn't text her today?

No. I don't think so. Give her some time to get over Jeremy.

But it will eat me up that she's upset.

I know. It makes me upset too. But she'll be OK. And she'll need a good man like you.

Marc smiled. He hoped he could be a good man for Ravyn.

OK. I'll wait until Monday. But it will kill me.

See, I knew you were a good man.

Ravyn went through the rest of the weekend in a fog. She was hurting from what she considered a betrayal from Jeremy. All she could hear in her head were those last words: "Jeremy, are we going to have some fun?" "Yes, baby, we are."

She could picture Tasha's red hair. She could picture Tasha naked, her red pubic hair, in her mind. The sign of a true redhead.

Ravyn was miserable. She spent most of Sunday in bed in her pajamas. She'd gotten up to feed Felix. She'd made a half pot of coffee, but then returned to her bed.

She slept off and on, but when she woke up, she felt lethargic, unable to fully wake up and when she finally got up, she reached for the red wine bottle.

Ravyn just didn't want to feel anything. She wanted to feel numb. She poured another glass when she heard her phone with a Tinder text message.

Hey Ravyn, how are you this evening?

Ugh. It was from Ed. Ravyn didn't want to talk to him. Not today. Maybe not ever. She didn't want to talk to another man again. But she did respond. It wasn't in her to be rude. And Ed had only ever been nice to her. He was harmless.

Hey, Ed. I'm not so good tonight.

What's wrong?

I broke up with my boyfriend Friday. I don't want to get into it, but it was bad.

Ravyn could feel the tears beginning again. She took a sip of the wine.

I'm so sorry, Marc said. He really was sorry. He could just sense Ravyn was hurting, even though he'd been hoping for the break-up. Is there anything I can do?

I don't think so. I just need to get through this. I just want to forget him.

Maybe I can help you forget about him. Can we meet for coffee soon? Just to meet. No expectations. I'd just really like to meet you.

Ravyn wasn't so sure. It felt too soon to meet anyone. She decided to decline Ed's offer.

Ed, I'm sorry. I'm just not ready to meet you for coffee. I hope you understand.

Of course. I'll wait.

Ed said he'd wait. Wait for her? Wait until she was ready? Was she missing out on a good man? One who was probably boring? But a good, loyal man? She wasn't sure. She was probably overthinking the whole thing.

OK. Thanks. I don't know what to think about this, she said.

Don't think anything about it. I'll just wait until you are ready to meet me. I'll wait. I think you are worth waiting for.

Ravyn was stunned. Was she worth waiting for? And for the first time that weekend, she smiled a sad smile.

Marc was a little nervous that he hadn't waited to text Ravyn until Monday, as Julie has suggested.

But he couldn't stop thinking about Ravyn since Julie had first texted him. He was worried about her.

He put his phone down but picked it up again to text Julie.

Hey, Julie. Is this a bad time? I texted Ravyn this evening. She's really upset. Have you talked to her?

Marc got no response from Julie, so he stood up, pacing his house.

Marc owned a small three-bedroom, two-bath bungalow in the Garden Hills area of Buckhead, an older part of the posh neighborhood of Atlanta.

Marc wandered from his master bedroom, then his guest bedroom, then into the kitchen. He opened the refrigerator, but he wasn't really hungry.

He had pent up energy. Maybe he should go to the gym for another workout. He looked at his watch and saw it was a little late for the gym.

Marc looked around this house. There were things about it he would like to change. It needed some sprucing up.

If the deal went through and he sold part of his company, LindMark Enterprises, he'd erase a lot of his debt and maybe he'd have some leftover to make some upgrades.

He got out a notepad and began listing things he'd like to change. He'd like to update the kitchen, maybe the master bathroom. He could put in some nice landscaping in the front of the house.

Maybe he'd tackle the garage in the back. He always parked in his front drive, because the detached garage was a bit uneven. His list was looking long. He could ask a contractor to at least take a look at his list and give him some estimates.

Marc put the pen down and looked around his house again. What he wanted was for his house to be somewhere Ravyn wanted to live.

Ravyn had a headache as she drove south to her office at *Cleopatra.* She'd had way too much red wine the night before, but she almost felt it was necessary. She needed to get Jeremy out of her system, even if that meant abusing her own.

She thought about her text conversation with Ed. She didn't feel she wasn't all that into him, although he didn't seem to be a bad guy.

Ravyn decided she would try again to meet someone else on Tinder. She'd keep Ed in the background, but she was looking for that spark on Tinder. She was hoping for a spark, at least.

Maybe she'd reach out to Evan. He seemed cute.

Ravyn put her handbag down on her desk. She was grateful she'd gotten in before Jennifer, who usually arrived at 10 a.m. She needed a chance to just get coffee and get her head together. And she needed to do that before Jennifer arrived.

Jennifer usually worked from 10 a.m. to 7 p.m. Ravyn liked to leave around 5:30 p.m., so she could go for a quick run through Piedmont Park or meet friends for dinner in Midtown or Buckhead.

But she often thought she was getting the stink eye from Jennifer if she left at 5:30 p.m. She'd put in her hours. She wasn't shirking her work. She worked hard and stayed late to get things done. She didn't like being made to feel like she wasn't pulling her weight.

Ravyn concentrated on her computer when Jennifer stuck her head in her office.

"How was the time management session Friday?" she asked.

"You mean the one where the time manager was late to my appointment?" Ravyn responded, not even hiding her sarcasm.

"Oh. She was late?"

"Not even a little late. A lot late," Ravyn said, looking up from her computer.

"But was it useful?"

"Not at all. I could have told her how to be more productive."

"Oh. Well, that's unfortunate."

"Jennifer, it was a complete waste of my time. But I was there, so I hope I get the 'team player' badge for this."

Ravyn was tired of Jennifer's passive-aggressive attitude. Her head hurt and she didn't want to dance around the inane corporate bullshit.

"As long as you attended the required meeting, corporate will mark you as attending," Jennifer said.

"I'm delighted," Ravyn responded with sarcasm.

Chapter 11

Jennifer Bagley knocked on Ravyn's door, startling her. She had been texting Evan for the first time on Tinder, she hadn't heard Jennifer approach. Ravyn almost dropped her phone.

"Busy?" Jennifer asked.

"Just texting someone," Ravyn lied.

"For work?"

"No, sorry. This was a personal conversation."

"Please try to keep personal conversations short, Ravyn," Jennifer chided. "I was just checking on the two stories that came in late. Did you get the editing done on them?"

"I'm done with one of them. I'll get on the other one right away," Ravyn said.

"Please do. They are late already."

Ravyn made a face at Jennifer's back as she walked out of her office.

Why was Jennifer so difficult to work with?

Ravyn opened the freelance article but decided she'd need another cup of coffee once she saw some grammatical errors in the first few lines. This article was going to take some work.

Ravyn got up from her desk and grabbed her coffee mug. It was one she got when she ran the Cooper River Bridge Run 10K in Charleston, South Carolina, one year with friends. She'd had a great time and remembered it every time she drank from it. But it needed a good wash.

She headed to the break room, passing Jennifer's office as she went. Ravyn had thought about walking the long way around to the break room to avoid Jennifer's office but decided that would be childish.

Ravyn peaked around the corner but could not see Jennifer in her office. She breathed a little sigh of relief.

Ravyn walked into the break room and went to the coffee pot. Thankfully, there was still coffee in it. She didn't think it was the best office coffee, but it was good when she needed a little boost.

She poured a cup and turned to find Jennifer staring at her. Ravyn almost dropped her mug.

"Oh, I didn't see you," Ravyn said.

"Obviously," she replied.

Ravyn reached up into the cabinet to get some creamer and sugar for her coffee. She'd never learned to drink it without a bit of sugar and milk.

"Have you finished editing the articles?"

"Not yet. One of them needs a little work, and I needed some coffee to get through it," Ravyn said, raising her coffee mug.

"Well, you better get on it," Jennifer said.

"Yes, I'll get on it right away," Ravyn said, leaving the break room as quickly as she could. Bitch, she thought to herself.

When got back to her office she was anxious to see if she'd heard from Evan. He had a very European look to him and had beautiful blue eyes. She was delighted to see a reply.

Hi Mizzou Gal. That can't be your real name, he texted.

It's not. My name is Ravyn.

Are you here in Atlanta?

Yes. In north Buckhead.

Great. I'm Midtown.

You have beautiful eyes.

Thanks, Evan.

I could get lost in your eyes.

Ravyn felt herself blush. She was a little worried Evan was going to begin quoting one of the great poets. "How do I love thee? Let me count the ways." She giggled.

Thank you, she texted but wanted to change the subject. How long have you been on Tinder?

Not long.

Have you been on Tinder long?

Not that long.

Have you been matched with a lot of men?

I've been matched with a few, but they haven't worked out.

Well, I'm glad for that. That means I can have you all to myself.

Ravyn's eyebrows raised. What did Evan mean by that? Was he going to end up being a stalker dude?

Have you been divorced long?

Oh, my wife died five years ago.

I'm sorry to hear that.

Yes, it was very sad. She died in a car accident. I have a young son, too. It was hard to tell him his mother wasn't coming back.

Ravyn felt her heart tug at that information.

How old is your son?

He's just six years old.

That's a terrible time to lose his mother.

Do you have children?

I do not, but I like children, she said. And she did. She always thought she would be a good mother.

You would like my son. He is a very loving child.

What is his name?

Kevin.

Do you have a picture of him?

I can't send a photo through Tinder. Will you text me on WhatsApp? Send me your number. I can send you a photo that way.

Ravyn hesitated for a moment, but then sent her phone number to Evan.

Within moments, a number that was not from Atlanta texted her on WhatsApp.

Hi Ravyn. This is Evan. This is better. I keep track of all of my overseas contacts this way.

Then Evan sent a photo of himself and a beaming young boy looking up at him.

Kevin is adorable. He obviously adores you, she said.

Ravyn could feel a lump in her throat. It saddened her that a young boy would lose his mother so young.

He is adapting. He is resilient, Evan texted back. And this has made us very close. I'd love for you to meet him.

I'd like to meet him, she responded.

Evan, what is your last name?

Evan Miller. What is yours?

Ravyn Shaw.

I'd love to get to know you better. I'd love to be the only one you talk to. Can you stop talking to other men on Tinder? Will you only talk to me? I feel such a connection to you.

Ravyn was skeptical. How could they make a connection in just a short text conversation? She wasn't going to agree to be exclusive just yet.

Well, maybe we should meet so we can see if we are compatible, she texted him.

I'd love that, but I'm headed over to Spain soon for work, Evan responded.

Spain? What do you do for a living?

I'm an engineer. I have a big construction project over there.

Oh, is that why you don't have an Atlanta number?

That is the number for the company I work for. It is in Pennsylvania.

Well, can we meet for coffee before you go overseas?

No, there will be no time. I have to leave this weekend and I have a lot to do.

Who will stay with Kevin? she asked, alarmed that he was leaving his son.

I have a nanny. She will take good care of him. I trust her completely. She's been with us since my wife died.

Ravyn was again skeptical. Why was Evan leaving the care of his young son to a nanny? And what kind of live-in nanny was she? She tried to picture the nanny as a severe older Russian woman. But a picture of a young Swedish au pair came to mind instead.

You can't even meet for coffee? It would only be about an hour, Ravyn persisted.

I'm so sorry, my love. I just can't meet right now. But soon. I won't be in Spain long. Just two weeks. And when I get back, we will meet. But it will be good this way. We can get to know each other by texting. You will see. I know we are meant for each other.

Evan and Ed. Neither man seemed to be her ideal man. One was off to Spain for at least two weeks and the other was a geeky IT guy. She'd keep searching on Tinder.

Ravyn sat down again at her desk and tried to concentrate on the freelance article. She got halfway through and needed to take a break. The article required a lot of rework.

These were the times she disliked. Most of the freelance writers were good and sent her clean, well-written articles. Those that had been run through spell check and a grammar check. But now and again, she felt like the writer missed the mark and she ended up writing and rewriting the work.

Ravyn's coffee had gone cold, but she dared not go back to the break room to reheat it in the microwave oven. She was afraid she'd run into Jennifer again. She didn't want to be chastised again.

Instead, she gulped down the dregs of her cold coffee and got back to work. A half-hour later, she was done and was ready to send the completed copies of the articles over to Jennifer.

Ravyn hesitated on hitting the send button to her email with the attachments. In truth, she was intimidated by Jennifer. She was hoping to have a good working relationship with Jennifer but had never felt that. She felt like Jennifer gave negative feedback on everything she did. How was she expected to work this way?

In the end, she hit the send button on her email, then sighed. I can't live my life on hold, she thought to herself.

She heard another ping on her cellphone.

Ravyn was surprised to see it was from Ed. She sighed. The geeky IT guy.

Hi Ravyn. I hope you are having a good day, Marc, as Ed, said.

I'm doing well today. How are you?

I'm good. Just at work but taking a little break.

Are you allowed to take breaks in IT? Ravyn tried to joke. I thought cybercriminals never sleep.

Well, little breaks. What are you doing?

I just finished editing a couple of articles for the magazine. One of them needed a lot of work. I just sent them off to my boss.

So, you get a little break now, too?

Yes, a little one.

That's good. Are you free for coffee later today?

Ravyn was surprised at Ed's persistence. Maybe it was time to let him down easy and unmatch him. She sighed again, before answering.

Ed, I'm not ready.

OK. Just asking. Let me know when you are. Marc was disappointed Ravyn didn't want to meet with him. He wondered if he should just come clean and tell her who he was. But what if she didn't speak to him again? At least through Tinder, she was still texting him. They were connecting. At least Marc hoped they were making a connection.

Well, have a great afternoon, Ravyn, Marc texted.

You too, Ed.

Ravyn's phone rang that afternoon and she was excited to see it was her sister, Jane.

She hadn't heard from her in a while and wanted details on the wedding and when she'd need to drive up to Greenville to help her pick a wedding dress. Before she'd know it, Jane's October wedding would be here. She hoped she'd have a new boyfriend to go with her.

"Jane! How are you? How are the wedding plans coming along?"

"Oh my God, Ravyn, there is so much to do! I had no idea there would be so much to plan. We have the venue booked, and I'm getting a florist and someone to do the cake. But I've got to get the dress and pick out bridesmaids' dresses. I'm thinking of a seafoam green for the bridesmaids' dresses. What do you think?"

"Jane, you should pick whatever color you want," Ravyn said.

"No, I mean would you look good in seafoam green? Can you come up next weekend? The weekend after July 4? I've got a couple of boutique bridal shops I'd like to visit."

"Of course. I'm running the Peachtree Road Race in Atlanta on July 4, so I couldn't come that weekend anyway. But I'll drive up next Friday night after work. Can I stay with you or should I stay with mom and dad and come up to your place Saturday morning?"

"We don't have a guest room, so you'd better stay with mom and dad. Otherwise, you'd have to sleep on the couch and it's not comfortable."

"OK. I'll call mom and let her know I'll be up Friday night. I'm looking forward to seeing you Saturday."

"Me too. Thanks, Ravyn. I love you."

"I love you, too, Jane."

Ravyn sat at her laptop drinking her coffee Saturday morning, dreading the email she would have to send. She was letting her landlord know she could not buy her condo. Ravyn's stomach was in knots and the acidic coffee wasn't helping.

"Dear Mr. Spanner, It is with great regret that I inform you I will not be able to purchase the condo. Unfortunately, I don't qualify for a loan for the price you are seeking. I will be out of the condo on August 31. Sincerely, Ravyn Shaw."

She hesitated to hit send. She had three more days before she'd have to let Keith Spanner know she couldn't buy her place. But no miracle was going to happen in three days. She hit send. There. It was done.

Ravyn could feel the tears begin to well in her eyes again. She looked around and realized she would miss this place. And it scared her that she didn't know where she would be living next. It scared the hell out of her.

Ravyn ran through Piedmont Park after work the Thursday before July 4, which fell on Saturday. She took a break watching the Atlanta Track Club volunteers setting up for the Peachtree Road Race in the meadow of the park.

The Peachtree Road Race is one of the largest 10K road races in the United States. Ravyn had Friday off, a three-day weekend when July 4 fell on a Saturday. She was planning to pick up her race number at the health expo on Friday.

She was a little leery of the forecast. July 4 promised to bring rain, and Ravyn was hoping the rain would hold off for the race.

If it did rain, she was hoping it would be light rain. Two years ago, a light rain during the race had felt good, keeping temperatures cool.

Ravyn kept her run easy. She wanted to save her legs for the race in two days.

She was glad she didn't have to set an alarm Friday morning. She'd be up very early for the race. She stretched and rolled over in bed.

Ravyn heard her phone ping a text message.

Hey, beautiful. It was Evan Miller. Ravyn needed to Google his name. Maybe he was on social media.

Hi Evan. How are you? How is Spain?

It is very busy. I am working all the time. I can't wait until I can be back in Atlanta.

I'm sorry you are having to work so much. Will you get the weekend off?

No. I have to work Saturday to do all the paperwork for the week.

So, you'll just have Sunday off?

Yes, but I'll get up early to go to church.

Oh, are you religious?

Yes. Are you?

Ravyn squirmed. She wasn't an agnostic. She considered herself a Christian, but she didn't attend church except for the major holidays — Easter and Christmas.

I attend church infrequently, Ravyn said, which was true.

Well, when we are together, we will attend every Sunday.

Ravyn blanched. When they were together? Were they a couple? Were they together? Evan seemed to think so. But from Ravyn's point of view, they were just texting.

I have dreams about you, Evan said.

Dreams about me? You've never met me.

But I see your picture in my dreams. And when I wake up, I'm sweaty.

Ravyn didn't know how to respond to that, so she didn't.

When do you think you'll be returning to Atlanta?

I'll be here for another two weeks. Things are delayed with my job. But I will be with you soon. What are you doing today? Evan asked.

I'm going to pick up my race number for the Peachtree Road Race. I'm running it tomorrow morning. And I'm hoping it doesn't rain.

You will run it in the rain? It's cool here in Spain. I wish I could snuggle next to you.

Ravyn wasn't sure how to reply to Evan, so she texted I will. I run it every year. I love that race.

Well, I've got to go, beautiful. Text me when you finish the race, will you?

I will, Ravyn answered. She put her phone down. What did Evan mean about 'when they were together'? What the hell was he talking about?

Ravyn got to the Georgia World Congress Center, Atlanta's convention center, shortly before 1 p.m. She thought about taking

MARTA, Atlanta's mass transit system, but since the day was pleasant, she decided to walk down.

It was kind of a long walk, but she dared not drive. The traffic to the convention center for the Peachtree health expo would be horrible.

Ravyn, decked out in the Peachtree Road Race T-shirt from 2011, one of her favorite designs, picked up her number and waved to her friend, Carolyn, who was volunteering at numbers pick up that day. She then wandered up and down the aisles of vendors, sampling some power bars and electrolyte water.

Ravyn could feel the excitement building. She was as ready for the race as she could be. The ultimate goal was crossing the finish line and collecting the Peachtree Road Race T-shirt.

Atlantans voted on five T-shirt designs, so runners only learned of the race T-shirt design when they collected the coveted prize. The Peachtree shirt was something of a badge of honor. Ravyn always wore it after she finished the race, whether she went to Julie's house for her family barbecue or at a bar later that week.

Ravyn even wore it when she visited Waffle House for breakfast later that week. Waffle House, a sponsor of the race, always inserted a coupon for a free waffle in the swag bag for the runners.

Ravyn's alarm went off at 5 a.m. July 4. The Peachtree Road race started at 7:30 a.m. Well, the elite runners started at 7:30. Ravyn was not an elite runner, so she would start about 8 a.m. in a later wave of runners. But she wanted to get there fairly early so she could stretch and take one last porta-potty break.

The skies overhead were cloudy as she got to the Midtown MARTA station. The platform was crowded with runners and Ravyn was glad she'd left her condo a little early. She'd need to take MARTA up to the Lenox Square station.

The Peachtree Road Race is a point-to-point race, so runners begin near Lenox Square and Phipps Plaza shopping malls, then run a southerly direction down to the finish at Piedmont Park.

Ravyn squeezed herself onto a MARTA train almost under the armpit of a tall man holding onto the grab bar hanging from the train's ceiling. She was glad he appeared to be wearing deodorant. There were years when she was nose to armpit with those who weren't.

There was nothing else to do, she knew. More runners would try to embark on the train at two more stops before they got to their destination.

Ravyn got off the MARTA train and felt the first raindrops beginning to fall. She was glad she remembered a running hat. She usually ran with just her hair pulled back in a ponytail.

She was dressed for the heat and humidity the Peachtree Road Race was known for. She wore a pink tank top and light gray shorts. The course would supply plenty of water and sports drink but she did carry two packs of sports beans for energy.

She chewed one small pack of the sugary beans as she got to her starting wave. She'd plan to eat the remaining pack around mile four.

As she got closer to the starting line, inching up as each wave ahead of her got its start, she saw the huge American flag hung from a crane. Ravyn felt a lump in her throat.

Before she knew it, she heard the air horn signaling the start of her race wave. The race start was always a little crowded as runners got bunched up.

Ravyn had to be careful, watching her feet and other runners until the field was sparser.

But just a half-hour into the race, Ravyn saw a bolt of lightning and heard a loud boom of thunder. She jumped. That was close, she thought. She looked around uncertain about what she should do. She knew it was dangerous to be running in lightning.

Ravyn put her head down and kept running. When she looked down, she saw her shorts were completely wet and had turned transparent.

Ravyn was mortified. She wasn't wearing any underwear. She'd put on shorts that had a little panty built-in, but she wasn't so sure she wasn't flashing everyone as she ran.

The lightning had caused her to pick up her pace. This may be one of the fastest Peachtree Road Races she'd ever do.

As Ravyn crossed the finish line she was spent. She'd run hard. Mostly out of fear.

She was about to step onto the meadow of Piedmont Park when she saw wooden boards put down. The meadow was a muddy, mucky mess.

Ravyn looked down and didn't want to ruin her running shoes. These were relatively new.

She leaned against a small tree and tried to untie her wet laces. They'd tightened up as they'd gotten wet. She worried she'd have a blister or two from her wet socks.

Ravyn finally got her shoes off and then stripped off her wet socks. She tucked her socks deep inside her wet shoes and walked through the chute to collect her finisher's T-shirt.

It was red and a performance shirt, the first year for that. In years past the finisher's shirt had been 100 percent cotton.

Ravyn had hoped to meet up with some friends after the race but with the muddy field and rain, she decided to head to Park Tavern and the Atlanta Track Club after party. She drank a beer with her running friends, then tried to get her socks and shoes on before making the slow trek back to her condo.

As she walked up Eighth Street, she wondered if she'd be close to Piedmont Park next year for the race.

Ravyn looked at her phone to see what time it was in Spain.

Hi Evan, I finished the race.

Did you win? he asked.

Well, I'm not an elite runner. But I did finish. That's kind of the point. Finishing.

I'm impressed you ran a marathon.

No, not a marathon. It was a 10K. A little over six miles.

I am missing you, Evan said.

Missing me?

I think you are so beautiful and funny. I think I'm falling in love with you.

In love? Ravyn thought. They hadn't even met!

Have I given offense? Evan asked. I just feel so strongly toward you.

No. It's just love is a very strong emotion.

I know. But I am feeling it. I love you, Ravyn. You are my soulmate.

I'm flattered. But I'm not quite there yet. I mean, I don't have those same feelings for you.

But you might? Are you feeling positive, or negative or neutral about us?

Positive, she replied truthfully.

So, you might love me? You see us together? I'm so glad you are off Tinder. I want you all to myself.

Once I meet you and get to know you, it would be better. I want to meet you. I want to get to know you.

Yes, I will be back in Atlanta soon to meet you and get to know you. These people here are driving me insane. They are crooks and so lazy! I am working such long hours. And on Saturday, too.

Crooks?

Yes, they are stealing supplies from my work and are so lazy. They don't even do all the work.

I'm sorry. It seems like you are under a lot of stress.

Yes. A lot of stress. There are equipment problems here, too. That adds to my stress. These lazy workers and the breaking equipment.

Is there anything I can do to help?

I wish you could. I have to return to work. Just know, Ravyn, there is someone in this world who loves you and cares for you.

Bye, Evan.

Ravyn ended the text conversation feeling very confused and a bit uncomfortable at how her relationship with Evan Miller was moving so fast. Too fast, she thought.

Chapter 12

Ravyn headed north on Interstate 85 toward Clemson, South Carolina — her ultimate goal being Greenville the next day to meet Jane.

She pulled into her parent's driveway and grabbed her weekend bag out of the trunk. Her mother, Kaye, met her at the front door.

"I was beginning to worry!" she said.

"I got a late start this evening and traffic out of Atlanta was terrible."

"I don't know how you live in that city," Kaye said. "Atlanta is too big for me."

Kaye closed the door behind her daughter, calling to her husband. "John! Ravyn's here. Please, come get her bag and bring it up to the guest room!"

Ravyn's father John came down the stairs and hugged her.

"How was your drive?" he asked.

"It was OK. Bad until I got a little farther up I-85. Then it was better."

"Well, you've missed dinner," her father said, "but your mother saved you a plate."

Ravyn's mouth watered. She was hungry.

"Thanks, Mom."

Kaye came out of the kitchen with a steaming plate of prime rib, mashed potatoes, and carrots. Ravyn's mother knew how to cook comfort food. Ravyn knew to bring a bottle of wine since her parents didn't drink.

Never sure what was on the menu, Ravyn brought a bottle of red and white.

She'd open the bottle of red and would save the white wine to bring up to Jane's house.

Ravyn's mother and father sat at the dinner table with her while she ate her meal and finished her glass of wine.

They chatted about her job and the Peachtree Road Race. Ravyn had worn her finisher's shirt on her drive up to South Carolina. Talk around the table was easy.

When Ravyn finished her meal, her mother cleared her plate, setting it in the dishwasher. She and her parents moved to the living room. Ravyn poured another glass of wine and settled in for some evening TV.

As she climbed the stairs at the end of the evening, she smiled. It was good to be home.

Ravyn drove north again to get to Greenville to see her sister Jane Saturday morning. Her mother had sent her off with a nice breakfast and some strong coffee. Ravyn got a later start than she intended, but she was sure Jane wasn't going to be up early either. Jane had never been an early riser, especially on the weekends.

Ravyn smiled to herself remembering their times in high school when Ravyn would hear Jane's morning alarm clock blaring. She'd enter Jane's bedroom to find Jane sound asleep and roused her for school.

"How can you not hear that alarm?!" Ravyn would shout at her sister. "It's right by your head!"

Jane would open one eye and stretch, unfazed by Ravyn's anger at having been awoken by Jane's alarm clock, not Ravyn's.

Ravyn had never been to Jane's new apartment that she shared with Nick. Ravyn slowed her Honda on the street but missed the driveway to the apartment complex and had to turn around.

Eventually, she pulled into the complex and found a free parking space. Jane had warned her not to park in a marked space or she'd get ticketed or towed.

Within an hour she and Jane were back in Ravyn's car headed to the first of two bridal shops they planned to visit Saturday afternoon.

At the first shop, Jane tried on four bridal gowns and Ravyn tried on one bridesmaid's dress. Jane's dress looked beautiful, but she wasn't convinced about any of them. Ravyn disliked the one dress she'd tried on.

At the second shop, Jane tried on three dresses and fell in love with the second dress. Ravyn tried on another bridesmaid's dress. It was better than the first one. The style was better, but Ravyn thought the dress's seafoam green color was unflattering on her.

But weren't all bridesmaid's dresses supposed to be hideous, so the bride is the one who looks wonderful?

Ravyn told her sister her dress was beautiful, which it was. And Ravyn would be happy to wear her bridesmaid's dress, but at $250 she just wished she'd liked it better.

She wasn't even sure she could cut it down for a cocktail dress. And with that color, why would she? Sigh, another bridesmaid's dress that would be stuffed in the back of her closet.

Ravyn gasped. This dress would end up being in some closet at her new place. The new place she didn't have yet.

"You don't look so good," Jane said. "You OK?"

"Well, I have to give up my condo."

"What? Why?"

"The investor who owns it wants to sell it. I don't have the money to buy it, so I've got to find another place."

"Oh, no! Why don't you ask Mom and Dad to help you?"

Ravyn didn't want to tell Jane she'd already asked them for help, but because of the wedding, they didn't have any help to give.

"I didn't want to ask," Ravyn lied.

"Well, you should. Hey, let's go get a drink to celebrate. We found dresses for the wedding!"

Jane and Ravyn enjoyed a glass of wine and split an appetizer. They didn't want to spoil their appetites since they were meeting Nick for dinner later that evening at The Lazy Goat in downtown Greenville.

They returned to Jane's apartment to pick up Nick before enjoying their dinner. The trio shared fried goat cheese and crispy Brussel sprouts and then shared a pair of pizzas and a bottle of wine before finally splitting a dessert.

They left the restaurant full of food and elan. They'd had fun. Ravyn felt like she was getting to know Nick better and she liked him more and more. He was a good match for Jane, she thought.

In the crowded restaurant, Ravyn hadn't heard the text pings on her phone. She was alarmed to see several from Evan, all seeming more and more desperate.

Hi gorgeous, are you there? I need some help, baby, please.

Darling, please help me. I need your help so much.

Ravyn, are you there? I need help so badly, my dear, the final one said.

Ravyn saw the last message had come in an hour ago, but she replied as quickly as she could.

What's wrong, Evan?

Are you there, my love? I need some help. Everything has gone wrong.

Wrong? What's wrong? What kind of help do you need? What can I do?

I have a financial situation. I need you to wire me some money. My equipment has broken down. My company has ordered new equipment but the invoice is delayed. I can pay you back, but I need the equipment fixed immediately or I'll be here another four weeks.

Wire you money?

Yes, I need you to wire me $5,000. Please baby. I don't want to be away from you any longer than I have to. Love you so much babe. I want us to be together always.

Ravyn was shocked. She didn't have $5,000 to spare. And why would she send it to Evan Miller?

With a pit in her stomach, Ravyn realized she'd fallen victim to a fake profile. Evan wasn't real. He was out for money. A catfisher. Ravyn had read up on "catfish," fake profiles that targeted the dating apps. Catfishers were only out for money. They were scam artists. She was so disappointed she'd been taken in.

Ravyn felt like such a fool. She could feel tears beginning to form. She went to her phone and deleted his texts and blocked him from texting her again.

"What's wrong?" Jane asked.

"Oh, just had someone ask me for a favor that I cannot do."

"What's the favor?"

"To send someone $5,000."

"That's a pretty big favor."

Ravyn felt a tear slipping down her face. She didn't want to cry in front of her sister. She took a big breath and sighed. "It's a scammer. I'm on Tinder trying to meet someone and I got matched with a person who is a fake profile. Who just wants money."

Jane was quiet.

"I was warned about the fake profiles who just want me for my money. They're called catfish. Except I have no money to give,"

Ravyn said with a bitter laugh. "If I had the money I could have stayed in my condo."

"I'm really sorry."

"Well, don't be. That guy, whoever he was, just picked the wrong fool."

"You're not a fool. You didn't fall for it. And you'll meet someone."

Ravyn gave her sister a weak smile. "I'm sure you're right." But Ravyn didn't feel so sure.

It was getting late and since they'd all had wine with dinner, Ravyn didn't want to drive back to Clemson, so she crashed on Jane and Nick's couch. She awoke stiff and sore. She hadn't slept well because she kept dreaming about Evan. Bad dreams. Dreams of him being on a construction site and falling to his death. Dreams of his son being kidnapped.

Dreams where he robbed her with a gun. Then the dream morphed and she realized her bank account was empty. Ravyn shook her head to clear the dreams.

She sat up on the couch, propping the pillow behind her back. She pulled the sheet up and pulled out her phone.

Ravyn was ready to delete her Tinder account. It was nothing but bad news, she thought.

She hesitated over the delete button. She had one match left with the geek Ed. Maybe she would meet him for coffee and then delete the dating app when it didn't work out.

Hi Ed. I'd like to have coffee with you next week if you are free. I'm in South Carolina this weekend, but I'll be back late Sunday night. Let me know when you are available.

She didn't see a response to her message on Tinder, but it was Sunday morning. Maybe Ed was at church. Another churchgoer, she thought. She'd give it a few hours. If he didn't respond by Monday, she'd delete her account on Tinder without meeting him.

Jane, Ravyn, and Nick enjoyed a nice lunch out on the patio of a trendy brunch spot before Ravyn headed home.

Ravyn hugged her sister hard.

"I'm so glad and proud to be your maid of honor," she said, tears in her eyes.

"Oh stop! If you start crying, I'll start crying!" Jane said.

Ravyn gave out a little cry and wiped her right eye with the back of her hand. "OK, I won't," she croaked. She hugged her sister again, tears spilling from her eyes.

"Love you, sis," Ravyn said.

"Love you, too. Drive safely. Call me when you get in."

Ravyn gave another smile. "You sound just like Mom. I've got to call her, too."

"OK. Call Mom first, but then call me," Jane said.

Ravyn smiled through her tears. "I will."

As Ravyn got on Interstate 85 south, she settled in for a 2 1/2 hour drive. She was listening to Taylor Swift on her iTunes through her Honda's Bluetooth system.

She heard a text chirp on her phone and glanced to see it. It was Ed on the Tinder app.

She opened the app to see what he said, trying to pay attention to the highway.

He said he'd love to meet her, but how about dinner on Tuesday. He'd come to meet her in Midtown.

Ravyn groaned inwardly. Dinner? With coffee, she'd be in and out in an hour if she didn't like him or felt no spark. Dinner could mean sitting with Ed for a couple of boring hours.

Maybe she could ask Julie to call her 20 minutes into the dinner so she could get out of staying longer. Ravyn smiled. That was a plan. Julie would do her a solid.

As soon as she stopped for gas, she'd send a text to Ed accepting his offer of dinner. A girl's gotta eat, right? she smiled.

Ed, I'd love to have dinner. When and where? I'm on the road returning to Atlanta. Just let me know what the plans are.

Then she'd text Julie to let her know of the emergency call plan.

Hey Jules. OK. Evan turned out to be a fake profile. He was a catfish. Google it. I've agreed to go on a dinner date with Ed, but I need an emergency call in case he's a weirdo. Let me know if you can do it.

Ravyn hadn't left the ladies' restroom at the Georgia welcome center near Hartwell, Georgia, when she got Julie's responding text.

Evan was a fake profile? WTF?

He wanted $5,000 from me. He picked the wrong fool for money. If I had that money it would go to buy my condo.

Oh, I'm so sorry. But you are going out with Ed?

Yes, I've told Ed I'd have dinner with him next week. I just need an emergency call in case he's a total loser.

Maybe you'll like him.

Maybe. But will you call me? I don't know our dinner plans yet.

I'll call you. I promise. I have a good feeling about Ed. Good luck.

Thanks.

Ravyn got back in her Honda and continued south, ready to be back in Atlanta and her home. She was also a little concerned about Felix. She'd left him alone that weekend, not asking Jake Palmer to cat sit him. Instead, she'd left extra food and water. She was only going to be gone for a weekend, after all.

Ravyn unlocked the front door of her condo, dropping her bag at the foot of her breakfast bar.

Felix came out of Ravyn's bedroom and chirped at her.

"Felix! I'm home, boy. Did you miss me?"

Ravyn realized how ridiculous her asking that question was. Most likely, Felix had slept all weekend, enjoyed himself in a sunny spot, licked himself inappropriately, and only needed the litter box changed.

Around 8 p.m., Ravyn's Tinder app chirped. It was Ed.

Hi Ravyn. I'm so glad you'd like to have dinner. I'm willing to come to you. How about Tin Lizzy's in Midtown? Do you know that restaurant?

Marc Linder certainly knew that restaurant. It was the first date he'd had with Ravyn. Although at the time, it hadn't been a date. He'd just met her for dinner to thank her for the profile she'd written on him for Atlanta Trend magazine.

But today, he liked to think of it as their first date. It was the start of their initial relationship.

Ravyn gave a little start when Ed suggested Tin Lizzy's. The last time she'd been there, she'd had dinner with Marc.

Marc. Was she missing him? Or was she missing the idea of him?

She shook her head, clearing Marc from her mind. It was Ed who wanted to have dinner with her. Ed was interested in her.

Sure, Ed. That restaurant is not far from my condo. I'd love to meet you there. What day and what time?

How about Tuesday at 7 p.m. Let's say the patio.

Sounds great. I'll meet you then.

Ravyn put down her phone. It was done. She was going to meet nerdy Ed. She hoped it went well, but she didn't think it would. Well, she'd walk down to the restaurant and order a pitcher of margaritas. If the date went badly at least she'd have a good buzz when she walked home.

If the date went well… Well, she'd see how that went.

She picked up her phone to text Julie for the emergency call.

Hey, I'm meeting Ed at 7 p.m. at Tin Lizzy's in Midtown. Call me at 7:20 or so?

Yes, I'll call you then. Good luck!

Ravyn wasn't so sure she'd need luck on that night.

Julie couldn't wait to call Marc as soon as she learned Ravyn agreed to have dinner with him. But she didn't want her husband Rob to know she was calling Marc.

She got her daughters to bed and saw Rob was engrossed in a TV detective program. NCIS something.

She slipped into the guest bedroom with her glass of red wine and called Marc.

"Hey. I see you have a date with Ravyn."

Marc was a bit startled that Julie just started talking. No greeting, no hello.

"Ah, yes. She agreed to meet with me. I'm not sure why."

"I know why," Julie said.

"So, tell me. Why?"

"She got matched with some guy named Evan, and he turned out to be a fake profile and asked her for money."

"She didn't give him money did she?"

"No! She doesn't have it. Marc, you know that."

"I know that."

"Where are you taking her for your date?"

"Tin Lizzy's in Midtown. It's where we first had dinner."

"That's very romantic, Marc. You need to know she misses you." Julie took another sip of her wine.

"I hope she misses me," Marc said. "I'm a little nervous about this. She's going to finally know it was me, not Ed, and that I was being deceitful. What if she sees me and walks right out of the restaurant?"

"Well, I don't know what she'll do in that case. But you need to convince her that you care for her so that she doesn't want to leave."

Julie jumped as her husband banged on the guest bedroom door.

"What are you doing in there?" Rob asked. He had heard Julie talking to someone, although he didn't know who. Rob rattled the doorknob. Why was the bedroom door locked? "Julie!"

"Hey, I've got to go," Julie whispered to Marc. "Call me tomorrow."

Julie walked over to the guest bedroom door and unlocked it, opening it to see her husband scowling.

"Who were you talking to?" Rob demanded.

"Just a friend with a personal problem. Am I not allowed a little privacy?" Julie asked, taking another sip of wine and starting to be annoyed with her husband.

"I just wanted to know where you were, that's all," Rob said, backing down.

"Well, I'm right here," Julie said as she drained her wine glass. "I'm out of wine," she added, walking past Rob and heading down the stairs to the kitchen, which is where she'd find more wine. She was ready for another glass of Cabernet.

Ravyn was glad to hear from her real estate agent first thing Monday morning that there was another property to look at, and could they meet that evening?

Cindy Freeman certainly was working to find her a new place to live. Ravyn was game and said so.

Do you want to meet at the property? Cindy texted.

Sure, what's the address?

Cindy sent the link to the condo property.

I'll be off work by 6 p.m. I'll leave for the condo right away.

Meet you there, Cindy texted.

Ravyn was able to leave work a few minutes early but since rain began earlier that day, she crawled up Peachtree Road. Cindy was waiting for her.

"Hi, Cindy. Sorry, I'm late," Ravyn said, shaking her umbrella off in the small foyer of the building.

"Don't worry about it. I know how it is. This is a one-bedroom, one-bath condo. It was converted from older apartments, but I think it has some character. It has some finishes you don't normally find in this price range."

Ravyn walked through the open door and smiled. There were lots of windows along one wall, giving the condo a lot of natural light. There was also a long mirror along the living room wall.

"What's with the mirror?"

"Well, these apartments were built in the 1970s. That was the style then. You can always remove it and paint the wall. This place probably needs a good coat of paint. It doesn't look like the owner has done that."

Ravyn saw she would have to repaint the place. The living room walls were dark green, with the kitchen a bright orange.

"Is the owner a Tennessee fan? Green and orange are not colors I'd pick for my home."

"You could be right," Cindy chuckled. "But I've seen worse."

"I bet. I remember that condo with the black walls. Yuck. You could probably write a book about it."

Ravyn walked into the bathroom, which was small, then entered the bedroom. It was small too, with a very small closet. She wasn't sure how she'd get some of her clothes and shoes to fit in this tiny closet.

"Is this a queen bed?" she asked, looking at the small bed.

"Hmm. I don't think it is. I think this is a double bed."

"Do you think I could get a queen bed and dresser in here?"

"I'm not sure. Maybe the bed, but probably not a dresser. But it depends how big your dresser is."

Cindy walked to the far wall of the bedroom, near the closet. "Could you put it here?"

"If I put it there, I'm not sure I could open the bedroom door all the way."

Ravyn walked into the kitchen. It was small, too, with outdated appliances and a white Formica countertop that had obvious stains.

"Well, this certainly has the charm of a 1970s-era apartment," Ravyn said, trying not to sound too disappointed. "But I can't see myself living here."

"Very well. It was in your price range, but I can see why. I'll keep looking."

"Thanks, Cindy. I know you are looking. I'm just afraid I won't find anything by the time I have to move out."

"Have you thought about getting a short-term apartment lease? That way you can keep searching without having to worry about getting locked into a full lease. I think you should look into that. We couldn't close in under a month."

"OK. I guess I better check that out, then."

"I don't mean to discourage you, Ravyn. You are just in a limited price range for this area. If you'd consider something outside the Perimeter, I could find something larger for you."

"Let me think about it," Ravyn sighed. "It's just I love living in Midtown."

"I know you do. Why don't I find a couple of properties outside the Perimeter just to show you what's out there."

"OK. I guess I should."

Chapter 13

Ravyn was nervous Tuesday knowing she would be meeting Ed. She'd asked for his phone number on the Tinder app. She could tell he'd seen the message, but he hadn't responded.

Marc saw Ravyn's message asking for his phone number and panicked. She knew his cell number. He couldn't give her that one. She'd know it was him.

He quickly called Julie for help.

"Julie? It's Marc. Ravyn has asked for my phone number. What do I do?"

"Hey, Marc. Just go down to Walmart and get one of those burner phones."

"Burner phones?"

"They're the phones that drug dealers use so they can't be traced by the police," Julie answered.

Marc stopped talking in stunned silence. "And how do you know that?" he asked tentatively.

"Oh, I watch all those cop shows. Or rather my husband Rob likes all those shows. The drug dealers use them all the time. Just go to Walmart and get a cheap phone with a cheap service."

"I don't have time to do that today," Marc stammered. He was meeting Ravyn in just a few hours and he didn't have time to drive to Walmart to get a phone.

"What about a Google number? One of my tennis partners has one so her husband doesn't know who she's having an affair with."

Once again Marc was stunned into silence. "What?"

"I'm kidding, Marc! She uses the Google number as her business phone so she doesn't have to give out her cell number."

Marc breathed a sigh of relief. "Of course! Why didn't I think of that? I can get that right away. Thanks, Julie."

"No problem. You know Ravyn has asked me to be her emergency call."

"Her what?"

"She's asked me to call her cell about 20 minutes into the date so she can bow out if it's going badly."

Inwardly, Marc groaned. It might go badly inside of two minutes if Ravyn gets mad at his deception.

"What do I do?"

"How about I call her a little early and calm her down if she's upset."

"Ah, she might be upset."

"Then I'd say you are going to have to wow her and talk fast," Julie advised. "Why don't you bring some flowers or something?"

"That's a great idea."

Julie rolled her eyes. Of course, it was a great idea and Marc hadn't thought of it.

"I think her favorite flowers are daisies. Gerbera daisies."

"Great. I can get those at Publix," Marc said.

Oh Lord, Julie thought. Ravyn's getting grocery store flowers.

"Hey, how about you stop at a florist and get a nice bouquet of daisies. You want to make a good impression, right?"

"Right."

"OK, go get her tiger," Julie said.

"Thanks, Julie. I appreciate all you've done for me."

Marc stopped at a florist near his Buckhead home. He ordered a nice Gerbera daisy spray and was just about to pay when he looked up and saw a small bouquet of roses. He'd get those for Julie as a way of thanking her.

"Would you like to send a card with this order?" the florist asked.

"Yes, I would."

"Julie, thanks for all you've done for me, M.," he wrote. Marc gave instructions for the delivery to Julie's house and left for his date with Ravyn.

Ravyn had gotten a message with Ed's phone number and texted that she was at Tin Lizzy's.

Ed said he was running just a little late and would be right there.

Marc had seen Ravyn enter the restaurant, but wanted her to be seated on the patio so she couldn't bolt without allowing him to explain why he was there and not the fictitious Ed.

Marc had tipped the hostess $20 to make sure Ravyn got a corner table on the patio.

Ravyn sat at the table feeling her palms sweat. She was nervous. She rubbed her palms on her jeans and scanned the patio for Ed.

Her eyes widened when she saw Marc walking toward her.

"Oh, hi Marc," she said. "Are you having dinner here tonight, too?"

"Yes."

Ravyn could see the flowers in his hand.

"On a date?" she asked.

"Yes," he replied.

Ravyn could feel a frozen smile on her face, trying not to show disappointment.

"These are for you," he said, handing her the Gerbera daisies and sitting down across from her.

Ravyn's frozen smile went from a shocked 'O' to a grimace with knitted brows.

"Marc, you can't sit here. I'm waiting on a date," she hissed.

"I know."

"Well, you have to leave. My date is about to get here."

"He is here."

"Where?" Ravyn looked around, craning to see if she saw Ed.

"I'm right here, Ravyn. I'm Ed."

Ravyn's eyes narrowed and she could feel her cheeks get hot.

Just then, her cell phone rang. It was Julie's emergency call. But it was early. Thank God, Ravyn thought.

"Let me just get this a minute," she said to Marc.

"Now Ravyn, don't be mad," Julie said immediately.

"What do you mean?"

"I mean don't be mad that Marc is Ed. We didn't know how else to get him matched to you."

Ravyn's eyes now widened again.

"You were in on this?" Then Ravyn remembered Julie taking her phone and "accidentally" matching her with Ed. "Julie!" she shouted at her friend.

She was now angry with Marc and angry with her best friend. She felt like she'd been betrayed.

Marc felt like he needed to intervene. He didn't want Julie and Ravyn to have a falling out.

"Ravyn, it was all my idea," he said, trying to interrupt.

"Oh, don't listen to him, it was all my idea," Julie said, hearing Marc trying to take the blame.

Ravyn didn't know what to say. She stood up, ready to leave the restaurant, but still held her phone, ready to yell at Julie.

Marc reached out to grab Ravyn's arm.

"Let go of me!" she shouted, jerking her arm away. She nearly dropped her phone. Other patrons were beginning to stare.

"Ravyn, Ravyn, calm down," Julie said. "Have dinner with Marc. Have a margarita, or three. Hear what he has to say. He's got big news about his company."

Ravyn glared at Marc, covering her phone. "You have big news about LindMark?"

Marc shook his head. "I do. I'd love to tell you about it. Please have dinner with me."

"I feel like I'm here under false pretenses."

"Bye!" Ravyn could hear Julie call out as she hung up.

"Who is Ed?" Ravyn asked as she sat back down. She was taking deep breaths, trying to calm down. "A friend? I mean where did you get those profile photos?"

"Those are some photos of my brother, Bruce," Marc said. He wasn't sure Ravyn wouldn't bolt from the restaurant. "And Edward is my middle name."

Of course, Ravyn remembered. She'd gotten him some low-ball glasses for his Scotch as a gift for Christmas two years ago and had them monogrammed: MEL.

"You and your brother don't look anything alike," she said, cocking her head at him.

"No. I take after my father. Bruce looks more like my mother."

The waitress came over and saw the bouquet of daisies on the chair next to Ravyn. "Would you like some water for those?" she asked.

"Oh, yes, that would be lovely," Ravyn said, looking over at the flowers. She couldn't let the flowers go to waste. "Gerbera daisies are my favorite, you know."

"I know. Julie told me."

Of course, she did, Ravyn thought.

The waitress disappeared, returning with a pitcher of water.

"And can we get a pitcher of house margaritas?" Marc said, turning to the waitress. "Margaritas are OK, right?"

"Oh, yes," Ravyn replied.

"Margaritas will be right up," she said. The waitress came back with the pitcher of margaritas in one hand and two frozen glasses in the other. "Are you celebrating anything tonight?" she asked as Ravyn was putting the daisies in the water.

"This is sort of our second first date," Marc said.

"Second first date?" the waitress questioned.

"We had our first date here several years ago. Now we're having our second first date," Marc explained.

"We broke up in between," Ravyn broke in.

"Oh," the waitress said. "Do you know what you'd like to order or do you need a minute?"

"I think we'll need just a minute," Marc said.

The waitress looked as if she couldn't leave the table fast enough.

"I think you scared her off," Marc said. "I hope she'll come back. I'm hungry."

Ravyn giggled. She hadn't meant to be so blunt.

"So, what's this big news about LindMark?"

Marc shifted uncomfortably. "Ravyn, I have to ask you to keep this in the strictest of confidence."

Ravyn nearly rolled her eyes. "Seriously, Marc? You can't trust me?"

"I'm sorry. It's just that if this gets out, the deal will be off. And I can't afford that. I really can't."

"Marc, we aren't together anymore but I'd never betray your confidence."

"Well, I have a majority buyer for LindMark."

Ravyn sat up, excited. "That's great! That's what you need, right?"

Just then the waitress walked over, pad in her hand. "Are you ready to order?"

"How about we order some chips and cheese dip. We haven't looked at the menu," Marc said.

"OK, sir," said the waitress as she walked away.

"The majority buyer is Black Kat Investors," he said, his voice lowered. "I'll be a minority owner though. I'm giving up control of my company."

Marc looked pained as he spoke those words. Ravyn furrowed her brows.

"But I thought you didn't want to give up control. I know you wanted investors, but not to give up control."

"I don't want to give up control," Marc said a little too loudly. He lowered his voice again. "But to get the investors I need, they want to call the shots. I have no choice."

Marc looked down, dejected. He looked up and tried to give a smile. "But tell me about you."

Now Ravyn looked down and frowned. "Well, I haven't had very good luck on Tinder, that's for sure."

"Well, you met me, didn't you?" Marc said with a grin.

Ravyn half-smiled. "Well, yes I did. I guess my big news is I'm losing my condo."

"Oh, Ravyn, I'm sorry. What happened?" Marc asked, knowing full well the story Julie had told him.

"Well, my landlord, my investor, has decided to sell the condo. And I can't afford to buy it. Plain and simple. Except I can't afford anything nice in Midtown," she said, her voice starting to shake.

"Oh, Ravyn," Marc said, feeling genuine concern for her. "Can you rent something?"

Just then, as if on a bad cue, the waitress appeared with the queso dip. "Are we ready to order?"

"I'm afraid we'll need more time," Marc said. He looked over at Ravyn, wiping her eyes.

The waitress glanced over at Ravyn and said, "Very good, sir."

"We really should decide on food. She's going to give up on us," Ravyn said.

"OK, what do you want," Marc said, picking up the menu. "And this is on me. No argument. This is supposed to be a Tinder date."

"OK. Can I order whatever is the most expensive thing on the menu?"

"In a Tex-Mex restaurant? Go ahead," Marc laughed.

In the end, they decided on fajitas, steak and shrimp.

They ordered another pitcher of margaritas and the evening got late. Just like their first date at Tin Lizzy's.

Ravyn was surprised at how easy it was to talk to Marc. Their conversation just flowed. She was at ease and relaxed by the end of the evening. It was a long time since she'd felt this way.

She found herself laughing at his easy jokes and his self-deprecating ways.

"Oh Marc, that didn't happen!" she exclaimed.

"Yes, it did! It really did!" he replied excitedly.

As the night got late, the fairy lights on the patio winked. The waitress walked over to clear their plates.

"Any dessert?" she asked.

Ravyn and Marc looked at each other with that too stuffed look.

"Check please," Marc said.

Marc and Ravyn stood at the front door of the restaurant, Ravyn holding the daisies with some paper towels wrapped on the ends to keep them from dripping.

"I walked over," she said. "Did you park nearby?"

"I'm right over there," he said, pointing to a surface lot. "May I walk you home?"

Ravyn hesitated. There were plenty of people on the sidewalks. She knew she'd be safe, but Marc was being gallant. "Sure. That would be lovely."

Ravyn was holding the flowers with two hands, making it impossible for Marc to hold her hand while they walked down Crescent Avenue before turning on 13th Street and again on Peachtree Road. It was just a few blocks to Ravyn's condo building.

She looked up at the tall building. "I'm going to miss this place," she sighed. "It was so convenient to everything."

"I know you will," he said. "I'm sorry you have to leave."

"Well, this was nice, Marc. I had a nice time despite the trickery."

"I didn't mean to trick you. I just wanted to have dinner with you."

Marc took one hand away from the flowers she was holding. "I've missed you. Really missed you. And I want to say I'm sorry."

"Marc…"

"No, Ravyn, let me finish. I should have believed you from the start. I let my anger get the better of me. And I lost the best thing that ever happened to me. I lost you. And I'm sorry."

Ravyn could see Marc had tears in his eyes. She'd forgotten how the gold flecks showed in his hazel eyes.

"Apology accepted."

"I'd really like to see you again."

"Marc, I'm just not sure…"

"I know we have to start over like we are dating for the first time. And you can take it as slow as you need to. I just don't want to lose you again. How about it?"

"We can go slow?"

"Yes."

"We don't have to get physical?"

"Not if you don't want to," Marc said, but inwardly he groaned. He desperately wanted to feel Ravyn's naked body next to his. He missed the smell of her perfume, the scent of her shampoo in her hair when she slept next to him.

"OK. If we can set those ground rules," she said.

"Great. Can you have dinner Friday?"

"Sure."

"No other Tinder dates?"

Ravyn smiled wanly. "No. Not right now. Just you, I guess."

"I'm glad," Marc whispered as he reached down and kissed Ravyn tenderly. "Good night, Ravyn. I enjoyed our second first date immensely."

"Good night, Marc," she said as she entered her condo's lobby.

Ravyn couldn't help but smile as she worked at *Cleopatra* Wednesday morning.

Jennifer Bagley walked by Ravyn's office and stopped.

"You're in a good mood," she said at the office door. "Have a hot date last night?"

"I had a very nice dinner with an old friend," she said, not wanting to share her personal life with Jennifer. "It was a nice way to reconnect."

"Yes, it always is good to reconnect with friends. Do you have a preliminary budget for the next issue? I'd like to have that by the end of the week."

"I'll have it on your desk Friday," Ravyn responded.

"Great."

Ravyn smiled as she thought about seeing Marc on Friday, too. She'd drop the budget on Jennifer's desk right before she left work to enjoy her weekend.

The florist was running late with her deliveries on Wednesday afternoon. The last one was to a Julie Montgomery in Buckhead.

She got out of her delivery truck and moved to the back to get the flowers.

As she started up the driveway a black Mercedes-Benz pulled up and a gentleman exited.

"May I help you?" Julie's husband Rob asked.

"I have a delivery for Julie Montgomery," the woman answered, ringing the front doorbell.

Rob stared at the flowers. Who the hell was sending his wife flowers? he wondered.

"I can take those for you," he started to say when Julie opened the door.

"Julie Montgomery?" the florist asked.

"Yes."

"These are for you," she said, handing over the flowers in a blue vase.

Julie looked puzzled. She wasn't expecting flowers. Then she saw the frown on Rob's face. Julie smiled brightly and took the flowers.

"Thank you so much," she said.

Rob entered their house. "Who is sending you flowers?" he demanded.

"Well hello to you too," Julie snapped. "I have no idea who they are from. Maybe I have a secret admirer."

"You'd better not!" he shouted.

"Keep your voice down!" Julie hissed. "Do you want the girls to hear you?"

Julie reached for the card to see who they were from, but Rob reached over and snatched it from her hand.

"Hey!" she yelled.

Rob read the card and waved it in front of her. "Who the hell is M?"

Julie grabbed the card back from her angry husband. "Let me see that."

Julie read the card and began laughing. She was laughing so hard she couldn't catch her breath.

"What's so funny?" Rob demanded. "Are you seeing someone?"

"I am not," she said, suddenly angry. "But it's nice to think you'd accuse me of that. You're the pot calling the kettle black! These are from Marc. Ravyn's Marc."

"Is Ravyn back with Marc? I thought they broke up. And why did he send flowers to you?"

"They did break up, you asshole. He wanted to get back with her. I helped."

Julie grabbed her car keys and turned to her husband. "You can fix dinner for your daughters tonight. I'm going out!"

"Please don't go," Rob said, grabbing her arm. "I thought," he stammered. "I just thought..."

He looked stricken, like he was going to cry. Julie felt her anger melt.

"I thought you were seeing someone," he said quietly. "You've been acting so secretive. I can't lose you, Julie. I just can't. I messed up, I know, but I can't lose you."

Julie turned and hugged her husband. They were both crying in the foyer when their daughters came down the stairs. "What's going on? Why are you crying? What's for dinner? Who gave you flowers? Daddy?"

Julie wiped her eyes with the back of her hand.

"Yes, your father gave these to me," she lied. "Aren't they beautiful? They are so beautiful they made me cry."

Ravyn walked down the corridor to Jennifer's office Friday afternoon but could hear raised voices as she got closer to Jennifer's closed office door.

"You are completely out of line here!" She could hear a man shout.

Was that Joel? It sounded like it, Ravyn thought.

"Well if I didn't have to keep cleaning up your mistakes, I wouldn't have to report this to corporate!" Jennifer shouted back.

That didn't sound good, Ravyn thought. Jennifer had reported Joel to corporate? Yikes. She wondered what Joel had done. He'd probably be in Ravyn's office Monday to bad mouth Jennifer and tell her what happened.

Ravyn didn't want to stand at the door eavesdropping, but she had told Jennifer she'd give her the budget. Ravyn walked back to her office and got a manila folder, sliding the budget in, then sliding it all under Jennifer's door.

The arguing stopped. Regretfully, they'd both now know she'd likely heard the argument, but she couldn't help that.

Ravyn practically sprinted to the elevator and gave a big sigh of relief as she pushed the down button.

Chapter 14

Marc had called Ravyn Thursday night and told her he had made reservations at Portofino in Buckhead for their dinner Friday.

She'd have to go home to get ready. Portofino was a fancy Italian restaurant and she'd need to change into a nice dress instead of her Friday casual attire. Her office let employees wear jeans and a nice shirt on Fridays, but she couldn't go like that on her date.

Ravyn found herself getting excited about seeing Marc and the dinner. He'd texted that he was coming to pick her up. He was putting in an effort, she'd give him that.

She glanced over at her Gerbera daisies in a nice vase she was glad she hadn't packed away yet. They were so pretty in the variety of colors: bright pink, yellow, orange, and red.

Around her were boxes she had collected from work — she loved the copy paper boxes with their lids — and a few boxes from the nearby liquor store. She was making a half-hearted effort to begin packing up her things and tossing out what she didn't want. She'd started a bag for donations as well.

But at the moment she was rushing around her condo, trying on one dress, then another. Both now were crumpled on the floor as she decided on a third. Strappy sandals were strewn across the floor as well.

Ravyn was now deciding on jewelry for her outfit when she got a text from Marc. Damn, she thought. He's on time!

I'll be right down, she texted. I'd invite you up but I'm starting to pack so it's a wreck.

No. I'm not in a real parking space.

OK. I'm on my way down.

Ravyn grabbed her lip gloss, threw it in her handbag, and ran out the door.

Marc unlocked the passenger side door before Ravyn slid into his car.

"Hey, you," Ravyn said. She had started to lean in to kiss him, then stopped herself.

"Hi," Marc said. "How was your day? Busy?"

"Not too busy. Kind of steady. I had to deliver the budget for the next issue to my boss and I heard her arguing with a coworker. Awkward," she said in a singsong voice.

"But you still really enjoy the job?" Marc asked.

"I like it most days. I like it a lot of days, but there have been some changes."

Marc slowed for traffic on Peachtree Road. It was Friday in Atlanta. Everyone seemed to be out for dinner and dates.

Marc looked at the clock on his dashboard.

"Are we going to be late?" Ravyn asked.

"We're going to be cutting it close, I think."

"Do you want me to call the restaurant?"

"Maybe you should. I thought by making the reservations for 8 p.m. we'd have plenty of time."

"You should have let me meet you at your house," Ravyn said.

"No. This is a new beginning. I wanted to pick you up. And it's nice just to talk in the car."

Ravyn looked up the restaurant number on her phone and called, explaining they were stuck in traffic but were coming. The hostess assured her the reservation would be held and thanked her for letting them know.

"We're good. They're holding the reservation."

"Thanks."

They suddenly drove on in silence. Marc staring straight ahead moving through the slow traffic. Ravyn didn't quite know where to look and what to say. It was getting awkward.

Marc turned onto Irby, and then in several turns ended up turning up into the short hilly drive to Portofino. A valet was waiting at the top of the crest of the driveway. Marc handed his keys to the valet and walked around to open the door for Ravyn.

He took her hand to help her out of the car. Ravyn felt like a princess. It was bringing back warm memories of Marc, of an earlier time.

Marc put his hand on the small of Ravyn's back as he led her to the front door of Portofino, the flagstone lining the way to the door.

They walked up the short incline to the hostess desk.

"Linder, party of two," Marc said.

"Right this way, Mr. and Mrs. Linder," the hostess said.

Marc smiled and Ravyn looked chagrined. They were led to their table, almost the same one they'd had about two years ago.

"Marc, you are taking us to the places of our first dates," Ravyn said.

"You noticed that did you?" Marc said.

Ravyn smiled. "Well, I did notice. I like that you are taking us back to some special places."

"I'm glad you think of these as special places. They are certainly special places for me. They are the places I fell in love with you."

Ravyn was shocked. "In love with me?"

"Yes, in love with you. Ravyn, I fell in love with you then, and I'm hoping we can fall in love with each other again."

Ravyn was quiet. This was overwhelming. "I…," she started.

"Ravyn, I don't expect you to feel the same way as back then," Marc said. "We're starting over. It's all new now."

Ravyn felt herself relax. She gave Marc a half-smile. "As long as we understand each other."

They ordered an appetizer to share, a bottle of pinot noir wine, and eventually dinner. Ravyn ordered her favorite lamb Bolognese. Marc, as usual, ordered his favorite, a braised short ribs dish.

Once the appetizer arrived, they found themselves downloading into some small talk, but then they moved into more substantial conversation.

Their dinners arrived and they began digging into their meals, each giving a small sample to the other.

But something had been bothering Marc. "So, you got fooled by fake profiles?" he asked.

Ravyn frowned. "Well, I wasn't sort of fooled. I was completely fooled. There was something about his story that seemed off, but I believed it."

"Well, I'm sorry you were hurt, but I'm not sorry you were hurt."

Ravyn widened her eyes. "What?"

"I'm not sorry he hurt you, Ravyn," Marc said. "If he had been great to you, we would not be having dinner together."

Marc reached over to pour Ravyn another glass of wine.

Ravyn took a long sip before answering. "Well, I never thought of it that way."

"Would you have ever returned my calls or gone to dinner with me if that con artist hadn't hurt you?" Marc asked pointedly.

Ravyn shifted uncomfortably in her chair. "No, probably not." She sighed. "Marc, it's not that I didn't want to see you again. It's just I was afraid — am afraid — I'll just get hurt again."

Marc took Ravyn's hand across the table and laced his fingers through hers.

"I don't intend to hurt you ever again."

Ravyn looked into his eyes. He looked so sincere. She had a sudden urge to kiss Marc. Instead, she withdrew her hand from his and drank more wine. She was glad he was driving tonight.

They ordered another bottle of wine as they finished their dinners.

As the waiter cleared their table, he asked if they wanted dessert. Marc and Ravyn looked at each other. There was about a quarter bottle of wine left, enough for a small glass for each of them.

"If I'm honest, I'd like some chocolate cake, and a decaf cappuccino," Ravyn said.

"That sounds great," he said. "I'll take a decaf coffee, instead."

The chocolate cake arrived and they finished the wine. The coffee arrived next. Marc and Ravyn ended the evening draining their coffee cups.

"Shall we go?" Marc asked.

"Sure. I've had a lovely evening, Marc."

"Me, too."

They walked toward the front door and waited for Marc's car to be brought around by the valet.

They got into Marc's older model BMW. "Do you want me to take you home? Or would you like to have a nightcap? Maybe even at my house?"

"Do you have wine at your house?"

"Yes."

"Well let's go there for a little while. You'll take me home later?" Ravyn asked.

"Of course."

They drove down on Peachtree almost in total silence again. Then they turned left onto Peachtree Avenue and then onto North Fulton Drive. They pulled into Marc's driveway shortly before 10 p.m.

Marc opened another bottle of red wine and handed Ravyn a glass. They talked until after midnight, about Ravyn's job, her search for a new condo, and the funny stories she had about some of the Tinder profiles that she'd looked at, Marc's concern about his company's sale, and stories of when they were together.

Ravyn stood up to use the restroom and found her legs were a little wobbly.

"Woah," she said. "I guess I better be going home."

Marc stood up as well. "Ravyn, I'm not sure I should drive now. I can call you an Uber," he said. He looked around his living room. "Or you can stay here."

"Marc! You said…"

"Ravyn, you can sleep in the master bedroom. I'll sleep in the guest room."

"I can't take your bedroom. Why don't I sleep in the guest room?"

"The guest bathroom isn't working well. You take the master. That bathroom is working right. These older houses…" he trailed off.

"I don't have anything to wear to sleep in."

"I'll get you a T-shirt. Will that be OK? And I think there's a robe here you left behind. I think I remember where I put it."

"That would be great."

"I think I even have an extra toothbrush."

Marc found Ravyn's leftover robe, an extra toothbrush, and a clean white T-shirt. He handed them all over to Ravyn as he tried to clean some dirty clothes off the master bedroom floor.

"Sorry, I didn't expect you to be here," he said.

"It's fine. Don't worry about it. I've seen your messy bedroom before. Good night, Marc. I had a nice time tonight."

She closed the door and changed into the T-shirt. She turned off the light and slid under the sheets. She inhaled, smelling Marc's cologne on the bedding. She smiled, rolled over, and fell asleep.

Marc closed the door to the guest bedroom. Ravyn was right next door. He felt a stirring he didn't want to feel. He wanted her.

He wanted to go to her. He wanted to take her in his arms and make love to her.

Marc sighed and sat at the end of the bed, removing his shoes, socks, shirt, and pants. He looked down to see an erection in his boxers. He was trying to think nonsexual thoughts.

He turned the light out and laid down on the bed but couldn't fall asleep. It was going to be a long night, Marc thought.

Ravyn awoke and slowly stretched. She inhaled the slight scent of Marc's cologne again. She was in his bed, but he wasn't.

It was nice of him to give her his bed. She looked at her phone, it was almost 8 a.m. She was surprised she'd slept so late. Well, she and Marc had been up late.

Now she felt a little awkward. Was Marc up? Should she wake him and ask him to drive her home? Maybe she should call an Uber and just leave.

No, that would be rude. She should at least tell him good-bye. She was glad she'd left the robe behind. She pulled it on and opened the bedroom door and could smell fresh-brewed coffee.

"You're up," Marc said. "I've got coffee on."

Marc stood at the counter in his sweatpants, but no shirt. Ravyn's heart did a little flutter.

"Yeah. I'll take a cup. You look tired. I'm sorry if you didn't sleep well in the guest bed."

"No, the bed is fine. I just didn't sleep well."

"Sorry about that. You'll have your bed back tonight," she said, taking a hot cup of coffee from Marc.

"Milk and sugar, right?"

"Yes, please."

Ravyn stirred some sugar and milk in her coffee. She leaned against the kitchen counter. "What are your plans for today?"

"I'll go to the gym and work out. What about you?"

"I'll probably go for a run in Piedmont Park. I need to take advantage while I can. If my real estate agent calls, I'll probably go look at some more condos. I guess by next week I'll start looking for apartments."

"Can I fix you breakfast? Or are you ready for me to take you home?"

"Breakfast would be nice, then I need to get home. I need to feed Felix."

"Oh, right, Felix. Well, I can scramble some eggs. That would be quick."

"Great. I'll go ahead and get dressed. Be right back."

Ravyn went back to the master bedroom and changed back into last night's clothes.

As she re-entered the kitchen, she said, "I'm going to do the walk of shame going back to the condo today."

"Excuse me?" Marc said, standing over the skillet with eggs at the ready.

"The walk of shame," she laughed. "I'm returning to the condo in last night's clothes."

"Oh, right," Marc smiled. "But your chastity remains intact, my lady."

Ravyn blushed, noticing a bulge in Marc's sweatpants. She was hoping her chastity would remain intact by the time she left.

"Yes, you were a perfect gentleman. Thank you. Thanks for letting us go slow."

"Of course," he said. "Are you ready for the eggs?"

Ravyn's cell phone rang Saturday afternoon. It was Julie.

"What's up?"

"You need to thank your boyfriend for sending the flowers to my house and making Rob jealous."

"What?"

"Marc sent me flowers as a thank you for helping get the two of you back together. The delivery arrived just as Rob got home and he went nuts. Accusing me of seeing someone."

"Oh my God, Julie! I'm so sorry that happened."

"Don't be. We got into a fight and I was ready to walk out the door to clear my head. He pulled me back into the house. The girls came down the stairs wondering what all the shouting was about."

"What did you tell them?"

"Well, they asked if their father had sent me the flowers, and I lied and said he did. And now he's being more attentive. You have to thank Marc for making my husband step up in the romance department. We're even planning to go out to dinner on a weeknight! He's booked a babysitter and everything."

"Wow! That's great."

"It is great. It makes me feel appreciated. And how's it going with Marc? Have you slept with him yet?"

"I have not. We came a little close this weekend. I stayed over at his house Friday night."

"And you didn't have sex?"

"No. We're taking it slow. Well, I want to take it slow."

"Well don't go too slow. I hear Laura Lucas has broken up with her man of the month and is on the prowl."

Laura Lucas, the public relations bitch who had been working for Marc when Ravyn and Marc had first met. Laura had done everything in her power to keep Ravyn and Marc apart.

They eventually broke up because of Laura's shenanigans, breaking into Marc's laptop and causing havoc with his company's financial numbers. That was nearly two years ago and Laura's name still made Ravyn's blood boil.

"Do not even speak her name to me. It's like saying Voldemort in the Harry Potter books."

"OK, OK. Just don't wait too long for him, Ravyn. Marc's a good man."

Ravyn was smiling as she arrived at her office Monday morning. She'd had a great date with Marc Friday night, and they'd talked for two hours on the phone Saturday evening. Then they talked on Sunday.

"You're in a happy mood," Joel said as Ravyn entered the break room for coffee. "Get laid this weekend?"

"Joel! That's not appropriate."

"Sorry, sorry," he said. "Did you hear what happened with me and Jennifer Friday?"

"I heard you arguing, but I have no idea why and I'm not sure I want to know."

"Well, I'll tell you. She reported me to corporate. Me! When really I could report her for harassing me."

"Harassing you? How is she harassing you?"

"She is constantly hounding me about ad sales. Says I'm not making my numbers."

"Well, are you?"

"No, but it's not my fault. I've just had a little slump in sales. But I've got a lot of leads."

"That's great. But why did Jennifer report you to corporate? It really couldn't have been for being down in your numbers."

Joel scowled. "I called her a bitch to her face. Well, not to her face. She was leaving my office and I didn't think she heard me."

"Joel, you've got to temper your temper. Ha ha. Say that three times fast."

"You are not funny."

"I'm not trying to be funny, Joel. I'm trying to give you a little advice. I know you and Jennifer don't get along, but don't antagonize her. You can think she's a bitch, but don't say it out loud."

"Well, thank you, Miss Manners."

"Hey, don't get mad at me. And don't call me a bitch as I leave the room," Ravyn said as she took her coffee and went back to her office.

Ravyn looked up two hours later to see Jennifer at her door.

"What's up?" she asked.

"I'm sorry you had to hear my argument with Joel Friday."

"Jennifer, I wasn't eavesdropping. I only heard raised voices through the door. I'm sorry I had to shove the budget under the door, but I wanted to be sure you got it."

"Well, I'm sorry you had to hear it. I won't tell you what it was about, that would be unprofessional."

"Oh, Joel told me," Ravyn blurted out.

"Joel told you?"

Ravyn was sorry she had said anything. She'd probably just gotten Joel in more trouble with Jennifer. This office drama was draining, she thought.

"Sorry, he caught me in the break room and asked if I'd heard your argument. I told him I'd heard it but I didn't know what it was about, and I didn't want to know. I didn't ask him to tell me. He just did."

"That would be just like him."

"Well, I'm not trying to be nosy."

"Do you want to have lunch today?" Jennifer asked.

"With me?" Ravyn said, trying to hide her surprise.

"Yes, with you. We've never been out to lunch. I'd like to get to know you better."

"Sure, that would be great."

"Say, around noon? That Thai place around the corner?"

"Perfect. I love that place."

"I'll meet you at the elevator."

As Jennifer left Ravyn's office she wondered what she'd done to warrant lunch with Jennifer. Was she hoping Ravyn would be her office best friend? Or did she want to know more about what Joel had said to Ravyn?

Ravyn was hoping the lunch would go well. She wasn't sure that it would.

At noon Ravyn headed to the elevator, finding Jennifer waiting on her.

"Ready to go?" Jennifer asked. "Hungry?"

"I am hungry. I didn't have time for breakfast this morning."

"Oh, breakfast is the most important meal of the day," Jennifer said as she pushed the down button in the elevator. "You should never skip breakfast. I have some cottage cheese and a hard-boiled egg every morning."

Ravyn knew that. She'd seen Jennifer in the break room with her breakfast. Ravyn knew it would be a long lunch.

As Jennifer and Ravyn got back on the elevator, Ravyn was a little surprised she'd had a nice lunch. There were some awkward moments, but then they began talking about their earlier careers and hobbies.

Jennifer had shared she'd lived in Oregon and worked in the private sector before coming into journalism. Ravyn had always been in journalism, with her brief detour into freelance work.

Jennifer enjoyed gardening and knitting. Ravyn shared her love of running and told Jennifer about her search for a new place to live.

"I'm sorry that you are having trouble with finding a new place," Jennifer said. "There are a lot of places where I live in Cobb County."

Jennifer lived in a northern suburb of Atlanta.

"Well, I'm trying to stay in Midtown. I just love it here."

"Suit yourself," Jennifer said with a shrug. "But you'll be able to afford the suburbs."

With that, Ravyn knew the lunch was over.

Chapter 15

Ravyn saw Marc twice more that week, once for a movie at Phipps Plaza. She had been wanting to see the blockbuster Marvel movie, "Ant-Man."

Now this was a Marvel movie she could follow. It was nice to hold Marc's hand in the darkened movie theater and eat popcorn.

She'd also had dinner with him at The Tavern at Phipps Plaza. They'd shared some calamari as an appetizer. Ravyn ordered a cheeseburger, while Marc ordered the pastrami sandwich, which came piled high with the classic deli meat.

"This will probably give me heartburn tonight, but I don't care," Marc said. "Have you ever had one of these sandwiches at Katz's Deli in New York?"

"Oh my God. I had one last year. Those are huge. Samantha and I had to split one."

"Samantha?"

"Samantha Hunt. My old boss in New York. My new boss is here in Atlanta. I liked it better when my boss lived in New York."

"How long have you had your new boss?"

"Not quite a year. We went to lunch this week. It was OK, but it was also weird. We're not really friends, but I kind of thought she was reaching out. Like she wanted to be friends. But it was so awkward."

"Sorry to hear that."

"Tell me about the sale of your company. Is it moving forward?"

"Yes, but slowly. I know it takes time when there is an M&A, but it seems to be going at glacier pace."

"I remember that from my days at the newspaper. Mergers and acquisitions can take a long time."

"Yeah. A really long time that I don't really have. My new boss will be Kyle Quitman. Did I tell you that?"

"No. I've never met him. Hey, I forgot to tell you, I'm out of town next weekend. I'm headed up to Greenville to do some stuff for my sister's wedding."

"But you are here this weekend? Do you want to do something? Come over to the house for dinner? I'll grill out."

"That sounds great."

"Come over Saturday. I'll grill some steaks, throw on a couple of baked potatoes."

"Let me bring the wine then," Ravyn said.

"Great. How about you come over at 7?"

"It's a date."

"I'm enjoying this, Ravyn," Marc said, holding out his hand. Ravyn reached across the table to take it. "I feel like I'm getting to know you even better now."

"I like it, too," she said and squeezed his hand.

That Saturday, Ravyn drove her Honda Civic to Marc's Garden Hills home. She always liked the look of his bungalow, a three-bedroom, two-bath house. It was small but cozy.

She pulled into his driveway and grabbed the two bottles of Cabernet Sauvignon she'd bought earlier that day. She knew it would pair well with the steaks.

"Right on time," Marc said at the front door, giving her a kiss. "I've been marinating the steaks all day. I think they'll be really good tonight."

"I can't wait. Is there anything I can do to help in the kitchen?"

"Nope. I've got it all covered. I've got the potatoes started in the oven and I'll steam the green beans at the end. And I'll open one of these," he said, taking the wine bottles. "I'll open both, so one can breathe. I've got a wine aerator, so this one will taste great right away."

Marc poured the wine, then moved out to his back deck where he kept the gas grill.

He had the grill up on high, then moved it down to a medium heat before putting the marinated steaks on. He had some extra marinade in a bowl to brush on the steaks when he turned them.

"How do you like your steaks?"

"Medium."

"Me, too. I would have cried if you said well done."

Ravyn laughed. "My grandmother liked her steaks well done. They were like a hockey puck. My grandfather used to complain he was ruining a good piece of meat for her, but she wouldn't eat it any other way. So, he ruined a good piece of meat for her every time."

"Your grandfather was right," Marc said. "Medium is the way to go."

The steaks were perfect, the potatoes were perfect, the steamed beans were perfect, the wine was perfect, the meal was perfect.

Ravyn pushed away from the dining room table. She and Marc had considered eating out on the patio table, but it was July in Atlanta. In the end, they decided it was too hot.

"Oh my God, I'm stuffed. This was so good, Marc."

"I'm glad you liked it."

"Let me help you clean up."

"I'm going to just load everything in the dishwasher."

"Well, I'll help."

They busied themselves in the kitchen, keeping their wine glasses full as they worked. When they were done, Marc moved them into the living room, taking the second bottle of wine with them.

"Any news on the sale of LindMark?" Ravyn asked.

"Nothing yet," he sighed. "But it won't erase all of my problems."

"Problems?"

"Well, it won't erase all of my debt. The sale will make me look good on paper, but I owe my father about a quarter of a million dollars, with interest."

Ravyn was silent. She had no idea that Marc owed his father that much. That was a lot, she thought.

"And I've got a second mortgage on this house," he said. "I couldn't sell it if I wanted to. I'd never get my money out of it."

"But it's a great house. You don't want to sell, do you?"

"No, I don't want to sell and I don't intend to. But the sale of the company will help clear my debt to my father and put a dent in the second mortgage."

"Well that's good news, right?"

"It's somewhat good news. My father never stopped being disappointed in my leaving the law practice at Kramer & Spelling and becoming an entrepreneur."

"But you were successful at it!"

"I'll be successful if I sell it at the right time, which is now," Marc said.

"I don't see it that way," she answered.

"Well, that's how my father sees it. Once I get most of my debt cleared, I'm going to have to live on my salary. I've got some stock options in the sale, but I can't cash them out for at least two years, and only if I stay with the company to help run it. Over the next 10 years, if I continue to stay with the company, I'll get more options, but I'll only be able to cash out a little at a time."

"Why are you telling me this?"

"Money was a factor at the end of my marriage, Ravyn," Marc said quietly. "I just want to be honest with you. Financially, I'll look good on paper if and when the company is sold. In reality, the next few years are going to be a struggle."

"Marc, you hardly ever talk about your marriage and your ex-wife."

Marc's face showed pain.

"I'm sorry, I shouldn't have brought her up."

"No, it's OK. I never talk about her, my ex-wife, Karen, because it is painful."

"I'm not trying to pry," Ravyn began.

"No, I want you to know. You deserve to know my life before you."

Marc and his wife Karen had met in his final year of law school at The University of Georgia, where Karen was an undergraduate.

Upon graduation, Marc moved to Atlanta, with Karen still in school in Athens. They tried to meet up every weekend, but he was with Kramer & Spelling, or K&S as it was known in Atlanta, working hard, working long hours.

Marc and Karen even broke up a couple of times, he explained, but they always got back together.

"She's from Valdosta, Georgia, straight down I-75 and near the Florida line. And her ambition in college was to get married," Marc said. "Among her friends, Karen had won the prize. She'd married an up-and-coming lawyer for K&S."

They married, but she spent far beyond their means, straining the marriage.

"Did you ever want children?" Ravyn asked.

Ravyn could see tears in Marc's eyes. "We did. Karen had two miscarriages and she never really recovered after them. We never recovered after them. Her spending got out of control after that. I have a lot of debt from my failed marriage, too. I sound like a real prize, don't I?"

"Marc, you're a great man. Don't kid yourself. Do you ever see her, after the divorce I mean?"

"No, she moved back to Valdosta. I never see her or hear from her. She took a chunk in the divorce settlement. I think she has remarried."

"Does it bother you that you didn't have children with her?"

"I want children," he said. He took a long sip from his wine. "I'm glad now we didn't have children together, but I sometimes think about the children we lost."

"I'm so sorry, Marc, I didn't mean to upset you."

"You didn't. It's good to get this off my chest."

"Well, you may want children but you might not want the tween years," Ravyn said. "Julie said her girls are really becoming a handful. Apparently, they know everything now."

"Tween years?"

"I guess it's between the ages from 9 to 12."

"That seems young," Marc said. "Why can't the just be fully formed adults, who have graduated from college?"

Ravyn laughed. "I'm sure my parents had wished me and my sister came out that way. Would have saved a lot of scream fests in our teens."

"Yeah, I know my folks wished that same thing. My brother, sister and I made three. We outnumbered my parents. We could kind of gang up on them when we wanted out way."

"And did you always get your way?"

"Rarely."

Ravyn was pensive, thinking about what Marc had said, about his ex and about his family.

She then slowly stood up, placing her wine glass on the side table and took Marc's glass from his hand, placing it next to her wine glass. She took his hand and led him into the master bedroom.

Ravyn began to pull up Marc's golf shirt.

"Are you sure about this? You said you wanted to go slow."

"I'm sure."

Marc took Ravyn's hands and stopped her from removing his shirt. "Slow down."

He began to pull up her V-necked shirt slowly. Ravyn could feel her skin prickle as Marc ran his hands over her outstretched arms and then down her back. He then unbuttoned her jeans and slowly undid her zipper.

Ravyn could feel the dampness in her panties. She was so glad she'd worn some sexy underwear tonight instead of her far more comfortable "granny panties."

Marc removed his shirt, but not his jeans. He held Ravyn close, smelling her hair and kissing her neck.

Ravyn could feel her nipples get erect. Marc was going so slowly it was making her want him more. She tried to move him to the bed, but he resisted.

He knelt before her, blowing on her panties, then began licking the outside of her panties.

Ravyn moaned and felt her knees go weak. "Marc," she groaned. "Oh, God. Please."

Marc moved up and removed Ravyn's bra, kissing her erect nipples, circling them, then knelt again, pulling her panties down. Ravyn moaned again. "I can't wait," she said. "Please." It was almost a plea.

"You will wait," he said, whispering into her labia. His tongue flicked over her, driving her wild. He pulled her labia open and flicked his tongue on her clit.

Ravyn gasped and her knees buckled. Marc finally placed her on the bed.

He removed his jeans, his erect penis straining behind his boxers.

Ravyn reached for it, but Marc pushed her hand away. "I want to make love to you, slowly."

Ravyn wasn't so sure she could wait for that. She wanted Marc now.

She tried to pull him on top of her. She tried to rush him. But Marc wouldn't be rushed.

He was aroused, but he continued to pleasure Ravyn with his fingers and his tongue. She could barely contain herself.

"Oh God, oh God," Ravyn shouted, climaxing.

"Now I can make love to you," Marc said, with a husky voice.

He put on a condom and moved on top of her and entered her slowly, deliberately. He began to thrust slowly.

Ravyn could feel herself getting aroused again. She was sure she was going to climax again. But she needed Marc to thrust faster, harder.

"Harder, Marc, harder. I need you," she implored.

"Slow, baby, slow. You said you wanted it slow," Marc teased her.

"Marc, Marc," Ravyn pleaded. "Harder, baby, harder."

Marc began to thrust faster and Ravyn responded with an intake of breath, then let out a gasp with her climax.

"Ah, ah," she cried out. Marc climaxed next and Ravyn pulled him on top of her, feeling their heat and sweat.

Ravyn and Marc made love once more that night.

When they awoke Sunday morning Marc had his arms curled around Ravyn. She tried to wiggle out to use the bathroom but ended up waking him.

"Sorry, I didn't mean to wake you. I just need to use the bathroom. I wish I'd left my robe here. It's chilly in the house."

"I like to sleep with the air turned way down. I've got it on a programmable thermostat. I can give you a T-shirt or something," Marc said, leaning on his arm as he watched Ravyn's naked body slip into the bathroom. "But I like to see you naked."

Ravyn made a face at him as she closed the door.

Ravyn crawled back under the sheets and Marc curled his arms around her.

"I'm hungry," she said, giggling. "I seem to have worked up an appetite."

"I can make scrambled eggs again," Marc said, snuggling into her. "I've missed this."

She turned to face him. "But what is this? Friends with benefits? Something serious? Because I'm not sure I'm ready for us to be serious."

"Why not? I'm willing to commit to you," he said, then quickly added, "you know to be exclusive. I want more stability in my life and I'd like for us to be exclusive. No more Tinder, no more dating. Just us."

"Marc, I'm just not sure…"

"Ravyn, I love you."

Ravyn was speechless. "You do?"

Marc looked her in the eyes. "I do. I've always loved you. I should have told you a long time ago."

"I don't know what to say. I mean, not yet. I can't say I love you back, yet."

"It's OK, Ravyn. I'll wait."

He pulled her in closer to him. She could feel herself becoming aroused and she could tell Marc was as well. Breakfast would have to wait, she thought.

Ravyn and Marc talked or texted almost every day that next week and went out again during the week. They ended up back at her place, amid half-packed boxes.

"And you haven't found anything you like?" Marc asked.

"Nothing in my price range is all that nice. I think I'm going to have to rent something. I hope I can afford rent in Midtown. Everything has gotten so expensive since the economy turned around."

"I believe it. What time do you leave Friday?"

"Right after work, but I'll be back Sunday afternoon. I've got another dress fitting for my bridesmaids dress and there's some bridal luncheon I've been invited to."

Ravyn sighed.

"Sounds like you aren't that excited."

"Well, I'm supposed to be getting the bachelorette party together and it's stressing me out. I know destination parties are a thing now, but I can't swing going to Las Vegas or anything."

"What are you going to do?"

"I'm going to ask my friends Celia and Lynne if I can rent the lake house for a weekend to host the party. Right after Labor Day would be great, and cheaper, I'm sure."

"That's a great idea."

"For the cost of cleaning at the end and gas for the SeaDoos, I could swing it. I'm sure it will cost a bit to rent the lake house, but I can ask the other girls to chip in."

"Have you decided on a date?"

"I don't have an exact date since I need to see if I can rent it in mid-September. And with my moving in August, it will kind of be a pain in the ass to organize. But it will be fun, I know. And I want to do it for Jane. I'll float the idea to Jane this weekend and find out who she might want to invite."

"Let me know if I can help. I mean, if you want help."

"I may take you up on that, thanks."

Marc was secretly hoping Ravyn would ask him to be her date for her sister's wedding, but he knew it was too early to broach the subject.

"Well, have a safe trip. I'll miss you."

"I'll miss you, too. And I'll call you when I get to my parents' house."

"Your parents' house? I thought you were staying with Jane."

"Her apartment is small and doesn't have a guest bedroom. I'll stay with my parents and drive up that next morning."

"Greenville sounds great. Have fun."

"I will. And I'll miss you."

Chapter 16

Ravyn enjoyed her weekend with her sister in Greenville. They had the bridal luncheon at The Lazy Goat, which Ravyn had enjoyed the last time she'd been to the city. As she drove back to Atlanta Sunday afternoon, she called Marc.

"Hey, I'm on my way back. How was your Sunday?"

"I went to the gym for about an hour and then I mowed the backyard. That's been the highlight of my day."

"Maybe I can improve your day."

"Oh really?"

"I'm about an hour and a half out. Can I come by?"

"Yes," Marc said, feeling aroused. "Do you need stress relief after your long drive?"

"I think I might."

"Well, I can help you with that."

"Great. I'll try not to speed."

"Drive safely. Don't speed. I want you here in one piece."

Ravyn hung up with Marc and felt dampness in her panties. Damn, he makes me wet, she thought. She tried not to speed too much. The drive was pretty boring until she got closer to Atlanta when traffic picked up and she had to pay attention.

She could tell people were coming back from Lake Lanier. She was a bit jealous of people who had enjoyed the lake that weekend. She realized she should call about renting the lake house.

Ravyn had cleared it with Jane about a bachelorette lake weekend so she just needed confirmation she'd be able to rent the house from Celia and Lynne in September.

Her sister Jane had been excited about the idea. They'd agreed on six friends, including the two of them, for a total of eight. There would be just enough bedrooms for eight women as long as they shared.

Ravyn decided to see if she could reach Celia to confirm the rental.

The phone rang several times before Celia answered.

"Hey Ravyn, what's up?"

"Hi, Celia. I'm planning a bachelorette party for my sister, Jane. She's getting married in October and I'm hoping I can rent your lake house the weekend after Labor Day, or maybe two weeks after Labor Day, for the party."

"Let me check those dates. If they are open it's yours."

"Oh, thank you. I've had such a good time at the lake and I've told my sister all about it. I think she's a little jealous," Ravyn laughed.

"Is your sister in Atlanta with you?"

"She's in Greenville, South Carolina, so she'd be driving down, and there would be eight of us. If you can, email me the particulars about the cleaning fee and what we'd need for gas for the SeaDoos."

"I can do that."

Ravyn was excited and relieved that she'd likely booked the house for the bachelorette party. She put her foot on the accelerator to face the excitement of seeing Marc.

Ravyn pulled into Marc's driveway shortly before 3 p.m. He met her at the door with a glass of wine, which he handed to her.

"I knew I liked you," she said, taking the glass from him.

"Have you had lunch?"

"I grabbed something on the road."

"Can you stay for dinner? I've got some chicken thawing out that I could put on the grill."

"That sounds great. Might have to work up a bit of an appetite before that."

Marc reached down to kiss her inside the doorway. "I can arrange that," he said as he led her to the master bedroom.

Ravyn followed him in, gulped her wine, and placed it on the end table by the bed. She smiled at him.

"Your smile looks a little devious," Marc said.

"Maybe. I'm feeling a little devilish. And in need of some stress relief. I've had a whole drive down Interstate 85 to think about what I'd like to do to you."

"Oh really? Why don't you tell me all about it?"

"Why don't I show you."

And she did, slowly pulling up his shirt. Then she pulled off her top and undid her bra. She pulled him close to her.

"I want to feel your skin on mine," she whispered.

Marc ran his hand through her hair and then moved his hands down her back.

"Like this?"

"Yes, yes. That feels so good."

"Is this better?" Marc said as he moved his hands over her breasts. Ravyn's nipples got erect at Marc's touch.

"I want you to suck my nipples," she moaned.

"Like this?" Marc said, moving down and sucked her right nipple, then licked and sucked her left nipple.

Ravyn groaned with pleasure. She held Marc against her. She knew she was going to get some great stress relief and work up an appetite for dinner.

Ravyn walked into her condo building later than she expected Sunday night. There had been one more round of "stress relief" after she and Marc had grilled the chicken.

Ravyn didn't want to leave Marc's place, but her neighbor Jack Parker had been feeding and watering her cat Felix and she'd told him she'd be back Sunday. Felix was probably hungry and annoyed.

Plus, Ravyn didn't have any clean work clothes with her. If she'd stayed over at Marc's Sunday night, she'd have to return home very early Monday to get ready for work.

As much as she disliked it, she wheeled her suitcase through the lobby. She stopped at the bank of mailboxes to grab her mail. There was a note taped to Ravyn's mailbox.

"Please see me Monday. I may have a rental for you." It was signed by Kevin, one of the assistant property managers.

Ravyn could hardly believe her eyes. A rental in her building! That would be perfect. She would only have to move her boxes several floors and not rent a truck for her furniture.

Ravyn wished she could call Kevin now, but no one was working the desk this late at night. She'd just have to wait until morning. She could hardly believe her luck.

Ravyn was up early Monday morning having not slept well thinking about the rental. Her mind turned over all night. Was it a one-bedroom condo or two bedrooms? Could she afford it? How long would the lease be? She hoped it was for a whole year.

She got up around 5 a.m. to make coffee. The property management office opened at 7 a.m. she thought. Or was it 8?

She'd go down at 7 just to check. She could be a little late for work today. Ravyn wanted to know about the rental.

Ravyn was there as Kevin was unlocking the office.

"Oh, hey," he said. "You got my note?"

"Yes. And I'm glad you left it. I've not had any luck finding a place to buy on my own in Midtown. My real estate agent wants me to look in the suburbs but that would mean a bad commute."

"Well maybe this will work out, at least until the end of the year," Kevin said.

"End of the year? It's not a long-term rental?"

"I'm afraid not. Jeanie Cooper in 1320 is a professor at Emory University. She just found out she will be teaching in Oxford for the fall semester. Some other professor was supposed to go but he broke his leg and can't travel. It's very last minute for her. Her place will be available August 10. I can give you her number so you can talk to her about it. It's really a sublet. We're not supposed to allow that, but we know you. It's not like she'd be subletting it to a rock band or something. We never have any complaints about you."

Kevin was smiling as he gave Ravyn the piece of paper with Jeanie Cooper's cell number. Then he saw her frown.

"What's the matter?"

"I was just hoping this would be long-term. I expect I won't even be able to move furniture or anything if it's a sublet. It will be kind of like living in a hotel. I'll have to put everything in storage and keep looking."

"Oh, if you don't want to call her, I get it," he said, withdrawing the paper.

"No, I'd better call or I'll be out on the street," Ravyn sighed. "Thanks for looking out for me. And who knows. Maybe something will come up later in the year."

Ravyn took the number and tried not to cry as she left the office. This was not going to work, she thought.

Ravyn got to her office in an unhappy mood. But she would call the woman about the sublet later that day. First, she needed more coffee.

She walked to the break room and grabbed her Mizzou mug. She'd had that mug since college.

Ravyn got her coffee and started back to her office. She could hear voices behind Jennifer's door. But Jennifer usually wasn't here this early. She came in around 10.

Ravyn could hear a man's voice and who she thought was Jennifer. But she couldn't hear detail. Then she heard what she thought was a loud moan. Shocked, Ravyn hustled back to her office. Did Jennifer have someone in her office? Who was in there with her? Curiouser and curiouser, she thought.

She tried to concentrate on work, but with what she'd heard, or maybe misheard, in Jennifer's office and her worry about the condo for rent made focus difficult.

Ravyn decided to call Jeanie Cooper and ask about the condo. She wasn't holding out hope that it would work out, but at least she wanted to hear the details.

"Hello?" Jeanie asked.

"Hi, Miss Cooper. This is Ravyn Shaw. Kevin gave me your number. I live in Spire and my investor is selling my condo, so I'm calling about your sublet."

"Oh, right. Kevin said you might call. Did he tell you I'm going to England to teach for a semester? I'd like someone to live in my condo, water my plants, get my mail. And I have a cat. I need someone to feed my cat."

"Oh. I have a cat too. Felix. He's a tomcat. And he'd have to come with me," Ravyn said.

"Oh. Hmm. That might present a problem. Unless we can integrate them. And I have two bedrooms. Maybe we can keep them separated in the bedrooms?"

"Kevin said you wanted the sublease to start August 10. I have to be out at the end of August. But I have furniture and stuff. I guess I could store everything," Ravyn's voice trailed off.

"Well, I'm gone until December 15. Kevin gave you a really good referral. Said you were quiet, not a partier, not a smoker. I can't have a smoker in my place. I'm allergic."

"Me too," Ravyn replied.

"Listen, because it's such a short lease, I'm willing to take a bit of a loss on my mortgage. I'm not asking you to cover it. And I'd make a deal on utilities. One rate for $800."

Ravyn was stunned. That was cheaper than her rent currently. And she'd have an extra bedroom? Maybe she could store some boxes in there and not rent a big storage unit.

"Are you home this evening? Maybe we could meet and discuss this further because I'm interested. I just need to work out some details."

"Sure. I'd love to meet. Why don't you come over tonight for some wine? Do you drink? I'm sorry, I didn't mean to presume."

"No, wine would be lovely."

"How about 7 o'clock? I've got some nice cheese and crackers and wine. We could talk and get to know one another then. I'm in 1320."

"I'll see you then."

Ravyn knocked on Jeanie Cooper's door at 7 p.m. sharp. When Jeanie opened the door, Ravyn recognized her from the building.

Jeanie was an older woman, with silver-gray hair and bright blue eyes. She was a thin woman with fine bone structure. She was probably in her late 50s or early 60s. But she was toned like maybe she did a lot of yoga.

Ravyn handed over a bottle of wine.

"Oh, you didn't have to do that," Jeanie said, inviting Ravyn in.

"Well, my mother would never forgive me if I came empty-handed. We are Southerners, after all."

Jeanie laughed. "Well, you will likely drink it while you are here. I'm not buying any more wine before I leave in two weeks.

"Well then, I'm glad it is one of my favorites!" Ravyn replied.

Jeanie showed Ravyn to the sofa. A tray of cheese and crackers was on the coffee table and two wine glasses sat empty.

"May I pour you some wine?"

"Please," Ravyn said as she sat down.

Jeanie poured a pinot noir from Willamette Valley. Ravyn recognized it was a good wine. She was impressed.

They settled onto the sofa and turned silent. Ravyn didn't realize this would be so awkward.

"So, tell me what you do," Jeanie finally said.

"I'm managing editor of *Cleopatra* magazine. It's a lifestyle magazine here in Atlanta. Before that, I was a freelancer after getting laid off from my newspaper job back in 2009."

"No playing drums in the middle of the night?"

Ravyn barked out a laugh. "No, no drumming. Or playing piano. I guess I'm kind of boring."

"Don't apologize for being boring. And I bet you aren't boring at all. Do you have hobbies? Quiet hobbies, I hope?"

Ravyn smiled. She was liking Jeanie more and more.

"I like to run. The whole reason I love this condo is how quickly I can be in Piedmont Park for a run."

"Did you do the Peachtree Road Race this year?"

"Of course. I love that race."

"I did it, too," Jeanie revealed.

"That's great. I can't imagine my Fourth of July without the Peachtree."

"Me neither. Well, let me show you the rest of the condo. Bring your wine."

Ravyn picked up her glass and followed Jeanie, who showed her the master bedroom, the guest bedroom, the bathroom, the washer/dryer area, and the kitchen. Jeanie also opened the balcony, which faced east. Ravyn's balcony faced south toward downtown, which she explained.

"I know, I don't have the downtown view, but I like sitting out here for my morning coffee to watch the sunrise."

"You watch the sunrise? You must get up early," Ravyn said.

"Well, I am up early to do yoga in the morning on the balcony, with the first of the morning light. And my college classes start pretty early too."

Ravyn gave a little inward cheer for guessing Jeanie was a yoga practitioner. Ravyn looked in the small storage unit off the balcony.

"Can I store some boxes in there? And your guest bedroom? I've got to move out at the end of August, but I've got furniture and stuff. I was trying to buy my unit, but prices in Midtown, for anything nice, are kind of prohibitive."

"I bet. I got this condo when the bottom fell out, so I got a pretty good deal."

"Yeah, I wish I could have bought mine way back when. The guy that owned it before me tried to get me to buy. I wish I could have done it, but I just didn't have the money. So, it went to an investor, and now he wants to sell at the top of the market. I can't blame him. It just puts me in a tight spot. I simply can't afford what he's asking for it."

"But there may be room for some of your things while you figure it all out," Jeanie said as they walked back into the living room. "I don't know the amount of furniture you have, but all of it probably won't fit in here. I hope you understand I don't want my condo being used as a storage unit."

"No, no. I think I'll have to rent a storage unit for a few months. I'll likely just bring clothes, a few boxes and my toiletries. And my cat, Felix."

Jeanie's cat Josie wandered into the living room. She was all black and had silky fur.

"Oh my gosh, she's so soft!" Ravyn said.

"She's my little black panther," Jeanie said. "I'm divorced. And I'm gay. That's what ended my marriage. I realized I didn't like men. I hope that doesn't shock you."

"Nope, not at all."

"Is there anyone in your life?"

"I'm in a complicated relationship," Ravyn started to say. "I'm back with an old boyfriend. And I'm a little conflicted about it."

"In what way?"

"Oh, Jeanie, it's almost too much to explain." But explain Ravyn did. She found Jeanie was a good listener. Ravyn felt she was meeting a new good friend.

"Well, it sounds like he's trying to make it up to you," Jeanie said, after hearing Ravyn's story.

"I hope so. I think he is. I'm just not sure yet."

"You're allowed to be uncertain. He hurt you initially. He has to rebuild that trust. But you have to be willing to accept that trust. Don't forget that. You have to be willing to trust again."

Ravyn sipped more of her wine. She really liked Jeanie. She was a wise woman.

"I know. It's just that…" she sighed. "It's hard to trust after what felt like a betrayal. He should have believed me."

"Yes, from what you said, he should. But people are imperfect, Ravyn. Marc will never be perfect. Don't expect him to be. I was not perfect in my husband's eyes. But I had to be true to myself. You have to be true to yourself. And you won't be perfect for Marc, either."

That struck Ravyn. She was likely not perfect for Marc. Yet he said he loved her. Did he love her imperfections? Maybe even despite her imperfections?

Ravyn and Jeanie had finished the bottle of wine. It had gotten late.

"Thank you for this evening, and for your insight," Ravyn said.

"I can open another bottle of pinot," Jeanie said.

"No but thank you. It was delicious."

"Do you think you want to sublet?"

Ravyn stood up. "I think I do. I need to work some things out, but I'd like to live here while I look for something more permanent. And who knows? I told Kevin maybe this sublet would help me find a long-term lease in this building. I really would like to keep living here. It's been my home for so long."

Jeanie came over and hugged Ravyn. "I'm glad you will be here. I'm glad you will be looking out for Josie. I have a very good feeling about you, Ravyn. You will get what you want. I just know it."

"Your lips to God's ear," Ravyn said and giggled. "That's what my grandmother used to say."

"She was a wise woman."

"She certainly was. So, will you send me over the paperwork about the sublet?"

"Yes, text me your email and I'll get it over to you tomorrow."

As late as it was, Ravyn found herself wanting to share her news on the sublet with Marc.

She texted him to see if he was awake, and he called her right back.

"So, you're going to take it?"

"I almost feel like I must. It's not ideal. It's not a long-term lease and I'll have to put my furniture and stuff in storage. But it buys me time. Maybe something permanent will open in the building that I can rent. Until I save up a bit more money to buy. I just don't want to buy something in the suburbs and be stuck with a commute I hate."

"When does the lease end?"

"In mid-December. She's going to England to teach for a semester. I'll be house sitting and cat sitting."

"Cat sitting?"

"She has a cat, too. Josie. I have no idea if Felix and her cat will get along. Marc, should I call her back and decline?"

"You have to go with what your gut tells you. Logically, as you said, this gives you a little more time to find something in the building. You've said you want to stay there."

"Yes. It's only for about five months. Less than that really. I don't know if four and a half months will make a difference, though."

"Listen, don't think that way. And you can come over here as much as you want if your sublet doesn't feel like home."

Ravyn smiled. "Thanks. I think you just want me to stay over there more."

"I wouldn't mind it. Why don't you sleep on it tonight? Maybe you'll feel better about it in the morning or you'll know it's not right for you."

"You're right. Thanks, Marc. Good night."

"Good night, Ravyn. I love you."

Ravyn opened her mouth to say she loved him, too, but stopped herself. She just wasn't ready.

Chapter 17

Ravyn didn't sleep well worrying about what she should do. She finally fell asleep late in the night and had to drag herself out of bed when her alarm went off.

Even Felix seemed grouchy that morning, yowling for his food.

"I'm getting it. I'm getting it," Ravyn said, testily, opening the plastic container that held his kibble. She wished she could call in sick and go back to bed for more sleep, but she knew Jennifer would question it since she had been feeling well the day before.

Ravyn also wanted to check in with Julie. Julie! She'd forgotten to tell Marc about the flowers he'd sent her. Well, now she'd definitely have to talk to Julie and Marc again.

Ravyn called Julie after she got to work.

"Hey Julie, need some advice."

"Keep dating Marc."

"Not that kind of advice. I called a woman about a sublet in my condo building, but it's only until mid-December. She's an Emory professor and teaching in England next semester. I'll be watching her cat and watering house plants. I'll have to move my stuff into storage. I thought I was going to accept it last night and now I'm unsure again."

"Do you have a place to stay now?"

"No."

"Do you have an apartment to move into?"

"No."

"And you want to stay in Midtown?"

"Yes."

"I think you have your answer. I know it's not ideal, but you get to stay in your building, at least for a little while longer. And Cindy hasn't found anything for you?"

"She's telling me to look OTP," Ravyn said, referring to the Atlanta term for "Outside the Perimeter," or the suburbs. "And I just can't see myself with an hour-long commute into downtown for work."

"Do you think you'll always work for *Cleopatra*? Maybe you'll get another job closer to where you eventually live."

"I'm not sure I want to buy a condo so far from where I work right now. I don't think I'll be happy. And then I'm stuck for a while. Maybe a good long while if the market turns sour again."

"Then take the sublet and keep looking in Midtown, even if it's just for another rental. You're bound to find something."

"I know you're right. Hey, I forgot to tell Marc about the flowers."

"Well, here's the surprise. Rob sent me more flowers this week! I can't believe it."

"That's good. I hope he keeps it up."

"I hope he doesn't. I see the credit card bills, remember? That's money I can use to shop at Phipps. Speaking of Phipps, we are overdue for lunch or dinner at Twist. Are you free this week or weekend?"

"I'm sure I could meet you this weekend for sure, but I might be able to swing a weeknight. Are you sure you can? With the girls, I mean?"

"Listen, I can feed them early and then meet you there for a late dinner. Rob can put them to bed."

"Sounds good. Oh, here comes my boss and I've already gotten a warning about 'personal calls' at work. Text me what day you want to meet. Bye."

Ravyn hung up quickly, but Jennifer walked by her office without stopping in. Ravyn couldn't be sure, but she thought she saw Jennifer smiling. Wonder what she's smiling about, she asked herself.

Julie texted shortly after they hung up suggesting Thursday night for dinner at Twist. Ravyn replied that it would be fine and they settled on a time.

The rest of the day went quickly, with Jeanie sending over a subletting contract. Ravyn read it through but didn't understand all of it. She'd ask her friend Henry Kolber, an attorney, to take a look at it.

Henry had been a source when Ravyn worked at the newspaper and became a friend after she'd been laid off. He'd given her some legal advice over the years when she needed it. He helped her draw up a basic contract when she'd been a freelance writer.

She emailed him and attached the subletting contract, asking if it looked fair.

By the end of the day, Henry had responded saying it was fair, but added that Ravyn ought to ask for a clause in case Jeanie returned home early. He didn't want her to be homeless.

Ravyn thanked him for the advice and promised to buy lunch if he was free next week.

Henry's advice was sound, Ravyn thought. She imagined Jeanie wouldn't return home early, but Henry was right, she'd have to add something into the contract so Jeanie couldn't kick her out without some compensation. Henry had even added the wording on the contract for her.

Ravyn sent the contract back to Jeanie asking for the addendum.

She called Marc on her way home, letting him know she was taking the sublet.

"Oh, and Julie wants to thank you for the flowers. Her husband thought she was seeing someone and got jealous."

"Oh no. I hope I didn't cause trouble."

"Julie's delighted. She explained it was you and now Rob is sending her flowers every week!"

"Is that good?" Marc asked.

"That's good."

"Will you need some help moving to the new condo?"

"If you are offering your big strong arms, yes."

Marc laughed. "Well, I was thinking I could borrow the hand truck from my office. I'm not sure my back could take all the boxes. What will you do with your furniture?"

"I'll have to put it in storage. I asked my new landlord if I could put some of my boxes in her guest bedroom."

"Guest bedroom?"

"Yes, it is a two-bedroom, two-bath condo. The master bedroom is kind of small. The guest bedroom is small too. I think I'll sleep in the guest bedroom. I don't want to sleep in the master. That's Jeanie's bedroom and I'm guessing there won't be room for my clothes unless I use the guest closet and dresser."

"How much furniture do you have?"

"Well, my couch, the end tables, and TV and TV stand from the living room. My bed and dresser from the bedroom. The washer and dryer set is mine. I should probably sell that. I can probably sell it to someone in the building. It's a stackable set."

Ravyn mentally went through the big items in her condo. "I have a microwave and all my pots and pans and plates and glassware from the kitchen. I've packed up some of the kitchen stuff already, but now there will be a lot more to do. Now I'll have to pack it all up."

"I can help you. I should get some boxes from the liquor store."

"That would be great. And can you grab any copy paper boxes from your office? The ones with lids? Those are great boxes for packing. I've been grabbing as many as I can from our office."

"I'll pick some up tomorrow. I think there are some empty ones ready for recycling."

"I need to find some old newspapers or something to pack things like my plates and glasses. I'm sorry the daily paper moved out to the suburbs. I could have gone right downtown to get some."

"I think U-Haul sells packing material."

"This feels overwhelming."

"I'll help you Ravyn. I can come over this evening if you want to get started tonight."

"I probably won't start tonight, but why don't you come over anyway. I might just need help getting myself organized. What do you want for takeout?"

"Why don't we go for burgers at Gordon Biersch."

"Oh yes. I can get those garlic fries."

"OK. See you in about an hour."

"Sounds great. Do you remember the code for the gate?"

"I do. See you soon."

Ravyn slowly got her condo packed and told her landlord Keith Spanner she'd be out by August 10. He'd have extra time to get it painted and show it.

She did a temporary change of address for her mail and moved several boxes and personal items into Jeanie Cooper's guest bedroom. As she stacked boxes along the wall, it felt surreal.

Ravyn tried to play with Jeanie's cat Josie each time she moved boxes so the cat would be used to her. She also wanted to bring Josie's scent back to her condo. Felix would sniff her down when she returned to her home.

Ravyn decided she'd wait to introduce Felix and Josie when she could be there to monitor how they got along. She knew she'd have to keep Felix in the guest bedroom and let the two cats smell each other under the door. She wasn't sure Felix would be happy about being confined to just the bedroom for all that long.

And she'd have to ask her neighbor Jack Parker to feed and water both cats when she was at the lake for the bachelorette party and when she was at the wedding in October. She might be gone for nearly a week for the nuptial activities.

The day came when Ravyn took the keys to her new, if temporary home, from Jeanie. Ravyn drove her to the Midtown MARTA station to catch a train to Hartsfield-Jackson Atlanta International Airport for her flight to England.

Ravyn cried when she got back to her condo. Boxes were everywhere, stacked neatly in the living room and all of her furniture was pushed in there, too. She and Marc would start moving things into her storage unit the next week.

Ravyn had taken the next two days off work to get everything moved. Marc took time off, even though he was in the last stages of selling a majority interest in LindMark Enterprises.

She'd even managed to find a couple of college guys from Georgia Tech to help move the bigger furniture, grateful she lived near the campus and young strong men.

Ravyn walked out onto her balcony to stare at her downtown view one more time. The sun was starting to set to her left. She pulled out her cell phone to get yet another sunset photo from her balcony. In the days left, she had taken so many sunset photos. She didn't want to ever forget this home.

The next day, Marc arrived early and knocked at Ravyn's new condo.

This is weird, he thought. He was so used to going up several more floors to her old place.

Ravyn opened the door and Marc handed her a coffee and a bagel bag from Einstein's Bagels.

"Oh! Thank you!"

"I wasn't sure if you had coffee or breakfast this morning, so I brought it. I hope you like plain cream cheese."

"That will be perfect. I have figured out how to work the coffee maker, but I was just going to have toast. This will be better. Thanks," she said, reaching up to kiss Marc.

"Are you ready to move? I have the hand truck in my trunk," Marc said, sipping his coffee. "I'll have to go back down to get it."

"I can't start moving until 10 a.m., per the condo rules. And we can only use the service elevator, but we can pretty well load it up. That hand truck will come in handy. I told the Georgia Tech guys to come at 10 a.m. With the four of us, I hope it doesn't take more than today. But I have the college kids tomorrow, too. I'm paying them for two days."

"Well can we take a few boxes out by hand? How will they know if you're just moving a couple of boxes at a time? We can put them in my car."

"Well, I guess they won't, but I need to go pick up the moving truck. I'll need that to get into the storage unit. We shouldn't use your car. Everything should go in the truck."

By mid-morning., Ravyn, Marc, and the college guys got to work, loading the service elevator to almost its top and then taking it down to the parking deck, where the moving truck sat. Back and forth they went.

At one point, Ravyn kept pushing her condo floor, rather than the floor to the parking deck, wondering why the service elevator didn't move. She was sore, tired and her brain seemed to have stopped working.

At 1 p.m. they stopped for lunch. Ravyn had ordered pizza delivery. She was glad she'd ordered two pies. She and Marc had eaten half of one and the college guys demolished one and a half.

By the end of the day, they were done moving everything into the storage unit. Ravyn paid the Georgia Tech students for both days, and she and Marc collapsed on Jeanie's sofa.

"Oh my God, I'm not sure I can move," Ravyn said.

"I'm so sore. And my back hurts."

"Oh no. I'm sorry." Ravyn was silent for a moment. "Hey, the master bathroom has a whirlpool bathtub."

"What?"

"Jets of love," Ravyn said. "Or at least jets of muscle release."

"Please tell me you aren't kidding."

"Nope. I saw it when Jeanie gave me a tour of the condo. It's so '80s, but right now, it sounds heavenly."

"Let's go."

"Do you want to get in first?" Ravyn asked.

"Can we both fit?"

"It's rather small. I think it's for one person. Maybe two people could fit."

"Let's find out," he said.

Marc snuggled next to Ravyn in the guest bedroom of her new place. He moved around, realizing this bed was not nearly as comfortable as Ravyn's bed.

He was just pleased he was wrapping his arms around her. He loved the fresh scent of her skin.

Marc was glad they had finished up with the move in one day. With the next day off, they'd have August 11 to spend together. They might have to use that whirlpool bathtub again, he thought as he rolled over and groaned. His back complained as he moved.

Ravyn let out a little mew as she rolled over.

"Are you awake?" Marc asked.

"I am now. Oh my God, I hurt. I think my hair hurts."

"Yeah, I'm pretty sore, too. Is there ibuprofen or Aleve around? I might need it."

"I seriously don't know what Jeanie's got in her medicine cabinet. I'm hoping she has opioid painkillers at this point. Percocet anyone?"

Marc pulled Ravyn closer. "I do know how you feel, but you know you don't mean that. Opioids aren't the answer. I can tell you from my experience with my brother Bruce."

"I'm sorry. I didn't mean to be insensitive."

"You weren't. But I'd settle for some ibuprofen right now. Do you want some? Is it in her master bath? I'll get up and go find it. In a minute. When I can move my muscles."

"I'd help you, but I don't think I can move. And yes, if you find it in her medicine cabinet, I'll take a couple of tablets. Or nine."

Marc rolled over to face Ravyn. They were naked. "Maybe we can work out this soreness in other ways," he said.

"Maybe. But seriously, I don't think I can climb on top of you."

"Let's just lay side by side," Marc said, his voice getting husky. "Throw your leg over me."

"Oooh," Ravyn said, feeling Marc's arousal and her own. "I like this. Lovemaking for the clinically sore."

Marc laughed. "Well, let's see if we can work out the soreness."

Chapter 18

Ravyn began spending a lot of time at Marc's house that summer. She'd noticed how uncomfortable Jeanie's guest bed was and wished she'd swapped out her mattress for the one in the guest bedroom.

But her mattress was safely stowed away in the storage unit. She'd have a hard time retrieving it now. She'd have to rent a truck again. That mattress would never fit in her Honda or Marc's BMW.

Ravyn spent Labor Day weekend at Marc's house. They grilled out, they drank wine, they made love. Over that three-day weekend, she went to Jeanie's condo once a day to feed Josie and Felix. The pair of cats were not friends, exactly, but they had declared some kind of detente, and no blood was shed over the holiday weekend.

"You know I'm headed up to Lake Lanier next weekend for my sister's bachelorette party," she told Marc.

"I remember. I'll miss you."

"I'll miss you, too."

"Will you?" he asked, moving in close to kiss her.

"Well, I'll miss you at night. I'm sure we'll be having too much fun during the day."

"Will you call me at night? We could have some phone sex."
"Oh, that would be nice."
"Well, it's a phone sex date then."
"Let's practice the real thing now so we know how to do it over the phone," Ravyn said.
"I like the way you think," Marc said, as he circled his arms around her.

Ravyn got to the lake house early Friday morning before everyone else was supposed to arrive. She'd gone to the grocery store to get a case of wine, snacks, some salad fixings, and a pack of chicken so they'd have dinner ready for that night. She'd also gotten eggs, orange juice, bacon, and bread, so they'd have breakfast.

They'd have to go for provisions later Saturday morning, but they could make a list of things they'd want and need for the next few days. Ravyn was hoping the wine would last the weekend, but with eight women, they'd probably need more.

Before she left Atlanta, she'd also gone to the liquor store for vodka and Bloody Mary mix. If any of them overindulged that weekend, maybe a bloody would help.

Jane arrived with her friends Dixie, Shannon, and Isabel, or Izzy.

Ravyn threw her arms around her sister. "I'm so glad you are here. We're going to have such fun this weekend!"

"I'm so excited. The other girls are behind us. They took a separate car. Oh my God! This place is great!"

Ravyn showed them into the lake house.

"What the hell is that?" Shannon asked, looking at the bison head above the fireplace.

"We like to call him Tom," Ravyn said.

"It gives me the creeps. And, I don't believe in killing animals for sport," Shannon huffed.

"Duly noted," Ravyn said, realizing Shannon was going to be the opinionated one of the weekend. Oh God, I hope she's not vegan! Ravyn thought suddenly.

No, she'd asked for food allergies and preferences. There had been no requests for vegans.

The women sorted themselves out to the bedrooms. Ravyn had been sure to take the bedroom in the back where she had been before. It was a queen bed and she hoped she wouldn't have anyone rooming with her. She wanted to be alone when she and Marc had phone sex later that night.

But Jane threw her overnight bag in Ravyn's bedroom.

"I'm bunking with you, right?" she asked. "It will be just like old times, sharing a bedroom with my big sister."

"Of course, Jane!" Ravyn responded, inwardly groaning. No phone sex with Marc this weekend.

The last three women, Stephanie, Joyce, and Raeanne, arrived about an hour later. "We got a bit turned around," Raeanne said. "We took a wrong turn, but we're here!"

"Come in and get a glass of wine!" Ravyn said. "This is a bachelorette party after all!"

Shannon, Izzy, and Dixie had strung party streamers and placed plastic male genitalia around the living room as decorations. They had ice cream and whipped cream as well. Ravyn had forgotten to get dessert, so she was glad they had brought that in a cooler.

Friday evening was shaping up to be a lot of fun.

Ravyn got the grill going and put the chicken on while others made the salad and pulled some frozen vegetables out of the freezer. Thank heavens Celia kept the lake house fairly well stocked.

They opened bottle after bottle of wine. Ravyn realized she was going to have to make a run tomorrow for another case of wine.

They played '90s music too loud, danced, and partied on the outside deck way into the small hours of the night. Dixie had been the deejay that night, playing music off her iPhone. The boy bands were in full force.

As they said good night and wobbled off to their rooms, Ravyn and her sister hugged in the kitchen.

"Thank you for this. It's just perfect," Jane said.

"I'm hoping we get good weather tomorrow. It looks a little iffy."

"I'm sure it will be fine."

"If not, there are tons of board games here in the house. And if the rain passes, we can get the SeaDoos out or go for a swim out to the buoy."

"You know I don't swim so well," Jane said, frowning.

"There are swim boards down at the boat dock. You can hold onto one of those as you swim and there are life jackets."

"OK. That's great."

"I'm so excited for you. Nick seems like a great guy."

"He is."

Ravyn and her sister hugged again before Ravyn and Jane toddled off to the bedroom.

Jane went to the bathroom to wash her face and Ravyn texted Marc. It was way past when she thought she'd be texting him.

Are you still up? she asked.

There was a delay in the response. Maybe he'd gone to sleep.

Ravyn put her phone down when Jane came out of the bathroom. Ravyn went in to take off her makeup and get ready for bed. She heard her phone ping.

I'm up. I'd given up on you. You must be having fun.

We are. Lots of dancing tonight. Lots of drinking tonight. I've got to make another wine run tomorrow.

Feeling frisky?

Sorry, babe. Jane and I are bunking in together. We'll have to wait.

I can wait for you Ravyn. I'll wait for you forever. I love you.

Good night, Marc. Sweet dreams.
My dreams will be filled with you.

Ravyn woke up with a hangover, an arm thrown over her sister Jane. Just like they'd done when they were young girls. Ravyn was very protective of her younger sister, even though they fought like cats and dogs as kids.

But no one was allowed to mess with Jane, only Ravyn.

Ravyn winced at the daylight peeking through the curtains. She'd had a lot to drink last night. She felt like she needed to get up and make coffee. When she'd been at the lake before she was always grateful that Celia had started coffee. She'd have to be the one this morning to make the sacrifice.

Ravyn got up and shuffled into the kitchen, starting the 12-cup Cuisinart coffee maker and making it a little stronger than she would have at home.

Shannon, Dixie, and Raeanne wandered out into the kitchen.

"I smelled coffee," Raeanne mumbled.

"I've got a full pot on," Ravyn said.

"I think Joyce and Izzy are still in bed. We may not see them until noon," Dixie said, her voice husky. She sounded like she'd smoked a pack of cigarettes.

Jane wandered out looking very hungover.

"Do you need coffee or a Bloody Mary?" Ravyn asked her sister.

"Well, I'd say coffee, but a Bloody Mary might be more appropriate."

"OK. I'll pour you one of each."

"Hey, if you're making them, I'll take one of those," Dixie said, blowing on her coffee cup.

"Same," Raeanne said.

Shannon just raised a finger.

Ravyn made several Bloody Marys and the other women staggered into the kitchen. She also poured coffee.

After breakfast and showers, the women reassembled in the living room.

"That thing still gives me the creeps," Shannon said, pointing to the bison head.

"Well, we can't take him down. I'm afraid you'll just have to put up with him this trip," Ravyn replied. "Who's up for a swim? We can swim out to the no-wake buoy and back. And there are two SeaDoos. They can hold four people. The rest of us can swim."

Raeanne and Shannon hopped on the first SeaDoo and Stephanie and Jane got on the second. They puttered out beyond the no-wake buoy and then roared off into Lake Lanier.

Dixie, Ravyn, Izzy, and Joyce decided on the buoy swim, which took a little more than a half-hour. Then made their lists for the grocery store.

There was some leftover chicken. They thought about a Thai stir fry for dinner. They'd pick up some lunch meat to go with the leftover bread.

Dixie had planned the bachelorette party for that afternoon. They'd have lunch and then have the party. Dixie had planned mimosas, a cake, and some heavy hors d'oeuvres, like meatballs and mini quiches.

Dixie had even planned some fun bachelorette party games. Ravyn got a peek at the list of games Dixie had found on the internet and some made Ravyn laugh out loud.

Ravyn, Stephanie, and Izzy went to the grocery store late-morning and returned shortly after noon, unpacking plastic bags and both putting things away and getting lunch prepared.

"Thanks for getting more orange juice," Dixie said. "I thought we'd have enough left over for the Prosecco. Although we can go right to the straight stuff. But I know we'll want it tomorrow morning for breakfast."

"And you can bring it home and just add vodka," Stephanie said, in a sing-song voice.

"Hell, depending who's driving we can make screwdrivers in the car to ward off the hangovers we'll have Sunday," Joyce said.

"We don't have to be out of the lake house until after lunch," Ravyn said. "We might have sobered up by then, and those of you in the passenger seats can have a screwdriver for the road."

"Hooray!" Izzy said.

"Oh, that's just because you aren't driving," Shannon said.

"Hell no. I'm going to enjoy that screwdriver, then sleep all the way the back to Greenville," Izzy said.

"Well, I'm going to be sleeping next to you in the back seat," Joyce said.

"Who's going to drive the car?" Raeanne asked.

"The one who is the least hungover," Joyce said.

"How do you know you won't be the least hungover tomorrow?" Raeanne asked.

"Because I'm going to have fun tonight!" Joyce exclaimed. "And that means you or Izzy are going to have to drive."

Ravyn just smiled. She knew she'd have to keep a more level head tonight. She expected to be holding someone's hair tonight as that woman prayed to a porcelain god. Maybe several women's hair.

The party games got started with the women each carving a cucumber into a phallic shape. Then came the panty game. Each woman brought a new pair of panties that reflected her personality and hung each pair on a string in the living room. Jane had to guess which woman brought which pair.

Jane guessed right away that Dixie brought the purple thong. Dixie was a huge fan of Prince. The other thong had to have come from Shannon. It was black with a chain across the front.

The others were bikini panties and Jane just had to guess who they came from. Ravyn gave her a pair with polka dots. Jane did guess her sister gave her those. Polka dots were Ravyn's favorite pattern.

The next activity was the ring hunt, where the women tried to find several plastic rings hidden around the living room, including one that looked like an engagement ring. The woman who found the engagement ring got a soy candle.

Ravyn hunted around the flagstone fireplace and finally found it close to Tom the bison. She smiled, thinking of the time she was with Julie, Celia, and Lynne and they knocked an eyeball out of the stuffed bison head.

Next, the women played a very X-rated version of Pictionary. The game seemed to devolve into sexual acts and simulated blow jobs.

Lastly, they played Prosecco pong, trying to get ping pong balls into a Solo cup half full of the bubbly drink. By the end of the game, most of the women were pretty drunk.

Ravyn thought she better get started on dinner to offset the alcohol.

"Hey, I'm going to make the Thai chicken," she said, attempting to stand up and feeling a little wobbly on her feet.

Ravyn pulled out the chicken, some frozen vegetables, a red curry sauce in a jar, and got some brown rice on to boil.

In about 45 minutes, dinner was ready. The women opened several bottles of chardonnay and the party continued.

After they cleared the dinner dishes, the music started and the women moved to the deck to dance. Tonight, they used Raeanne's iPhone, dancing to Motown and '70s music. The Jackson 5, the BeeGees, Queen, Abba, Rod Stewart, and everybody's favorite, the Village People's YMCA.

The women threw their hands in the air to make the Y, the M, the C, and the A. They ended up crashing into each other and when the song ended, they collapsed into deck chairs laughing and poured more wine.

"Hey, what about a late-night swim tonight?" Izzy asked.

"No. We've had too much to drink," Ravyn said, shutting down that idea.

"What about the SeaDoos? We could take those out," Shannon said.

"No. We've had too much to drink," Ravyn said, hardly believing she was having to explain that to them. "I'm not bailing your ass out for BUI," she added, referring to boating under the influence.

"No one will know," Joyce said.

"Not happening," Ravyn said, flatly.

"Party pooper," Joyce said, pouting.

"Hey, just play more music and get on the dance floor!" Jane said.

Ravyn smiled. She knew Jane had her back when the women wanted to do something unsafe.

Raeanne quickly pulled up some Fleetwood Mac, and the women danced to "Go Your Own Way" and then Abba's "Dancing Queen."

Around 1 a.m. the women began to flag. Several white wine bottles were empty and one bottle of vodka was empty, too. Thankfully, there was a small bottle of vodka for tomorrow's screwdrivers or Bloody Marys.

As the women said goodnight, Ravyn kept her eyes on anyone who might be in trouble. In the end, she ended up steering Jane into the bedroom.

"I don't feel so good," Jane said.

"Are you going to be sick?"

"I'm not sure."

"Let's get you in your pajamas and then go into the bathroom, just in case," Ravyn said.

Ravyn had to pull Jane's top off and get her shorts off. She helped Jane into a night shirt, then got her to the toilet. She was afraid Jane was going to be sick.

"I'm OK. I'm OK," Jane kept saying, but she kept close to the toilet. "Can I tell you something?"

"Of course."

"I'm not sure I want to marry Nick."

Ravyn sucked in a breath. "Why not?"

"Well, he snores, for one."

"Snoring is not a non-marrying offense. Dad complains all the time about Mom snoring. And they've been married for over 35 years."

"I'm not sure I love him."

Ravyn took another deep breath. Not love Nick? She seemed crazy about him.

"Why not? You seem to be perfect together."

"I know. I feel like we're too perfect."

"Too perfect? I don't think that's possible. But if you are having doubts, maybe you should postpone the wedding."

Jane started to cry. "I can't postpone it. We've invited everyone. The invitations are sent out."

"Jane, if you need more time, then you need to take more time. I'll support you with whatever you want to do."

Inwardly, Ravyn thought if this wedding was canceled she wouldn't have to wear that unattractive maid of honor dress. Then she frowned. She didn't want her sister to be unhappy. And to cancel the wedding, in Ravyn's mind, would be a mistake.

Suddenly, Jane vomited into the toilet. Ravyn quickly pulled back her hair. Ravyn held Jane's hair as she threw up again.

Ravyn got a washcloth and wetted it with cold water, pressing it against Jane's neck and forehead. "There, there. You're OK," she said, as she wiped Jane's neck and head.

After a few minutes, Jane looked up, bleary-eyed.

"Are you OK? Do you think you're done?" Ravyn asked. "Can you get in the bed? I can get you some water. You need some water to keep from dehydrating."

Jane shook her head yes.

Ravyn went out to the kitchen and filled a glass of water from the sink. Raeanne came out to the kitchen.

"Jane not feeling too well?" she asked.

"Nope. How about Izzy?"

"Nope," Raeanne said, filling a glass of water.

"Good night," Ravyn said.

"Good night."

Jane and Izzy didn't show up for breakfast the next morning.

The rest of the women sauntered into the kitchen, reaching for coffee and Bloody Marys.

Dixie and Joyce made omelets with the leftover vegetables and spinach from the previous meals. Ham, turkey, and cheese from the lunch fixings also made it in the omelets.

The women were slow and sluggish as they packed their cars for their respective rides home.

Ravyn went into the bedroom to check on Jane.

"Hey, sweet sister," Ravyn said, rubbing Jane's back. "Are you OK?"

Jane groaned and rolled over. "Not really."

"Do you remember what we talked about last night?"

"Not really."

"You were concerned about marrying Nick. You still feel that way?"

"Not really."

"Jane, I will support you in whatever you decide."

Jane started to cry.

Ravyn rubbed her back again. "What's wrong?"

"I just don't know. I don't know what I want."

"Do you want to marry Nick?"

"Yes, I do."

"Then what's the problem?"

"I just wish I knew we were right for each other. That we were going to have the kind of marriage Mom and Dad have."

"Jane, Mom and Dad don't have a perfect marriage. No marriage is perfect. They've had to work hard for what they have."

Jane looked up. "What do you mean?"

"Do you not remember hearing them argue after we went to bed as kids?"

"Not really."

"They aired out their differences and I think it made their marriage stronger. They didn't let things fester. And as painful as it was to hear them argue, I think they worked on their marriage. And you need to stand up for yourself when you disagree with Nick."

"Do you do that with Marc?"

Ravyn didn't answer right away. "I'm not sure how I feel about Marc."

"Really? You can't stop talking about him. You love him."

"I'm not sure."

"What are you not sure about?"

"He's hurt me before. I'm afraid he'll hurt me again. And I just don't want to be hurt again."

"Ravyn, what are you really afraid of? That he loves you?"

"Yes. I guess I am afraid of that. He's been telling me that he loves me and I can't say it back to him. I'm just afraid," Ravyn said.

Jane held her tight. "Don't be afraid of a good man."

"I could say the same to you."

The sisters held each other tight as they cried in each other's arms.

Chapter 19

Ravyn and Jane hugged each other hard as they stood in the driveway of the lake house.

Jane and Izzy got up so late, they ate their omelets as brunch. There were a few mimosas with the little bit of orange juice and Prosecco left and few Bloody Marys with the mix and vodka left. Mostly, the women drank water and coffee and nursed hangovers.

They'd cleaned up, brought the garbage out to the outside bins, and hugged each other as they said goodbye.

"Thank you so much for getting the house this weekend," Raeanne said.

"This was so wonderful. It was an incredible weekend," Joyce said.

"I don't like that bison head," Shannon said, smiling through tears.

They went slowly to their cars after loading bags and gifts for Jane into their cars.

And so Ravyn and Jane clung to each other outside Jane's car.

"I love you, little sis," Ravyn said.

"I love you, too."

Ravyn once again drove south on Interstate 85, feeling worn out from the emotion of the weekend with Jane and tired from all the drinking she'd done.

Marc called about halfway to Atlanta. "Are you on the road yet?"

"Yes. I'm about 40 minutes from Atlanta."

"Did you have a good time?"

"It got a little heavy. I think Jane is having doubts about the wedding. Maybe it's just cold feet, but I'm a little worried."

"Oh."

"Yeah, I know."

"Do you want to come to my house? Will you come? I missed you this weekend."

"I missed you, too. I can come. I have some clean clothes."

"Come. Do your laundry at my house tonight. Do you have anything to wear to work tomorrow?"

Ravyn smiled. Marc wanted her to stay over. She'd need to bring some work clothes to Marc's house. "I have something I can wear to work tomorrow."

"I'll fix dinner for us. Is grilled chicken OK?"

"Sounds good."

"You sound tired."

"I am tired. I didn't get a whole lot of sleep this weekend. A lot of drinking, a lot of dancing. We had fun, but I'm really tired."

"OK. We'll make it an early night. Love you."

"I'll see you soon."

Ravyn pulled into Marc's driveway around 3:30 p.m. feeling drained. She just wanted to crawl into bed — her bed. She missed her condo and bed. She felt the tears begin to fall as she sat in the driveway.

Marc came out on his short front porch and looked at Ravyn, her arms draped over her steering wheel, sobbing.

He walked over to her driver's door and motioned for her to unlock her door. Ravyn sat in the driver's seat, unmoved. She wasn't ready to let him in. She pulled herself together, wiping her eyes with the back of her hands.

She looked up at Marc and unlocked her car door.

"Are you OK?" Marc asked, clearly concerned.

"I'm OK. I'm just wiped out."

"Open your trunk. Let me get your bag in the house. We'll start your laundry. Can I get you bottled water?"

Marc offered his hand to Ravyn and helped her out of the car. He got her bag out of the trunk and helped her up to the front door.

"Thanks," she said as she went up the three steps. "Water would be great."

"Do you want to take a nap?"

Ravyn felt her face go slack. "That would be wonderful."

Marc steered her into the house and down to the master bedroom. Ravyn flopped on the bed on her back.

Marc reached down and pulled Ravyn's sandals off and helped her get under the covers. Ravyn, fully clothed, was asleep within minutes.

When she awoke it was about 5:30 p.m. She looked at her iPhone for the time. She felt sluggish, but she knew she needed to get up. Ravyn laid in the bed for a little while. She could hear some soft music in the living room.

She sat up and swung her legs over the bed. She went into the bathroom, splashing some water on her face.

Ravyn came out into the living room, seeing Marc laying on the leather couch.

"You're up," he said, sitting up.

"Did you want to nap? I'm sorry. I took your bed."

"No, I was just resting. Are you hungry? I can get dinner on."

"I really should start my laundry."

"I did it. I think everything is out of the dryer."

Ravyn was shocked. Marc did her laundry? Did he touch her underwear? Oh my God, she thought. He touched her unflattering underwear!

Half the time she came to his house and found his clothes strewn about his bedroom. She'd certainly seen his underwear. Thank God he wore boxers. She didn't want to see "tighty whities."

"I can fold the laundry," she said, blanching.

"Oh, I folded it.

Ravyn had no words. She couldn't believe Marc folded her laundry and was being so domestic. Was he changing? Was he being more metrosexual?

"Thanks. I am kind of hungry now."

"Great. I'm a little hungry now, too. I've had the chicken marinating while you napped. I can get it on the grill."

"Let's just wait a minute."

"Wait?"

Ravyn took Marc's hand. All of his domesticity got Ravyn's libido moving. "Let's go back to the bedroom," she said.

"Really?"

"Really," she said, pulling him back to the master bedroom.

Marc didn't argue and had a smile as Ravyn led him back to bed.

The couple emerged from the bedroom nearly three hours later. They'd made love and then slept. As they awoke, Ravyn and Marc both stretched, the dusk starting to surround them.

"I am really hungry, now," Marc said.

"Me too."

"I'll get up and throw the chicken on the grill. Should be done in about 20 minutes."

"Can I help?" Ravyn asked, not wanting to move. She could have stayed in bed, making love to Marc for the rest of the night.

"If you can start the vegetables and the rice for tonight, that would help."

Ravyn reached for some clothes. “I can do that.”

Nearly an hour later she and Marc were sitting at a small bistro table in his breakfast nook, eating their dinner. Marc had poured some wine, a Chardonnay that was not too oaky.

“This is delicious,” Ravyn said, wearing a T-shirt and yoga pants.

“You look delicious.”

“No, I don’t. I’m a mess. I have no makeup and my hair is a mess. My clothes are completely slouchy.”

“To me, you look beautiful.”

Ravyn paused, wondering if she should have a serious discussion with Marc. She decided she needed to clear the air with him.

“Marc,” she paused. “I’d like to know where we are in this relationship. I know you have been trying. Really trying. You have been a generous lover and trying hard. You’d done my laundry and made dinner. You’ve been great.”

Marc said nothing, just blinked at Ravyn. “What are you getting at?” he asked, hesitantly.

“This weekend Jane was questioning her relationship with Nick. It got me thinking about us.”

“Ravyn, I’ve told you I love you. I can’t make myself any clearer than that. And I know you can’t say you love me back...”

“I do love you,” Ravyn said, quietly.

“You do?” Marc asked, surprised.

“I guess I do. No, I really do.”

Marc sighed with relief. “It was kind of hard telling you that I love you and not getting any response. It kind of hurt my feelings. I was putting myself out there, and nothing from you.”

Ravyn lowered her eyes, then raised them to meet his. “I know. I just wasn’t ready. But in talking with Jane, she said I shouldn’t let a good man get away. And you are a good man, Marc. I know that. My God, you did my laundry and folded it!”

Marc smiled. “And I got to see your underwear.”

Ravyn smiled. "That's not all of it. You've changed."

Marc paused. "Well, I hope I've changed. And grown. I'd like to think I'm a better man, Ravyn. I'd like to think I'm a better man because of you."

She could feel the tears behind her eyes, then welling to spill over. "I love you, Marc."

Marc stood up and grabbed Ravyn's hand, leaving the dirty dishes on the table. He led her back into the bedroom and they didn't emerge until the Monday sunlight broke through the curtains.

Ravyn arrived at her office and walked to the break room for some coffee. Even though there were a couple of Starbucks coffee stops on her way, she felt like she'd gotten a late start, especially since she'd had to stop at her temporary condo to feed Felix and Josie.

Felix had a scrape across his nose, so Ravyn realized the detente between the two cats hadn't gone smoothly while she was away this weekend. She scooped dry kibble into two bowls and refilled the cats' water bowls.

"Be nice to each other! No fighting!" she called out as she grabbed her keys and she sailed back out of the condo.

As Ravyn exited the break room, blowing on her coffee mug, she saw Jennifer's office door was closed, but she could see the light was on under the door. Then she heard voices. A female and a male voice. Once again, she thought they sounded like noises she and Marc made in the bedroom. Ravyn hurried off to her office. She was probably imagining things.

Ravyn kept her head down that day but wandered back to the break room for more coffee. She passed Jennifer's office as she went, but the door was open, without Jennifer inside.

Ravyn felt like that was strange but kept her thoughts to herself. Mostly, she was thinking about Marc and her feelings toward him.

Now that she'd said she loved him, she felt a bit of lightness. Like it was all out in the open. But she was unsure what her future held.

Ravyn still needed a place to live. She couldn't rely on whether she and Marc would be a permanent couple. It was too early, she thought. After all, she was an independent woman. But she hadn't been trying to find a new apartment.

She'd already told Cindy Freeman she'd have to put her condo dreams on hold. Ravyn was hoping against hope she'd fall into another lease at her condo building.

When she got back to her condo after work, she rushed over to the property manager's office, asking if any new leases were available.

Ravyn was relieved to see Kevin working the desk. "Hey, Kevin, have you heard of any leases in the building? My lease at Jeanie's place runs out in a couple of months, and I'd like to find something more permanent."

"I haven't heard of anything lately, but I'll be sure to let you know. You are first on my list."

"Great. Thanks," she said, trying to smile. Ravyn went up the elevator frowning.

She pushed the button to the 13th floor, pulled out her keys, and when the elevator stopped, she turned to her condo.

Ravyn opened her door and automatically tried to put her keys in the bowl she used to have on her breakfast bar. Only this condo had no bowl for her keys. There was a hook by the front door. Ravyn turned back toward the door and hung her keys.

She looked in her refrigerator for dinner. There wasn't much there. She decided to order a pizza and called Marc.

"Have you had dinner yet?"

"Not yet. Are you coming over?"

"I was going to order a pizza, and maybe wings. Do you want to come over here?"

"Are you ordering wet wings or dry wings?"

"I can order dry wings. I'll make it two orders. I know you like wings. What do you want?"

"Lemon pepper sounds good. What are you ordering on your pizza?"

"My college roommate always loved Canadian bacon and black olives. She ordered it all the time. Now I order it too."

"I guess that sounds good. Want me to bring the wine?"

"That sounds great. It will probably be about 45 minutes to an hour before the pizza arrives."

"I'll get showered and come over."

"Did you go to the gym after work?"

"Yeah. Upper body tonight. Strong arms. All the better to hold you tight tonight."

Ravyn laughed. "Well, bring an overnight bag then. See you soon."

"Love you."

"Love you, too."

When Marc arrived at Ravyn's condo, he had two bottles of pinot noir, handing them over before planting a kiss on her lips and putting down his bag.

"I have some news," he said.

"What's up?"

"I have a closing date for the sale of my company."

Ravyn's eyes got wide. "Really?"

"Yes. I'll officially sell the company September 30 to Black Kat Investors. The announcement will be made on October 1. They will make a fresh start in the fourth quarter."

"Marc, are you ready for this? I know this company is your baby."

Marc sighed. "I thought I was ready. Now that it's 10 days away, I'm not so sure."

Ravyn came over and wrapped her arms around him. "I know this will be hard for you. But there will be less pressure on you, right?"

"Yes."

"And you will continue to be part of LindMark, right?"

"Right."

"You'll still make important decisions and be able to take vacations like a normal person, right?"

Marc smiled. "I guess so."

"Well, can you take a vacation in early October?"

Marc tried not to hide his excitement. He was hoping Ravyn would invite him to her sister Jane's wedding.

"Early October? I don't know that I can take a vacation right after I sell the company."

Ravyn's face fell. "Oh. I was hoping you could come with me to my sister's wedding."

"Well, if it's your sister's wedding, I'm sure I can take time off."

"Oh, I'm so glad. I told my sister I was bringing you to the wedding. You are my plus one."

"I've never been a plus one before."

"Never?"

"Well, I might have gone as a couple to weddings with my ex-wife."

Ravyn was silent. Marc had been married before and he'd just begun to talk about his ex-wife with her, but she had trouble imagining him in his previous life.

Marc sensed her mood change. "I'd love to be your plus one. I'd love to meet your family."

Ravyn brightened. She would be introducing him to her family. She supposed she'd better tell her parents they were a couple again, so they weren't surprised.

"What date is it?" he asked.

"Saturday, October 10. I have a hotel room for a few days leading up to the weekend. I'll have a lot of stuff to do before the weekend. I'm just not sure if Jane will be staying with me the night before the wedding. I have to figure that out."

"I can get a separate room."

"Would you? Then she can stay in my room the night before the wedding, but we will have most of the weekend together."

"Give me the name of the hotel and I'll book it tomorrow."

"Be sure to say you are with the Shaw wedding party so you get the discount."

Marc laughed. "I know I said I wouldn't make that much money on the sale of my company, but I may not need the discount."

"Ha ha. No, we booked a block of hotel rooms so we all get the discount."

"I'm glad to be going with you. Do I need a tuxedo?"

"Do you have a tuxedo?"

"No, but I can rent one."

"Just a nice suit will be fine. Maybe that dark gray one?"

"You remember that?" Marc said with surprise. He didn't know she'd paid attention to his wardrobe.

"Of course, I remember that. You wore it to the New Year's Eve event we went to. You looked great in that."

Ravyn's cell phone rang. She looked down. "It's the pizza delivery."

"Great. I'm hungry."

"Me too. I've got to go down to the lobby to get the food. See you in a second," she said, kissing Marc deeply, their tongues touching.

"Don't be long."

Ravyn arrived back at her door with two plastic bags, filled with the wings and some dipping sauce, and a pizza box.

Marc and Ravyn enjoyed the pizza, wings, and wine, ending the evening in the bedroom, locked in each other's arms.

Chapter 20

The September 30 sale of LindMark arrived and Marc signed the paperwork with a heavy heart. The ink dried on the legal documents, and Marc smiled, but it was a false smile.

He wished the company was still under his control. He wished he didn't need the majority funding of Kyle Quitman, the man behind Black Kat Investors, that necessitated the sale.

The October 1 press release appeared on Business Wire, showing LindMark Enterprises sold to Black Kat Investors LLC for nearly three million dollars. Marc fielded a lot of phone calls from friends and even a few media requests for interviews.

Toward the end of the day, he got a call from Laura Lucas.

"Hey rich man," she cooed.

"Laura, what can I do for you?"

"Buy me dinner. An expensive dinner. Three million dollars! You can afford it."

"Sorry, that's not going to happen."

"Why not?" Laura asked.

"Well, I plan on celebrating with Ravyn, for one."

"That loser? I thought you fired her. Are you seeing her again? She must be good in bed."

"I am seeing her. And you need to watch your mouth."

"Why?"

"Well, I love her."

"Love her? Are you kidding? What the hell?"

"I know you find this hard to believe, you heartless bitch, but I love her. I'm sorry I ever trusted you and I'm sorry I ever met you. You nearly ruined my life with Ravyn. I see my life with Ravyn. She's a good woman. I never saw my life with you, Laura. Never. You were just a fast fling."

Marc hung up. He didn't have anything else to say to Laura.

Laura was pissed that Marc had hung up on her. She'd invested a lot of energy into her relationship with Marc when she was his public relations person at LindMark.

Or at least her idea of a relationship with Marc. After all, she'd made sure she moved her PR relationship into a sexual relationship. She was good at that with handsome men.

She remembered making love to him in public places. She remembered them making love in Piedmont Park. It was so exciting. She loved the thrill of making love in the open, where they might be caught. That got her off. That turned her on.

But seriously, now that he was worth three million dollars, that made him far more interesting to her. Even if he was a dick. And a lousy lover. Hell, she could put up with a lousy lover for three million.

She read the press release again. Hmm, she wondered. If Kyle Quitman had three million to buy Marc's company, he must have plenty more money to spare.

Laura made it a point to find a number for Black Kat Investors. She'd be sure to reach out. Kyle Quitman surely needed her to provide public relations help.

Ravyn focused on her sister's wedding that first week of October and drove up to Greenville on October 3. She'd taken the full week off from work for the festivities.

Ravyn ran errands for her sister, checking on the wedding cake, the flowers, picking up the rings, and making sure the marriage license was in a safe place.

Ravyn got a text from Julie on October 6. OMG. Twist has closed.

What?

It's closed.

Closed? For good?

Yes. It's in the paper. All the restaurants in that restaurant group closed yesterday. Prime, Strip, Smash. And Twist!

Ravyn texted a sad emoji. We didn't even get one last meal!

I'm so sad.

Me too.

How's the wedding stuff going?

It's been busy. Marc comes up Thursday. We have the rehearsal dinner Friday night, then the wedding at 4 p.m. Saturday.

Have fun. Give Jane my good wishes.

Ravyn was shocked. She'd read about the divorce of Twist's chef/owner and his wife and knew the wife had taken over the operations of the company of restaurants. Some restaurants in the group, like Shout, the Midtown sister restaurant to Twist, had closed last year.

But Ravyn had no idea all of the restaurants were going to close.

"Why so glum, chum?" Ravyn's mother, Kaye, asked.

"My friend Julie just texted me. Our favorite restaurant just closed for good."

"Oh, that's too bad. What time will Marc be here? I'm excited to meet him. Are you two getting serious?"

"He'll be here Thursday, right after lunch. He just sold his company and he's got a morning meeting he's got to attend that morning."

"Sold his company? That's exciting. Now what will he do? Will he go back to being an attorney?"

"No. He's still working for the company, kind of as a consultant. But he's a little down that he sold it. It was his baby. You know, kind of like when dad couldn't expand his tire stores."

Kaye looked concerned. Her husband John had been saddled with debt and unable to expand his tire stores when they'd first met.

"So, he didn't make any money selling the company? He has a lot of debt?"

"No, no. He did make money with the sale, but he owes his father money for helping to keep the company afloat during the lean times. I think the sale of the company pretty well clears his debt to his father, though. That's good."

"Have you found a new apartment yet?"

"Not yet. Next week, as soon as the wedding is over, I'm going to find one. I was hoping I could find a rental in my building, but it's not looking good. And I need a lease that begins December 1, since the woman who owns the condo will be back in mid-December. There are other properties in Midtown that I'll look at. One's just up the street on Peachtree. Another high-rise. It's just a pain to move all of my stuff again."

"You like living in a high-rise? It would make me nervous. What if there's a fire?"

"Mom, all of the condos have sprinkler systems to suppress fires."

"But think of the Twin Towers. All those people who couldn't get out in the fires. What if you got stuck on a high floor," Kaye said with alarm.

"Mom, it's fine. The building is safe. It was built 10 years ago. It has all the latest fire safety."

"Why don't you take one on the first or second floor? Then I'll feel better."

Ravyn tried not to roll her eyes at her mother.

Marc realized he was nervous as he drove north to Greenville. He'd gotten a later start than he thought he would, and traffic out of Atlanta was surprisingly heavy.

In all the time he'd dated Ravyn nearly two years ago, they'd never met each other's parents. He wasn't looking forward to introducing Ravyn to his parents. Well, not to his father. And not his brother, Bruce.

Marc's mother would love Ravyn. And his sister Brooke would, too. But Brooke lived in Phoenix, busy with her family, and rarely visited Atlanta anymore.

In a way, Ravyn reminded him of his sister Brooke — always positive, loving, hard-working. He thought that's what his mother would see in Ravyn, too.

Maybe he'd arrange lunch at a nice restaurant for his mother and Ravyn. Then he could introduce her to the rest of his dysfunctional family.

Marc pulled his BMW into the parking lot of the hotel where the wedding guests were staying. He grabbed his garment bag with his suit from behind the driver's seat and then opened the trunk for his overnight bag. Ravyn had already texted her room number.

He walked into the lobby and checked in for two nights. Ravyn had arranged it so he'd be staying with Ravyn the night of the wedding in her room.

Marc got his keycard and went to the elevator, pushing the button to the fourth floor. He opened his hotel room and hung up his garment bag, placing his overnight bag on the luggage stand in the room.

He sat on the end of the king bed and texted Ravyn.

I'm here in room 405.

Great. I'll be right up. We're in 217. You'll be in my room on Saturday, right?

I plan to. I'll bring my bag down to your room before the wedding ceremony.

OK. On my way up.

A few moments later, Marc heard a knock at the door. He opened it to Ravyn, who hugged him hard.

"I'm glad you are here. My family is excited to meet you."

"I'm ready to meet them too. Here's a key card for you," he said, handing her the credit card-sized key.

"Just in case I want to sneak up to your room tonight?"

"Is there a chance that will happen?" Marc said, raising an eyebrow. He took Ravyn in his arms and kissed her.

"If you keep kissing me like that, maybe. Or maybe we'll be late for dinner tonight. Have you had lunch?"

"I grabbed something on the road."

"So not hungry?"

"Not for food," Marc replied, smiling, pulling up Ravyn's shirt. His hand slipped under her bra, circling her nipples.

"Well, what are you hungry for?"

"You," he whispered.

They awoke around 4:30 p.m. when Ravyn's phone began ringing.

"Where are you?" Ravyn's mother asked.

Ravyn sat up in the bed, untangling herself from Marc and the sheets.

"What?" she asked sleepily.

"We're going to head to the restaurant for dinner."

"Mom, that's not until 6 p.m."

"Well, where are you? Your sister said she didn't know where you went."

"I'm with Marc."

"Oh," Kaye said. There was a long silence. "How long will it take you to get ready?"

"I'll be at the restaurant in less than an hour."

"Be sure that you are," Kaye said, flatly. "We have reservations."

"Oh God, Marc. We're supposed to be having dinner with my parents and Jane and her fiancé tonight. I should have set my alarm," Ravyn said, looking at her phone.

"I'll be ready in about a half-hour. I'll take a quick shower and get dressed. I don't have to wear my suit, do I?"

"No, you can wear a nice shirt and sports coat," she said, collecting her clothes off the floor. "It will be more casual tonight. I've got to get back to my room to get ready. I take longer than you to get ready."

"Call me when you're ready and I'll come down to get you. We can go together. You're in room 217, right?"

"Right," Ravyn said, pulling on her clothes and kissing him at the door. "See you soon."

Less than an hour later, Ravyn texted Marc she was ready. She showed up at her hotel door, and she answered with damp hair, but with a nice dress and her makeup perfect. He kissed her.

"Hey, you're going to ruin my makeup. Or at least my lipstick."

"I wouldn't mind that," Marc smiled.

"My hair isn't quite dry, but I'm hoping the drive over to the Thai restaurant will help."

He dropped Ravyn off in front of the restaurant and parked in the lot nearby. Ravyn was waiting for him at the entryway.

"We have a private room toward the back. I didn't want you to wonder where I went."

She took his hand as they walked toward the back.

"Hi everyone! This is Marc," she said.

The conversation stopped and everyone looked at the couple. Marc put his hand up in greeting.

"We've heard a lot about you, Marc," Jane said, coming toward them. "Or at least I have."

Ravyn could feel herself blushing.

"Marc, this is my sister, Jane." They started to shake hands, but Jane pulled him in for a hug.

"Congratulations on your wedding."

Ravyn went around introducing Nick, the groom, and her parents, John and Kaye.

"It's good to finally meet you, Marc. Come sit next to me," Kaye said.

Ravyn shot Marc a glance and made sure she stayed by his side so she'd be sure to sit on the other side of him. Ravyn didn't want her mother to monopolize the conversation.

They settled around a round table. The room was small and intimate, red and gold decorations on the walls.

A waitress arrived to take drink orders. John ordered a beer, but Kaye stuck with water and ordered hot tea. Ravyn and Marc ordered wine, while Nick ordered a beer as well and Jane ordered a fruity cocktail.

They enjoyed their dinner, Kaye asking about Marc's business and family, while Ravyn chatted with Nick to her right.

The waitress asked if they wanted dessert, and Jane and Ravyn split some green tea ice cream. Kaye ordered grilled coconut cake. The men declined dessert, John ordering a coffee.

"No coffee, Marc?" John asked.

"No. Not for me. Too late in the evening. I don't want to be up all night. Big day tomorrow, right? The rehearsal? Will it be at a church?"

"No, we'll have it at the park downtown. We're getting married there, too," Jane said.

"It's Falls Park on the Reedy," Ravyn said. "It's really nice."

"I've never been to Greenville," Marc said.

"Well, we'll have to show you around before the rehearsal. Downtown is nice," Jane said.

"Wonderful. I look forward to it."

They arrived back at the hotel, Ravyn's parents bidding their daughters goodnight in the lobby. Jane had ridden back to the hotel with Marc and Ravyn. Nick had gone back alone to the apartment he shared with Jane.

"Good night, you two. Love you both," Kaye said.

John hugged his daughters and then held Jane tight. "Won't be long now," he said.

"Don't stay up late," Kaye admonished as she and her husband headed toward the elevator bank.

The hotel didn't have a bar, but Jane said she and Ravyn had a bottle of wine in the hotel room. Did Marc want to come up for a nightcap?

"Sure."

They went up to room 217, which was a suite, and Jane took the twist top off of the wine bottle. "We may need to rinse out some glasses."

"I'll do that," Ravyn said, rinsing several glasses before placing them on a coffee table in front of the small sofa. There was an armchair next to the sofa as well.

Marc sat on the sofa with Ravyn sitting next to him.

Jane filled the glasses halfway with the red wine and relaxed back into the armchair.

"Nick seems very nice," Marc said. "Where did you two meet?"

"We met through mutual friends," Jane said. "Ravyn said you sold your company."

"I did. Signed the final paperwork last week, but I had a meeting this morning."

"What will you do now?" she asked.

"That's a great question," Marc paused, thinking before he spoke. "For now, I'll be there, more as a consultant in the transition. I expect that will be for a couple of years. After that, I'm not sure."

Marc was silent then and the women were silent too. Marc drained his glass, then stood up.

"Thanks, ladies. This has been nice, but I'll let you two gossip about me when I leave," he said, smiling.

Ravyn laughed, walking him to the door. She kissed him.

"Goodnight, Marc. I love you," she whispered.

"I love you more," he responded.

Ravyn shut the door behind Marc. Jane's eyes were on her.

"It's love is it?"

"It's love."

"You've forgiven him for that nonsense from before? Him accusing you of trying to ruin his company?"

"He's apologized for all that, many times. And seems to be trying to be a better boyfriend."

"I hope so."

"Me, too."

Chapter 21

Friday morning dawned overcast and it looked like it might rain.

"Oh no!" Jane cried, looking out the window of the hotel. "It can't rain! I want to walk around downtown. I certainly don't want rain for the rehearsal. And it better not rain for the wedding!"

Jane ranted as if she could summon the sun god and drive the clouds away.

Marc, Ravyn, Jane, John, and Kaye met down in the lobby of the hotel for the continental breakfast. John went for oatmeal and fruit, while the rest of them loaded up their plates with eggs, bacon, and pancakes.

After breakfast, they decided to go to Greenville's downtown and visit the shops. Ravyn was glad she packed her umbrella because they got caught briefly in a shower as they walked up and down Main Street.

They then walked over to Falls Park on the Reedy in Greenville's Historic West End.

"This is a lovely park," Marc said. "It will be beautiful for the wedding."

"It will," Jane gushed. "I'm so glad we got a slot for the wedding. That's why it will be a bit early tomorrow. We have to be gone before the next wedding at 6."

Nick joined them around 11 a.m. and by the time they sat down for lunch, the clouds were clearing and the sun was peeking out.

"We need to be back at Falls Park this afternoon for the rehearsal," Ravyn told Marc. "But I wouldn't mind going back to the hotel for a nap."

"With me?" he said, whispering in her hair.

"Yes, with you," she whispered back.

"Well, we're going to head back to the hotel to rest up before the rehearsal," Kaye said. "Will you four stay downtown?"

"No, we'll head back, too," Ravyn said, holding Marc's hand.

"Nick and I will go back to our apartment," Jane said. "We've still got gift bags to put together. We'll meet you back here at 4 p.m."

"We'll see you later this afternoon then," Ravyn said. She could feel herself sprinting to the car with Marc on her heels.

They arrived at Falls Park on the Reedy in Greenville's Historic West End shortly before 4 p.m. Marc dropped her off near the park then spent a few minutes looking for a place to park. He finally found a parking garage.

Ravyn was waiting for him on the sidewalk. They walked down to where her family had congregated at an intimate spot below the waterfall.

The wedding party was there with the minister. Marc and Ravyn met the best man Andrew and his date Sherry. Ravyn and Marc also met Nick's father and stepmother, Scott and Stefanie, and his mother and stepfather, June and Butch. Jane's other bridesmaid Patti was there, along with another of Andrew's groomsmen, Peter.

As they milled about before getting started, Kaye pulled Marc aside. "Marc, would you mind taking a few photos of the rehearsal?"

"I'd be happy to," he said, pulling his phone out from his jacket pocket.

"No, no, I have my 35mm camera. It's digital."

Marc took the small silver camera from her. He hadn't seen one in a long time, and it had been even longer since he'd used one.

"There's a zoom lens, too," Kaye said. "I just want some candids but try to take a lot. Thank you."

The minister walked the family through the rehearsal ceremony, having each of them stand in their places, talking them through what he'd say and their responses.

Then they stood for photos at the falls, Marc taking pictures of the sisters together, Jane with Nick, Andrew with Sherry, Nick with his parents and stepparents, Ravyn and Jane with their parents, the bride and her two bridesmaids, and the groom and his two groomsmen.

After about 90 minutes the wedding party was ready to head to a family-style Italian restaurant for the rehearsal dinner.

"My God, even though it's October, I'm sweating through my shirt," Marc said, as he and Ravyn walked hand in hand back to the parking deck to collect his car. "I didn't even think to bring another shirt. I wish I had. Do we have time to run back to the hotel?"

"I'm not sure. Turn up the air conditioner on high. Maybe you can cool off before we get there."

"How far is it to the restaurant?"

"I don't think it's far from downtown," Ravyn said. She looked at her map app again and guided Marc there.

When they arrived, Marc again let Ravyn out in front of the restaurant and parked at a nearby paid lot.

He walked up to the front door pulling his sports jacket back on, trying to hide his sweaty shirt.

"We're at a table in the back. It's packed tonight," Ravyn said.

"Like Atlanta on a Friday night," Marc observed.

Both families were standing around a sturdy wooden table that could seat the entire wedding party and their various dates. Ravyn and Marc sat together, with Nick's stepmother Stefanie to Marc's left and the best man, Andrew, to Ravyn's right. Ravyn's father, John, was at the head of the table on one end, and Nick's father, Scott, at the other end of the table.

John and Scott agreed to order some appetizers for the table, then ordered large entrees that could be shared with the table: eggplant parmesan, stuffed shells, chicken piccata, and meat lasagna.

The appetizers arrived, followed by salads with breadsticks, then the real food arrived. Several sides of spaghetti with marinara and green beans also were placed on the table.

Bottles of Chianti were ordered. Ravyn lost count of all of it but was afraid she'd have trouble zipping up her maid of honor dress the next afternoon.

As two waiters cleared the table, dessert menus were passed around.

Ravyn didn't want dessert, but then she saw tiramisu was on the menu. "Marc, will you split this with me?"

"Oh, honey, I'm not sure I can eat another thing." Marc saw the disappointment in Ravyn's face. "But I'm sure going to try."

Ravyn's face brightened as she ordered the coffee dessert and a decaf coffee to go with it. Marc ordered decaf as well.

The conversation around the table began to soften, now down to a dull murmur. They were full and getting tired.

The fathers split the bill for the dinner and they moved toward their cars.

The families stood out in the parking lot, saying their goodbyes and agreeing to meet the next morning for breakfast before the nuptials.

Ravyn and Jane got into their hotel room, with Ravyn flopping on the small sofa. She put her feet up on the coffee table.

"My God, I ate too much," Ravyn moaned. "My dress feels tight. I'm a little worried about getting into my dress tomorrow."

"I know. My wedding dress has been a little snug this past week. But I think it's just because I've had my period. I've been bloated."

"Are you nervous about tomorrow?"

"Not really."

"No second thoughts?"

"No. None. I know Nick is the man for me."

"I'm glad. I want you to be happy."

Jane moved into the bathroom, disrobing, but keeping the door open so the sisters could talk. "I am happy. I just think I was having doubts at the bachelorette party."

"As long as you're sure."

Jane came out of the bathroom in a T-shirt and shorts. "All yours," she said, tossing her head toward the bathroom.

"Great. I need out of this dress and into yoga pants."

Ravyn changed and came back to the suite. "Do you want more wine? I bought another bottle when we were out today."

"I'll take one more glass. Is it red?"

"Yes," Ravyn said, twisting off the cap.

Ravyn poured some of the ruby liquid in each glass. "Cheers," she said. "Here's to you and Nick."

They clinked their glasses.

"Are you excited for your honeymoon? Tahiti. I'm jealous."

"I'm glad we're not leaving until Sunday afternoon. I've got some packing to do."

"You are flying through Atlanta?"

"Yeah," Jane said, reaching to refill her glass. She held the wine bottle up for Ravyn, who nodded. Jane then refilled her sister's glass.

"I know you'll have a great time."

"I'm so ready for a vacation. All of this wedding stuff has been stressful."

"Well, it's all over tomorrow."

"Thank God. What are you doing about your condo?"

"I've got to find a place by the end of this month or no later than early November. I want to sign a lease for December 1. I've got to be out of the new place by December 15. But I swear I'm hardly ever there now. I'm almost living with Marc."

Jane's eyebrows raised. "You are? Living with Marc?"

"Not really. I'm just spending a lot of time at his house because Jeanie's condo doesn't feel like mine. It doesn't feel like home. Does that make sense? I hardly have any of my stuff there. I don't have any art on the walls or pictures. Everything's packed away. I just want a place of my own. Where I can have my things."

"I get it."

Ravyn drained her glass. "We shouldn't stay up too late. I don't want to have to cover up any dark circles under your eyes."

"Ha! You won't. I've got a hair and makeup woman coming at 11. She'll do your hair and makeup too if you want."

"I think I'll be fine. I don't want her to rush. The focus is on you tomorrow, little sister."

Jane stood up and walked over to hug her sister. "Love you, Ravyn."

"Love you, too."

Ravyn woke up the morning of the wedding to see sunlight peeking through the slit in the blackout curtains of the hotel. She woke up five minutes before her phone's alarm.

She looked over to see her sister asleep — the deep sleep of the dead.

Ravyn smiled. She remembered their childhood and school years. Jane would set her alarm earlier than Ravyn's but would sleep right through it. Ravyn would hear the alarm clock blaring, that annoying beep of the old digital clocks, but Jane never heard it.

Ravyn would get up, turn on the lights in Jane's room, and yell for her to get up. Even their father would shout for Jane to get up.

Jane would shake off her sluggish slumber slowly, then yell at Ravyn to stop shouting.

Ravyn was hoping there wasn't going to be a repeat of that today. It was Jane's wedding day, after all. If it had been her wedding day, Ravyn wasn't sure she would have slept at all the night before. She'd have been the one using foundation and undercover eye makeup to hide dark circles.

"Jane. Hey sleepyhead. Time to get up for the big day," Ravyn said, putting her hand on Jane's shoulder and gently shaking her. "Wakey, wakey."

Jane didn't move. Ravyn shook her shoulder a little harder. "Wake up, Jane. It's time to get up."

Again, Jane kept sleeping. Ravyn went to the hotel curtains and pulled them open, filling the room with bright light.

"Jane!" Ravyn shouted at her. "Get up!"

Jane rolled over, then opened her eyes, but shielded them from the light.

"What time is it?"

"It's 7 a.m. You need to get in the shower, and then I will. We're supposed to be downstairs by 9 for breakfast, then we need to come back up here for your hair and makeup friend."

"Marilyn will be here at 11," Jane said, getting up and making coffee in the small coffee maker. "I'll get into the dress right after I have a bite of lunch. I'm ordering a box lunch from Panera. Let Mom know what you want. She's going to pick it up and bring it here."

"I'll text her. I always get the same thing."

"After we eat, I'll put the dress on. I don't want to get anything on it. Marilyn will do my hair first and then my makeup. I'll have to put a towel over the dress so I don't get makeup on it. I should be ready to head to the park at 2 or 2:30."

"You seem to have it timed out," Ravyn said, stirring her coffee. "God, this coffee is horrible. Want me to go down to the lobby and get some real coffee?"

"Would you?"

"Let me just put some yoga pants on. You want a squirt of that flavored creamer in yours?"

"Yes. Put some French vanilla in it if they have it."

Ravyn pulled on her athletic pants and pulled a baggy T-shirt over her sleep shirt. "I'll be back in a few. Don't go back to sleep!"

"I'll hop in the shower now. Thanks."

Ravyn pushed the button for the elevator and pulled out her phone to text Marc.

Hey, are you up? she asked Marc.

I'm up. Where are you?

I'm headed to the hotel lobby to get some coffee. The stuff in the room isn't as good as the coffee in the lobby.

Give me just a second. I'll meet you there.

Ravyn milled around the lobby waiting for Marc, texting her mother her order for a Panera sandwich. She scoped out the breakfast buffet that the family would surround in a few hours.

"Good morning, beautiful," Marc said, coming up behind Ravyn.

She turned and kissed Marc. "You need to have your eyes checked, my friend. I'm hardly beautiful right now. I haven't even showered yet."

"You look beautiful to me."

"Have you been up long?" she asked.

"I woke up when I got your text."

"Sorry, I didn't mean to wake you."

"No, I wanted to see you. We won't have much time alone together today. You'll be busy."

"Yeah, I will. But I'll see you tonight, after the wedding. Jane and Nick will be in the bridal suite and you'll come to stay with me in the suite. Be sure to bring your bags down this afternoon before we leave for the wedding."

Marc nuzzled Ravyn's neck. "Is it wrong that I want tonight to be right now? I miss you. I want to make love to you."

"Shit. You're going to make me want to go to your room."

"Let's go," Marc said.

"Don't tempt me. Jane and I are on a strict schedule today. I'll have to take a rain check."

Ravyn fixed her coffee, then fixed one for Jane. Marc stood beside her, fixing his own.

"You need help?" he asked.

"I just need you to push the elevator button."

"What about opening your hotel door?"

"Oh, yeah. I will need help with that."

They got on the elevator, stopping on the second floor, and walked to her room. Ravyn handed her coffee over to Marc and got the keycard out of her pocket to open the door. She pushed the heavy door open and took her coffee cup back.

Marc leaned in and kissed Ravyn. "See you in a couple of hours."

The morning seemed to fly by and soon she and Jane were at the park, Jane in her wedding dress and Ravyn in her seafoam green maid of honor dress. Even though she hadn't been wild about the color of the dress, when she put it on this morning and had a little help from Marilyn with her makeup, she realized she didn't look terrible in it.

Ravyn saw her father in his tuxedo at the top of the aisle, looking nervous. Ravyn's mother kept dabbing her eyes with a tissue.

"She's so beautiful," her mother cried. "She's such a beautiful bride."

"She is Mom," Ravyn said, holding her hand.

"And you look beautiful, too. My two beautiful girls." Kaye began to weep again.

"Mom, you'll ruin your makeup. And if you start crying, I'll start crying. And then my makeup will be ruined."

Kaye could only shake her head but dabbed her eyes even more.

In a few moments, Ravyn walked down the aisle with Andrew as her escort before they parted and took their positions in front of the minister.

Jane stood at the top of the outdoor aisle holding her father's arm. Ravyn could feel tears come to her eyes as Jane began the processional. She did look beautiful, and happy. She was beaming.

In what seemed like a blink, the ceremony was over. The minister had pronounced Nick and Jane husband and wife.

The bride and groom departed in a limousine back to the hotel, where a meeting room had been set up for the reception. A catered buffet and a drinks station were against one wall and a deejay had already cranked up the music when Ravyn and Marc arrived.

With about 100 people at the reception, the din of conversation got loud, with people trying to talk over the music. But a spoon against a glass got the crowd to quiet and the toasts to the happy couple began.

"Nick and I have known each other since we were freshmen in high school," began Andrew. "We did just about everything together. We played football together, had classes together, and skipped class together. Sorry, Mrs. Montalto. English wasn't our favorite subject."

The audience tittered with laughter.

"We told each other our dreams," the best man continued. "We wanted to go to college, maybe play college ball, and maybe play professional ball. Maybe we should have stayed in English class."

That got more laughs.

"We shared with each other the women we wanted to marry. I can honestly say, Nick has found the woman he talked about. One who is kind, caring, smart, and funny. And beautiful. Nick, our dreams may not have all come true, but today, I can say without a doubt, that one of yours has. Congratulations, buddy."

The audience cheered and clapped.

Now it was Ravyn's turn. She'd been nervous about giving this speech, and she was hoping she would make it through without breaking down to cry.

"My sister," she said, her voice a little shaky. "My sister, Jane," she said again with more strength this time. "Who could have known when we were kids, me mooning over Marky Mark and you mooning over Carey Elwes from The Princess Bride, that you would find your one true love? True love."

Ravyn took a deep breath and began to mimic the priest from the Princess Bride. "Mawage. Mawage is wot bwings us togeder today. Mawage, that bwessed awangment, that dweam wifin a dweam… And wuv, tru wuv, will fowow you foweva… So tweasure your wuv."

The audience began laughing and Ravyn fought hard not to laugh herself. She kept looking down at her sheet of paper with her speech on it. When the room quieted, she continued. "Yes, Jane and Nick, treasure your true love. My wish for you both is that it follows you forever."

Jane's new husband took her garter off with his teeth, to the delight and howls of the crowd. Nick shot the garter off into the crowd, with it bouncing off Marc's shoulder. He reached down to pick up the delicate blue garter.

Then came time for Jane to toss her bouquet. She looked back to see where Ravyn was standing and threw it high into the air, hoping her sister would catch it.

The bouquet caught Ravyn square in the chest. She grabbed it before all the other single women, including two aggressive 12-year-olds, could snatch it from her.

"Back, off kids, this is mine," Ravyn said, holding the bouquet aloft.

The couple enjoyed their first dance to John Legend's "All of Me."

Ravyn watched her sister. Jane's face was so full of love. She was beaming and only had eyes for Nick.

"May I have this dance?" Marc asked, coming up behind her.

"Of course," she said, as they moved to the small dance floor.

"I know it's not polite to say, but your sister isn't the most beautiful woman in this room. You are."

"I think you are biased."

"And what if I am? How much longer before I can take that dress off of you?"

"I don't think it will be much longer. My feet hurt in these shoes and I'm getting tired."

"So, a foot rub when we get to the room?"

"A foot rub would be heavenly. I think we have to wait for the happy couple to cut the cake and for the bride and groom to leave though. It's bad form to leave before the bride and groom. We have this room until 11. Any longer and my father will have to pay extra. I think my father will be ready to clear the room on time."

Marc laughed. "I'll be happy to help him."

Now it was Ravyn's turn to laugh.

Chapter 22

Just after midnight, Ravyn and Marc were headed to room 217. Ravyn held her shoes in her hand. A blister had formed on her big toe.

Ravyn went over and flopped on one of the queen beds, not even wanting to remove her dress.

"Sir, you said there'd be a foot rub?" she teased.

"Can I interest you in a little bubbly?"

Ravyn rolled over and sat up on her right elbow. There was champagne chilling in a wine cooler and a tray of chocolate-covered strawberries on a small stand near the flat-screen television.

Marc twisted the cork and they both heard the pop of the champagne bottle. Marc filled one flute and handed it to Ravyn, then filled his glass. "To us," he said, clinking her glass.

"To us," she repeated.

"I want to ask you something, and I'd like you to seriously think about it," Marc said.

"What's that?"

"I'd like you to move in with me."

Ravyn nearly choked on the sip of champagne in her mouth. "Move in with you?"

"Yes. I don't want you to lease another apartment or condo. Please move in with me. I love you and I love how much time we've spent together lately. It's made me realize I want to spend all my time with you, not just a night here or an hour there. And it would solve your problem of where to live."

Ravyn realized he was very serious. She began to list the reasons why she wasn't sure about living with him. She wasn't sure she wanted to give up her independence; Marc didn't live in Midtown; Her commute would be worse to her office. And she had her cat, Felix. Marc had leather furniture.

"I just don't know if I'm ready," she said, finally.

"Well, why don't you sleep on it," Marc said, taking her glass. He pulled her up from the bed and began to unzip her dress.

The couple woke late. Ravyn was sure everyone would be slow to get up that morning.

She got a text from her father about 10:30. Your mother wants to know if you will join us for breakfast. She found a breakfast buffet she wants to try.

"My parents want to know if we want to join them for the breakfast buffet."

"Here in the hotel?"

"No, some restaurant my mother wants to try."

"Do we have to?" he asked.

"No, we don't."

She texted her father back, declining the invitation.

"What time is check out? 11?" Marc asked. "We'd better hustle."

"I got a late checkout. We can stay until noon."

"Perfect."

"But if you think we need to hustle, maybe we should save time and shower together," she said.

"Well, that would save water."

In the end, they were nearly late checking out.

They stopped at a barbecue restaurant near the interstate to have lunch together before heading back to Atlanta.

"Wish I could drive back with you," Ravyn said.

"Me, too," he said, kissing her in the parking lot in front of Ravyn's Honda Civic. "Drive safely."

"I will."

"No, I know how fast you drive. Please drive safely. I love you."

"Love you, too."

The glow of the wedding week wore off quickly when she arrived back at *Cleopatra*'s office Monday. Ravyn had stayed in her sublet condo Sunday night and hadn't slept well.

She'd tossed and turned thinking about moving in with Marc. It would be nice to come home to someone every night, to discuss her day, to snuggle with at night. She discussed her day with Felix, but he either licked his butt or ignored her.

But Ravyn liked her alone time, too. And where should she put her things? Marc had barely made room in his closet and drawers for her extra clothes and toiletries.

Where would she put all of her bathroom stuff? Ravyn realized she had a lot of bathroom stuff.

Ravyn kept looking at her phone, watching the hours creep by. She thought she fell asleep around 4 and her alarm began trilling at 6:30.

If she hadn't just taken a week's vacation, she might have called in sick that morning.

She padded out to the kitchen and poured a cup of coffee. She was grateful that Jeanie had a programmable coffee maker. Ravyn was definitely putting that on her Christmas list.

Ravyn got to the office shortly before 9 and was grateful her boss Jennifer wouldn't arrive until later. She needed to go through a week's work of emails and voicemail messages.

But by 11, Jennifer hadn't poked her head in Ravyn's office, which was her custom.

Ravyn was ready for another cup of coffee, so she stood up from her desk, stretched, grabbed her mug, and walked to the break room.

She got her coffee and as she walked by the door to the fire escape stairwell, she heard a noise.

Puzzled, Ravyn opened the stairwell door and dropped her coffee cup. Jennifer and Joel were locked in a compromising position, Jennifer's blouse open and Joel with his hand on her breast.

"Oh!" said Ravyn, startled. "I'm so sorry." She quickly shut the door, picked her coffee cup off the carpeted floor, and ran to her office, closing the door.

What the hell had she just seen? Those two hated each other.

She grabbed her phone and texted Julie.

You're not going to believe what I just saw.

What?

Jennifer and Joel were in the stairwell and Joel was copping a feel.

What?

They were making out in the stairwell.

Didn't you say they didn't get along?

They hated each other.

Well, it's a fine line between love and hate.

Oh shit, here comes Jennifer.

Jennifer knocked on Ravyn's door, opened it, and let herself in.

Ravyn didn't know where to look, so she just looked straight ahead at her computer.

"I think we need to talk," Jennifer said.

Oh no we don't, Ravyn thought to herself. We don't need to talk about this, ever.

Ravyn said nothing.

"Joel and I are seeing each other," Jennifer said slowly.

"I see."

"And we have to be careful because corporate policy frowns on inter-office relationships."

Now Ravyn really did see. Jennifer wanted Ravyn to keep her mouth shut. "I see," she repeated.

"I hope I can count on you to keep my confidence."

And if she didn't would Jennifer get her fired? "Does my job depend on it?" Ravyn asked, angry that she was being put in a difficult position.

Jennifer pressed her lips into a thin line. "Of course not. I would just rather this not become company gossip. That's all."

Ravyn's stomach suddenly felt sour. She didn't like this situation at all. She wished Jennifer and Joel would go back to hating each other. That was easier to deal with.

Ravyn really couldn't speak, so she just nodded.

"Thank you. I knew I could count on your discretion," Jennifer said as she left the office.

Ravyn avoided both Jennifer and Joel the rest of the day, but as she was leaving, Joel caught her at the elevator, getting into the elevator when she did.

"Hey, Jennifer said you wouldn't say anything about us. It's just our little secret."

"Joel, you hated her. What happened? No, don't tell me. I don't want to know."

"We both stayed late one night, we started arguing and the next thing you know we were on my office couch fucking."

"I'm so sorry I asked."

"Now we can't get enough of each other."

"Stop, Joel. I don't want any more details."

"I'm very happy, Ravyn. And I haven't been in a long time. I was hoping you'd be happy for me, too."

Ravyn looked at him. He did seem calmer, more relaxed.

The elevator stopped at the lobby and the doors opened. Joel grabbed Ravyn by the arm, pulling her back. "I think I love her."

Ravyn was shocked. "Well, congratulations then."

Joel just looked a little sheepish and shrugged his shoulders before exiting the building.

Atlanta's summer heat began to dissipate and the mornings turned cooler, perfect for running.

Ravyn tried to get as many runs to Piedmont Park as she could and ran a 10-mile race sponsored by the Atlanta Track Club in mid-October. The course was hilly and challenging, with mile 7 the same uphill, called Cardiac Hill, as the Peachtree Road Race.

Ravyn finished just under 2 hours and then texted Marc. She knew he was in the crowd near the finish line.

"There you are!" he said. "How'd you do?"

"I felt strong pretty much the entire way, except that hill at mile 7. Felt like it would go on forever. Maybe because I was getting tired."

"Well, let's get you home and warmed up."

Home. Ravyn was still struggling with whether she wanted to move in with Marc. They had discussed it several times, but he wasn't pressuring her.

There were days when she was sure she wanted to move in with him and days she wanted her own place. Ravyn would have to decide soon, if she wanted to find a place and sign a lease by December 1.

"I think it will be cool enough tonight for a fire," Marc said.

An evening by the fireplace, with wine and a good meal. Ravyn smiled to herself thinking this was the way to get her to move in immediately.

"Why are you smiling?" he asked.

"Just thinking how cozy the fire will be tonight."

"It would be cozy every night if you move in."

"Don't start, Marc. We just end up talking in circles."

"I'm not trying to start a fight with you. I just wish I understood why you don't want to live with me."

Ravyn was silent as they continued to drive to his house. As they pulled into the driveway, Ravyn turned to him. "I think I need a trial cohabitation. You know how some couples need a trial separation? I need a trial cohabitation. I'll give it three months. And if I want to move out and get my own place and space, you have to let me go."

Marc turned the car off. "If that's what you want, I'll have to agree. But I won't want you to go."

"But that will be my decision. Deal?"

"Deal," he sighed.

"OK. I'll start when my sublet is up in December. Then I'll go until about mid-March. The Ides of March. How about that?"

"Deal."

"I guess I'll keep my stuff in storage until I know for sure."

"Won't you need your winter coat and things like that?"

"Hmm. Maybe you're right. I guess I will need to go to the storage unit and try to find a few things. Maybe next weekend?"

"You want me to help you?"

"I might need some help moving stuff around in there."

"Just so long and I get a good back rub after for my sore back."

"Deal."

Ravyn and Marc arrived at the storage unit mid-morning that Saturday afternoon.

She walked up to her unit and pointed to some mouse traps along one wall.

"That doesn't look good," she said.

"No, it doesn't. When was the last time you visited your unit?"

"I haven't been since we moved everything in August. Why?"

Ravyn opened the unit's door and heard scurrying. "Oh God! Mice! And the smell!"

Marc pulled his jacket over his nose as Ravyn flicked on the light. Out of the corner of her eye, she saw movement.

Marc waved his arm to get her to stay back as he eased into the storage unit. He could see holes in her fabric couch and gnaw marks on several cardboard boxes.

"Honey, I think the mice have gotten to some of your things."

Ravyn's eyes widened. "My things? Are they OK?"

Marc eased back toward the unit's door. "Some boxes are chewed up and I can see holes in your couch. I can only see on one side, but that might be a loss. Do you store any food in here?"

"No, no food. My things! Can I sue for damages?"

Marc, who hadn't practiced law for several years, still knew the contract for the storage unit would have a lot of fine print, including that the owner of the property was liable for any damage in the unit, including pests.

"Probably not. Did you get rental insurance for the unit?"

"Did I need that?"

"You probably should have gotten some, and I didn't think to ask you when you were moving your stuff in."

Ravyn looked like she was going to cry. "Can anything be saved?"

"I'm sure there are some things that are OK. We just have to go through this unit and pull out what can be saved and dump anything we can't."

Ravyn felt sick. Most of her condo contents were in this unit. And now much of it was gone?

"Let me go find the property manager and see what we can do," Marc said, as he walked back to the office.

Ravyn poked her head in the unit, trying to ignore the smell of urine. She could see mouse droppings all over the floor. She could see boxes with "kitchen," "bedroom," "living room" on the sides. She found one labeled winter clothes and tried to open it, but a gray mouse ran across her hand. She shrieked.

Marc and the property manager ran up to the unit.

"Are you OK?" Marc asked.

"A mouse ran out of my box with my winter clothes. It scared me."

"I'm sorry, ma'am," the property manager said. "Mice and insects are hard to keep out, especially this time of year as it gets colder. They're looking for a warm, dry place, too. You can make a claim with your insurer."

"I didn't get insurance," Ravyn said weakly.

"I'm sorry to hear that. We can fumigate this unit on Monday and you can come back and go through your things. But you have to be careful because there will be dead things in here."

Ravyn blanched and shuddered. She didn't particularly want to go through her boxes to find dead mice inside. She started to cry.

Marc hugged her to him. "It will be OK. We'll come back with gloves and masks and go through and keep what we can."

To the property manager, he asked, "Is there a dumpster we can use if we can't save some things?"

"Yes, there's a charge for that, but you can use it."

Marc nodded. To Ravyn he asked, "Is there anything you want me to try to collect now? Any clothes?"

"I don't want to bring any boxes back right now. I just want to go."

"OK. Let's go then."

Marc closed up the storage unit, locked it, and drove Ravyn back to his house.

A few days later, they were back at the unit, sorting through boxes and putting what wasn't ruined into large garbage bags.

Ravyn screamed when she found the first dead mouse among her clothing. She got over it by the fourth one.

Some clothes, like her sweaters, had holes in them, used, she supposed, for nests. Ravyn pulled out the teal cashmere sweater Marc had given her for Christmas two years ago. It had been stored in a plastic storage box. She was relieved it was intact.

"Well, they didn't get the Christmas present you gave me," she said, holding up the garment.

"I hope that's a good sign," he said.

In the end, her mattress, couch, chair, and dresser all had to be tossed. Her coffee table and an end table had gnaw marks on them, so she decided to toss those, too. She was grateful that her bedroom furniture was made out of metal. The mouse bastards couldn't eat that, she thought.

Her small kitchen appliances were fine, as were her dishes, silverware, and glasses, but she'd be sure to wash everything thoroughly. She pulled out a wooden spoon that had been half-eaten.

"Well, I guess it's good I'm moving in with you," Ravyn said, with a little disgust. "I wouldn't have been able to furnish an apartment now."

"Ravyn, it will be OK. We're not throwing out too many items."

"I haven't even begun to sort the boxes with my photos. I hope they didn't get in those."

Marc stayed silent. He was hoping there wasn't damage as well.

"Oh! My Halloween decorations!" Ravyn exclaimed, opening the box labeled "holidays." She'd had a wooden wreath with ghosts and pumpkins. "And my little Christmas tree is OK, but the string lights might be chewed up. I can't tell until I plug them in. Looks like my ornaments are OK, too."

"Give me the box and I'll put it in the car. Want me to take these bags as well?"

"Sure."

Ravyn stood up, surveying the damage. They were close to emptying the storage unit and had saved maybe half of the items in there. The rest were headed for the dump. Another tear slipped down her face.

"What was the total damage?" Julie asked.

"About half of my things were ruined."

"Well, I need to take you out for dinner and drinks," she said. "How about tonight?"

"Where will we go now? I hate we can't just meet at Twist. And with me at Marc's so much, it's easier for me to get there."

"How about Davio's? You like Italian, right?" Julie asked.

"That sounds good. Have you had their gnocchi?"

"No."

"It's really good."

"Let's meet tonight at 7. I'll make reservations."

Despite being a Thursday, the restaurant at Phipps Plaza was busy.

Davio's was a short distance from where Twist once stood, its sign still on the outside of Phipps Plaza.

They decided to wait at the bar for their table. Julie hopped on a bar stool with Ravyn next to her.

"What are you drinking?" Julie asked.

"I'm thinking of red tonight. How about pinot noir."

The bartender arrived and Julie asked for two pinots.

"So is Rob still sending you flowers?"

"Not every week. More like every other week now," she said.

"You're not getting tired of it, are you?"

"Oh, hell no. You are moving in with Marc?"

"Shit, I almost have to. Now that half of my belongings got ruined. Stupid mice."

"Can you sue for damages?"

"No, I didn't get insurance. Marc explained there's a lot of fine print in the contract for the storage unit and one of those fine print items says I'm responsible for damage to my property."

"That sucks."

"It really does."

The hostess signaled that their table was ready. Julie paid for the wine and they were seated.

"When do you move in with Marc?"

"Since my stuff got ruined, I can practically move in now. But I'll move in mid-December. And my trial cohabitation ends on the Ides of March."

"What's a trial cohabitation?"

"This seems like a big commitment to me, so I want to try it out for three months."

"And then what?"

"If I feel overwhelmed, I'll get an apartment back in Midtown. Of course, I'll need to get a furnished place now, which will be more expensive."

"You're not breaking up with Marc, are you?"

"No, I just might not want to live with him forever."

"Ravyn, you need to work on your commitment issues."

Chapter 23

Ravyn was looking forward to the Thanksgiving holiday. Four days away from work.

She'd been stressed out every time she passed both Joel and Jennifer in the hall.

A week before Thanksgiving, Jennifer came storming into Ravyn's office.

"Why did you say something?" she shouted.

Perplexed, Ravyn asked, "What are you talking about?"

"I thought we had an agreement. I thought we were friends. You ratted me out to corporate! I'm getting transferred to Dallas!"

Ravyn was shocked and angry. "Jennifer, I did not tell corporate about you and Joel. Someone else must have told, but it wasn't me."

"Well, who did?"

"Jennifer, I have no idea. You're going to have to ask others in this office."

Jennifer turned and stormed out of Ravyn's office.

Ravyn was curious about what the change would mean, and who among her coworkers had tipped off corporate. She wondered what Joel would do as well.

She caught Chase Riley, the art director, at the coffee machine that afternoon.

"Did you hear about Jennifer?" Ravyn asked. "She's being transferred to the Dallas magazine."

"I heard. I'm not unhappy. She should have kept her hands off Joel. Can you believe she went at it with that old goat?"

Ravyn frowned. "Did you say something to the higher-ups?"

"Yeah. I went straight to HR. Me and Gavin caught them in Joel's office being overly friendly, if you catch my drift."

"Do you know when she's leaving?"

"End of the year is what I hear."

"Are we getting a new editor?" Ravyn asked.

"I think she's just going to oversee us from the Dallas office."

"I wonder how Joel is taking this."

"He'll get over it. He'll have a new girlfriend before the week is out," Chase said.

Ravyn doubted it but nodded her head anyway.

Ravyn's family invited Marc to share Thanksgiving with them and Marc agreed.

"I hope you're not bored while you're in Clemson," Ravyn said.

"I'm sure I'll be fine," Marc said as they drove north to South Carolina.

"Now, my Dad likes to watch football after dinner. Are you a big football fan?"

"I like football."

"Well good. Jane and Nick are coming, too, so you won't have to watch it with just my Dad. And Nick is a real fan."

"Does your Mom go all out with the meal?"

"Oh yes. We probably should have stopped eating last week."

"My mother is the same way."

"I'm looking forward to lunch with her next week. Have you told her I'm moving in?"

"Yes. That's why she's excited to meet you."

"When will I get to meet the rest of your family?"

"Well, I wanted to see if you'd come over for Christmas unless you had plans with your family."

"I think that will be OK. Nick and Jane are celebrating Christmas with his father and stepmother. I'll let my mother know we'll be celebrating in Atlanta this year."

The holiday weekend seemed to go quickly. They ate too much, watched a lot of football, played cards, and talked late into the night. They even went out to see the movie "Bridge of Spies" with Tom Hanks. They all agreed it was a good drama.

The next week, Ravyn met Marc and his mother Carol for lunch.

"Ravyn, it's so nice to finally meet you. Marc's talked a lot about you."

"Good things, I hope."

"Only good things," Marc chimed in.

Marc had made reservations at Atlanta Fish Market, an upscale Buckhead seafood restaurant. They each ordered seafood dishes and shared small samples.

"Are you packed up to move in with Marc?" Carol asked.

"I've got some boxes packed. I'm sure Marc told you about the fiasco at my storage unit. I don't have nearly as much to move. We moved everything we could salvage from the unit to Marc's already."

"Well, I'm just glad he's found you. He needs a woman's touch."

"Mother!" Marc protested.

"Well, you do. You knock around that house like an old bachelor. You need a woman in your life."

Carol looked at Ravyn and smiled. Ravyn could feel herself blushing.

Marc and Ravyn drove back to his house after lunch.

"OK, my mother is not normally that embarrassing. I can't believe she said I need a woman. I'm sorry."

"I just think she's worried about you. When I first met you, you were knocking around that house like a bachelor. And it does need a woman's touch."

"What do you mean?"

"It means your home could use some upgrades. New curtains, maybe some new carpet, some new paint. Not right away. But eventually, it could use a boost."

Marc tried not to look shocked. He didn't think anything was wrong with his house. It was comfortable. And new paint? He liked the beige walls. It went with his dark brown leather couch.

"When was the last time you changed anything in your house?" Ravyn asked.

"I guess it was when I was married."

"And how long ago was that?"

"It's been a while."

"It looks like it's been a long while. Have you done anything to your house since your divorce?"

"No."

"It shows. Your house needs brighter colors, new art on the walls," Ravyn said.

Marc's face showed a flash of anger. Was Ravyn going to make him over too?

"You look like a deer in the headlights, Marc. Nothing needs to be done now. Just think about it."

The day arrived when Jeanie came back from England. Ravyn had offered to pick her up at Hartsfield-Jackson Atlanta International Airport, but Jeanie had said she'd take the train from the airport and then take a ride share service.

Jeanie got in late that night. She entered the condo and put down her bags.

"Can I get you a glass of wine? Or dinner? There are some leftovers in the fridge," Ravyn said. "I can heat them up."

Jeanie sat down hard in the living room chair. "I'd love a glass of wine. It will probably make me too tired for anything else. It took forever to get through customs. I landed and waited more than an hour before I got to the front."

Ravyn poured a glass and handed it over to her. "Do you mind if I stay here tonight? I'm moving in with my boyfriend tomorrow."

"No, please stay tonight. I'm not going to stay up much longer. I'm dead on my feet. You're moving in with your boyfriend? The one you were conflicted about? You need to fill me in."

Ravyn could tell Jeanie was tired, so she gave her the abbreviated version, but did explain it was only a three-month trial.

Jeanie frowned. "Ravyn, don't put an expiration date on it. This is a man you love. It's not a gallon of milk."

"It's just I'm so overwhelmed and scared."

"Change can be overwhelming and scary. But it can also be wonderful. Embrace the change, Ravyn."

Jeanie stood and stretched. "I'm tired. I'm going to bed."

Ravyn stood up and the women embraced. "Thanks for your advice."

Once again, Ravyn tossed and turned for most of the night. She was moving in with Marc tomorrow and she was filled with anxiety.

Her mind raced with "what ifs." What if she didn't like living with him? What if she was uncomfortable in his house? What if they broke up? Where would she go? What if, what if, what if.

Her alarm went off and she groggily arose. She'd once again need lots of coffee to make it through her day.

Ravyn packed the last of her bags and toiletries. She was glad she'd dropped Felix at Marc's house the day before, leaving Felix locked in Marc's guest bedroom. She hated leaving without saying goodbye to Jeanie and thanking her for allowing her to live here for almost five months. But Ravyn heard no stirring from Jeanie's bedroom, so wrote a note and left it on the breakfast table. She'd call her later that day.

Ravyn locked the door behind her and rolled her bags to the elevator, down to the parking garage, and loaded them into her Honda. She'd waved to Kevin as she left, fighting back tears.

When she got into the driver's seat, she started crying. She was leaving the building she'd called home for so many years.

Ravyn tried dabbing her eyes with a tissue but realized she was messing up her mascara. She'd get to the office looking like she'd been crying.

Come on, Ravyn. Get a grip, she told herself.

When she got to work, she had trouble concentrating. Her anxiety mounted. Two and a half cups of coffee hadn't helped. Now she was anxious and jittery. Bad combination.

Marc called shortly before noon.

"I wanted to see how you were doing. I know today's a tough day," he said.

Ravyn began sobbing. "I am just so sad about leaving that place."

"I know, honey. But I hope you'll be happy here. We can even pick out paint colors tonight if you want," he said, trying to cheer her.

Ravyn gave a choking laugh. "You're just trying to ply me with redecorating ideas."

"Whatever works," he quipped.

Ravyn smiled. Marc was trying, and now he seemed to be open to allowing her to put her touches in his home.

"I want this to be our home," he continued. "You got me thinking when you talked about my house. It is dated. It does need a woman's touch. It needs you. I need you."

"I should be home around 6 o'clock if the traffic isn't bad," she said.

"I'll try to be there around then, too. Do you want me to fix dinner or do you feel like going out tonight?"

"I'll probably want to stay in. I didn't sleep well last night and I'm sure I'll be really tired tonight."

"OK. I'll pick up a rotisserie chicken on the way home," he said.

"Sounds great."

"Love you, Ravyn."

"Love you, too."

By mid-afternoon, Ravyn could barely keep her eyes open. She headed to the break room for more coffee, finding Joel at the coffee maker.

"Hey Joel, how are you?"

"Why did you say anything?" he asked.

"I didn't. Someone else did. You and Jennifer weren't as discreet in your relationship as you thought."

"Who told?"

"Joel, I'm not saying. It wasn't me, though. What are you going to do? Will you go to Dallas, too?"

Joel sighed. "I can't. I can't follow her there. I need this job to pay my alimony and corporate won't let me transfer now that they know we've been seeing each other."

"I'm really sorry. Will you try the long-distance thing?"

"I expect we'll try, but you know those never really work out," Joel said.

He looked so sad, defeated, Ravyn thought. Joel could be a real jerk and sometimes very inappropriate, but now she felt sorry for the guy.

"I am sorry, Joel. I hope you two can make it work."

Ravyn got her coffee and left, feeling tired and depressed.

The *Cleopatra* holiday party was hardly festive that year. The company had catered in a lunch for the employees and the freelance writers the magazine hired, but Jennifer didn't show up and Joel sulked in the corner of the conference room.

Chase Riley and Gavin Owens, the staff photographer, stayed as far away from Joel as they could. Now and again Joel glared at them. The men were sure it had gotten around that they'd been the ones to tell human resources about his relationship with Jennifer.

Ravyn stayed close to the freelancers, chatting about having been one herself. She introduced them to Chase and Gavin, as well as some of the production team and sales staff.

After the party, Ravyn helped clean up the conference room when Jennifer stuck her head in.

"Oh, I was just putting the food away," Ravyn said. "Do you want a plate?"

"Yes, but I was looking for Joel."

"He was here earlier, looking pretty glum. I know he's going to miss you."

Jennifer remained silent, putting a sandwich on a plate and taking some salad. "I know it was Chase and Gavin," she finally said. "I'm sorry I accused you."

"Apology accepted."

"I'm not sure I am going to move to Dallas permanently."

That surprised Ravyn. "Are you leaving the company? Will you stay in Atlanta?"

"I'm not sure yet, to either thing. I'm going to go to Dallas but rent an executive apartment. I'll give it a few months and if it's not right for me I'll part ways with the company and come back."

"Kind of sounds like me," Ravyn said. "I moved in with my boyfriend recently but I told him I'd give it three months to see if I need my own space."

"And how is it going?"

"Really well so far. It's kind of surprised me."

"Well, I'm happy for you, Ravyn."

"I hope you find what makes you happy, too, Jennifer."

Ravyn and Marc celebrated Christmas with his family.

It was a quiet dinner, with Bruce showing up clean and sober. It was a pleasant afternoon and Ravyn even explained to Marc's brother the ruse Marc had used for the fake Tinder profile.

"You used my photo?" Bruce asked his brother.

"I did. I was afraid to use my own. Ravyn would have swiped left," Marc laughed.

"What?"

"She would have passed on my profile," he explained. "When you pass up a person on Tinder you swipe left."

"But you liked what you saw, right?" Bruce asked Ravyn.

"I did. You're a handsome guy."

"Can you help me do one of those dating profiles?"

"Sure."

"And show me how it works?"

"I can do that, too. You just need to watch out for the fake profiles," Ravyn said with a laugh, holding Marc's hand. "They'll get you every time.